Wired to the Moon

Sarah Kavanagh

FLAME
Hodder & Stoughton

First published in Great Britain in 1998
by Hodder and Stoughton
First published in paperback in 1999
by Hodder and Stoughton
A division of Hodder Headline PLC

A Flame Paperback

10 9 8 7 6 5 4 3 2 1

A CIP catalogue record for this title is available
from the British Library.

ISBN 0 340 71262 7

Printed and bound in Great Britain by
Mackays of Chatham plc, Chatham, Kent.

Hodder and Stoughton
A division of Hodder Headline PLC
338 Euston Road
London NW1 3BH

For Auntie Pegs and Uncle Dee

Acknowledgements

Jailhouse Rock by Jerry Leiber and Mike Stoller © 1957 Gladys Music Inc. for the world excluding USA – Lyric reproduction by kind permission of Carlin Music Corp.

Trouble by Jerry Leiber and Mike Stoller © 1958 Gladys Music Inc. for the world excluding USA – Lyric reproduction by kind permission of Carlin Music Corp.

(You're The) Devil In Disguise by Bill Giant, Bernie Baum and Florence Kaye © 1963 Elvis Presley Music Inc. for the world – Lyric reproduction by kind permission of Carlin Music Corp.

My Way – French Words by Gilles Thibaut, English Words by Paul Anka, Music by Claude Francois and Jacques Revaux © 1967 Editions Jenne Musique and Warner Chappell Music, France and Warner Chappell Music Ltd, London W1Y 3FA. Reproduced by permission of International Music Publications Ltd.

Have You Seen Her? – Words & Music by Record, Eugene/ Acklin, Barbara © 1982 Angel Shell-Music/Six Continents Music Publishing Inc., USA & Warner/Chappell Music Ltd, London W6 8BS. Reproduced by permission of International Music Publications Ltd.

I Fall To Pieces – Words & Music by Hank Cochran and Harlan Howard © 1960 Tree Publishing Company Incorporated, USA & Acuff-Rose Opryland Music Limited, London W1.

Rand, Lionel © Music by Rand, Lionel – © 1941 Shapiro Bernstein & Co Inc., USA Warner/Chappell Music Ltd, London W1Y 3FA. Reproduced by permission of International Music Publications Ltd.

Don't Let The Stars Get In Your Eyes – Words & Music by Slim Willet © copyright 1952 renewed 1980 Acuff-Rose Music Incorporated, USA & Acuff-Rose Music Limited, London W1. Used by kind permission of Music Sales Ltd. All Rights Reserved. International Copyright Secured.

Home and Away Theme – Words and Music by Mike Perjanik. Reproduced by kind permission.

I Useta Lover – P. Cuniffe/D. Carton/L. Moran/P. Stevens, copyright control. *I Useta Lover*, performed by the Saw Doctors, was the No 1 record in Ireland for nine weeks in 1990.

Guitar Man – Reed © Vector Music USA. Used by kind permission.

Pump Up The Volume – Words and Music by Steve Young and Andrew Biggs © copyright 1987 MNS Music Limited, Blue Mountain Music Limited, 8 Kensington Park Road, London W1.

So Lonely – Words and Music by Sting © 1978, G M Sumner, UK – Reproduced by permission of EMI Music Publishing Ltd/Magnetic Publishing Ltd, London WC2H 0EA.

The Way We Were – Music by Marvin Hamlisch and Words by Alan Bergman and Marilyn Bergman © 1973, Colgems-EMI Music Inc., USA – Reproduced by permission of Screen Gems-EMI Music Ltd, London WC2H 0EA.

Don't Be Cruel – by Otis Blackwell and Elvis Presley © 1956 Elvis Presley Music Inc. for the world. Lyric reproduction by kind permission of Carlin Music Corp.

Special thanks to Dad, Mum, Fee and all the family. To cousin Claire, and the many unsung comedians of Waterford. Craig and the City Lit writing group. Rachel, Lorraine and all my colleagues. Grahame and Kath for research materials. Ken the DHL man and to Catherine and Simon. Without the help and encouragement I received from these and many others, *Wired to the Moon* would never have been realised.

PART ONE

The Soap Opera

Spider Murphy played the tenor saxophone
Little Joe was blowing on the slide trombone.

He was swinging. His hips swivelled. His shoulders popped up and down. His legs shuddered. Damp hair slapped
against his forehead, and on every second beat he tossed the
microphone from one hand to the other. Behind him, the
Jordanaires were swaying in their plaid jackets and clicking their fingers. They didn't matter, because nobody was
looking at them. Everyone was looking at him; watching
the 'one, two, a-one, two, three' way he was moving. The
young girls in the front row screamed and pulled at their
hair as he stood in front of them and worked that pelvis.
He was stark naked.

The search was on for the Irish Elvis and Frankie Shaw
knew that they need look no further than a shower unit
in Loughfergus, County Wexford. It didn't matter that he
was only singing along to the record and that if his dream
came true the Jordanaires would be standing in next door's

kitchen. Frankie was bound for Graceland. The Lourdes of Rock and Roll.

Elvis Presley boomed out of the bathroom door and bounced up the staircase and rattled the flap on the letterbox. Frankie emerged from the steam. 'It's about time you made it, sonny boy!' he shouted to his reflection, making a circle in the fogged-up glass with the end of his towel. He didn't hear the click of the latch. He didn't see the black scarf as it was flipped over the coats hanging inside the door. Frankie was looking at the patch of grey hair above his left ear. The steam was clearing now, revealing a chin that was a little too square and a nose that was a little too long. Lips that didn't pout and eyes that were more green than blue. 'Buck up, man,' he mumbled, 'they didn't say it was a look-alike contest.' He scooped hair gel from a pot and curled his top lip into a sneer. His arms swirled towards his face, combing and preening and he sang:

> If you're looking for trouble . . . ta, da, da, da, dum!
> You've come to the right place.
> If you're looking for trouble . . . ta, da, da, da, dum!
> Just look right in my face.

'If you're looking for halfwits, more like,' said his mother from the doorway. 'Look at the state of the bathroom! You do it on purpose, Frank. I swear you do.'

'Sorry.' He reached for the mat and put it over the puddle around his feet.

'Too late for sorry. You've no consideration for others, that's your problem.' To Eileen Shaw, the bathroom was sacred. She had lived so many years without one. She breathed in deeply, a sound of utter disappointment that sent his stomach down to his kneecaps. As the kettle boiled in the kitchen, Frankie stood alone with his arms folded across his chest. He felt like a right bastard. Stepping into his jeans, he hummed: *Because I'm evil. My middle name is misery.* He stopped as his mother went past the door on her way to the lounge. His middle name was Dermot.

Elvis Presley was in the lounge, too. He was in a triple photo frame with Christ and the Pope, replacing the picture of President Kennedy which had smiled at Frankie through his childhood. Eileen wasn't pleased, even when Frankie pointed out the many religious songs that Elvis had recorded before his death. Rumours about Marilyn Monroe didn't stop her from including JFK in her prayers. To her, he was at the Lord's right hand, acting as his political adviser. Frankie crouched and lit the fire as she blew ripples on her cup of tea. 'Mum,' he said, 'they're having an Elvis competition on the telly.'

'The man's dead.'

'Well, so was John McCormack, but Dad tried to sing like him.'

Joe Shaw sang while he was shaving. Stopping and starting as he moved the blade. His voice sounded perfect coming out of the windows on bright, summer days; warm and wavering like the heat haze off the grass. At the time, Eileen had tutted, but now she remembered it like a Hollywood musical. Frankie could see his own shape reflected against the window in the lenses of her glasses. 'The finals are in Dublin,' he said. 'Loads of people impersonating all the stars and there's a separate section just for Elvis. Guys from all over the country will be getting up and singing like him.'

'God help us! One is bad enough, but a whole load of fellas doing that hup-a-hup-a stuff!'

Frankie pulled the net curtain aside and looked out at the front garden. His bum was twitchy with frustration. He wanted to be see-through, like the clock on the mantelpiece, so she could know the way he was inside. She had never seen him sing on the makeshift stage at the pub, so what could she know of the magic he felt when that voice came belting out of him. Magic that had them all believing that he was the King of Rock and Roll. To her, he was the only son of the late, great Joe Shaw, and if anyone had to oust JFK from his blessed neighbours, it should have been Joe.

Eileen looked up. 'Frank. Stop twitching the curtain. People might see.'

The Man in the Elvis T-Shirt

The clock above the door of the Lone Star Garage was bang on time at twenty past two in the morning and at twenty past two in the afternoon. That was how Michael liked to look at it. To Michael, Loughfergus was on the up. The local football team was heading for the Cup, his kids were future presidents and Frankie Shaw was a better singer than Daniel O'Donnel. Michael was Frankie's cousin and his employer. He was forty-one, short and skinny and starting to lose his hair. Michael could make anything work. Anything mechanical, that is. He had trouble with Frankie sometimes, when his head was in the clouds.

Michael left the morning jumble of breakfast and school bags and clicked the door behind him. Over the road, a trail bike was buzzing across the wasteland where the pitch and putt course still lay unfinished. The engine sputtered and roared as the tyres picked their way through the sandless bunkers, splashing up the mud that gathered every time it rained. He made his way along Finney Road, pulling his collar up in preparation for the moment when he had passed the last of the plain grey cottages and reached the crossroads where the wind battered you on the corner. 'Twenty past two,' he said as he passed Dec Ryan's shop and crossed the Enniscorthy road. 'Better get a move on.' He said it most mornings. His little joke. Nobody heard it, because there was never anybody around at eight thirty in the morning.

Back in the heydays of Elvis Presley and Joe Shaw, things had been very different. There was a factory two miles up the road, a social club with a spinning glitter ball and a line of shops. Each morning had a sense of purpose to it. Doors clicked and shoes scuffed and cars started. The air was sweet with pipe tobacco and the bread which Paul Macnamara unloaded from his van and laid out in the cake-shop window. There were dances every Saturday and a fair every summer when the streets were filled with music and swathed in bunting. It had everything but Judy Garland walking along, singing at the top of her voice about how great it was to live there.

Michael was standing with his hands on his hips, looking out of the door, when he spotted Frankie in front of the corner shop. The wind was bitter, blowing the rain down in arcs like handfuls of chicken feed. 'Surfin' USA' was on the radio. 'What a joke!'

Frankie was looking worried. He had a magazine tucked inside his jacket and his shoulders were shrugged against the wind. He looked up to the heavens, then over the road at Michael, then up again. 'Go on, Frankie, you can do it,' he mumbled. 'Get your bloody hair wet for once in your life.' Frankie unrolled the magazine, as if he were going to put it over his head, but he thought better of it and pressed it to his chest again. He ran with his head down and his jacket wrapped tight around him and didn't stop until he was standing in front of the smeared mirror in the back office.

The lettering on the front of the TV guide was big and red.

'NATIONAL TALENT QUEST.' Frankie had paced around the shop for five minutes, watching it out of the corner of his eye; half hoping someone else would rush in and buy every copy. He wanted to keep it hidden in his jacket so Michael wouldn't see it, but it was like driving past a terrible accident. He just couldn't help looking and Michael just couldn't help looking over his shoulder and saying: 'You'll walk it, you're a natural. Didn't I always tell you that you were a natural?' Frankie stared at the picture in the magazine. A collection of star-spangled look-alikes, posing with microphones. 'What on earth would I wear?' he said through his daze. 'They'll all be in those white suits. All I have are my decorating overalls.'

'Nonsense. You can wear your Elvis T-shirt.'

Frankie snapped out of it and turned to Michael. 'What Elvis T-shirt?'

'You know. The pale blue one with the black writing. The one you wore to the football on Saturday.'

'That says Levi's!' He hit Michael over the head with the magazine. 'So, do you think they'll look like Elvis? The other contestants?'

'Some of them maybe.' Michael opened his lunch box and pressed two cream crackers together so that the little worms of margarine squeezed out through the holes. 'I've seen Japanese and Indian fellas do it on the telly. It's all confidence, I reckon. If you believe in yourself, you will be Elvis all right.'

'Right.' Frankie got up. 'Think Elvis. I am Elvis!' He stopped and turned around. 'Yeah, but which one? Am I the young Elvis or the old one? The younger Elvis was better, but he jiggled around a lot, like this.' Frankie bounced up and down, holding an imaginary guitar against his hip. 'I have tried to do it, but I felt a bit stupid. Most people choose the older one. There was more to look at.'

'Yeah, he was a right fat bastard by the end.' Michael started on his sandwiches.

'No, I mean he was more of a showman.' Frankie flicked through the magazine. His hair was starting to curl in the damp air.

'Which song will you do?'

'I don't know. "Devil In Disguise" maybe. It's on the tape at the Palace.'

'How does that go again?'

'Oh, you know.' Frankie reached for his tools.

'No I don't. Go on. Sing it.'

'I'm not singing in here.' He grinned and looked around him. 'Someone might walk in.'

Michael picked up the magazine. 'Frankie, there will be hundreds of people walking into this theatre, to say nothing of those that will be watching it on the telly. They won't just take your word for it. Come on, now. Sing it like you mean it. I promise I won't laugh.'

You look like an angel, sang Frankie in barely more than a whisper. Elvis with the volume turned down. Michael cupped his hand behind his ear. *Walk like an angel.* He sang under the tractor bonnet, looking at the engine. It gave his voice an echo. *Talk like an angel. But I got wise.* Suddenly his body sprang to life. Frankie could hear it in his head. The whole band was behind him, slapping at the bass and popping on the drums. He shuffled and swung his hips. The soles of his shoes scraped on the concrete floor like maracas and he tapped the bonnet with his palms, sending raw, metallic thuds up into the roof. Against the quiet of the rainy day, Frankie became Elvis. The young and beautiful Elvis, singing for the love of it. *You're the devil in disguise, oh yes you are.*

Michael clapped enthusiastically. 'Come on, Frankie,' he shouted. 'Why don't you have a go? I tell you, you're great. You'd be mad not to go in for it.'

'The others will be miles better. I'd need a miracle.'

Frankie headed for the office door. Michael followed him. 'I think what you need is a manager. Someone to take that talent of yours and knock it into shape.'

'Oh yeah, and I suppose you're just the man for the job, being such a musical genius and all.'

Michael held a spanner up to his mouth. *Regrets. I've had a few*, he sang, all out of tune. *But then again.* He looked at himself in the mirror. 'I think I'll go in for it myself as Big Frank. What do you think? I've certainly got the hairline for it. Betty reckons I was a bit of a bobby-dazzler in my day, proving we've both got an eye for talent.' He wiggled his eyebrows.

Frankie laughed out loud. 'Jesus, you wouldn't know talent if it bit you on the arse.'

'That's no way to talk to your manager.' Michael turned on the radio and Frankie picked up a wrench and the day slid by with the crackle and flash of the soldering iron.

The Sunset Strip

'Caesar's Palace' was written in big, bold neon capitals. It glowed pink against the white pebbledashed walls and on rainy nights the colour covered the pavement like spilled milk-shake. The pub had stood at the crossroads for eighty-five years. 'H. Mehans' was its first name, then 'The Happy Wanderer', then 'The Jewel'. There were a few ruffled feathers when Hank Green came back to Loughfergus after nine years away, ripped down the old sign and called up the electricians, but nobody could stay angry with him for long. Hank was the man. The man with the drink and the chat and the music. He was the Saturday night hop and the social club and the summer fête rolled into one. The Palace held snooker contests and line dances and karaoke nights. They came from miles around to hang their hats in the Wild West saloon, to mosey on up to the bar and say: 'Gimme somethin' for the pain, big man,' and the big man never let them down. Everything about Hank was big. His hands, his stomach, his grey-bearded face, even his voice. The kind of voice to make women melt, though he was well over forty and still single. Old women teased him. Tugged on his sleeve and said, 'What a waste of a man, you are, Hank Green!' They had watched him for years, walking by himself on the hills around the village in his Stetson hat like the beginning of *Oklahoma*. Swiping at bushes with a blackthorn stick and staring off into the distance as if he were waiting for something. Something more than a bright golden haze on the meadow.

Michael's wife, Betty, was in the Palace every Monday with the Countrywomen's Association. A small, olive-skinned woman with cropped black hair. She came up behind Frankie and put her hands around his arms and told him not to worry about what to wear on stage. Steven, their eldest, had a lumberjack shirt that would be just right. He was still her little Frankie. The awkward boy they baby-sat when she was first going out with Michael.

'Thanks, Betty,' he mumbled, 'but I don't think I'll go in for it. I only do the karaoke for a bit of craic on a Saturday night.'

'Well, it's up to you, love. Nobody's going to laugh at you if you don't win. It might be something you can tell your grandchildren about. Oh, by the way . . .' She squeezed his arm. 'I'm surprised we didn't see you at the funeral today. Did you forget?'

Frankie felt like someone had just taken a shovel full of ice and stuffed it down his throat. So, that was the last of Mary Macnamara, the baker's wife. A nice woman, considering what happened to her. He should have gone to the funeral. He had spent a lot of time at her house when he was younger. She was the mother of Siobhan, Katie and Carmel. He shivered, wondering if, behind one of the raindroppy car windows in the funeral cortège, Carmel had sat on a worn, leather seat next to her husband, Billy. Holding his hand. Crying on the shoulder of his suit. Regretting the day she went away. Regret felt like ice in the stomach. Frankie could have told her that.

He had been suffering from it on and off for the last twelve years.

His wrist twitched and a slop of beer ran over the rim and on to his fingers. He sidestepped away from Betty, desperate to change the subject. Over at the bar, Hank was all animated. 'Talking of funerals,' he was saying to Michael, 'did you see the thing that was on the other night?' He gestured to the telly in the far corner of the bar. 'There were these fellas in Africa who were sort of undertakers. They made these amazing coffins in all kinds of shapes and colours. A farmer was buried in a yellow pod and a fisherman was put in this little boat. It was brilliant. I wish they did that over here. It would cheer things up no end.'

Frankie put his drink on the bar. 'What would you have suggested for poor old Mrs Mac, then,' he grinned. 'A loaf?'

'Nah,' said Michael. 'We could have got some of the ladies from the ICA to crochet her a coffin. A little blue one with a poodle on top. Like the things you put over the spare toilet roll. It would have been lovely.'

'Would you listen to yourselves,' said Betty. 'I can see the day when we're walking behind the two of you laid out in six-foot beer barrels.'

Everybody roared and said, 'Jeez, that's classic, Betty!' and all the ice in Frankie's stomach melted away.

On the way home, he picked bits from bushes on the roadside and threw them ahead of him. He smiled. 'Jesus, what a sad life,' he said. 'Carried out in my mother's shower unit.'

ʃ

Stewing

Wednesday was scone day and the house had a pretend warmth from the smell of baking. Eileen had her blue overall on and her rings were in the soap dish. They were playing Deanna Durbin on the afternoon melody show. He stood in the doorway and put a plastic bag on the dresser. 'What's that?' she said.

'Bacon. You asked me to get bacon.'

'I did,' she said at last, 'but I forgot and went out for stewing steak. That stupid Dec Ryan never told me you were in. Did he think we would be eating twice?' She opened the bag and peered in, sniffing. Frankie laughed and went over to the sink to wash his hands. She stayed stony-faced, cut too deep to see the lighter side. He watched her as she jiggled the pressure cooker on the stove and put the cool scones in the tin. When he was a child, he longed for her to slip up and make a fool of herself, but not now. They sat at the kitchen table in silence as the rain ran down the steamy windows. Eventually, Eileen said: 'I saw Betty in the shop today. She told me that the Macnamara girl is living up at the cottage again. Just until it's sold.'

'Carmel?' said Frankie nonchalantly. The thought of her made his earlobes prickle.

Eileen nodded. 'It's the money. That's why she's here. They're worth a bit, those cottages.' Frankie opened his mouth and closed it again. Oh, here we go! he thought. Eileen sniffed. 'That's the way with the young ones nowadays,' she said. 'Off to England and God knows where and good luck to them, I suppose.' She placed her knife and fork together on the cleared plate. 'The poor woman could have been lying paralysed for days and nobody would have known.'

Frankie sighed. 'You know full well that it happened on the bus. They went straight to the hospital. Passengers and all.'

'Lucky for her that she was.' She looked over at Frankie as he pushed his food around. 'And you'll be off soon to do your singing. I had to fight my way through your adoring public in the post office today. All saying you're heading for Dublin, and why shouldn't you? A young man with your own life to lead.'

Frankie was dying to say that he would have left a lot sooner if his father had lived. He stopped himself, because he could feel her ear-splitting, overwhelming fear coming back at him over the table. 'I'm sure Carmel's very upset about her mum,' he said, gently. 'Anyway, she's been back loads of times over the years. Much more than Katie or Siobhan. She was always a very nice girl.'

'Oh yes, I remember just how nice you thought she was.' Eileen raised her eyebrows. 'The state of her! Dyeing her hair all the colours of the rainbow and riding around on the back of motorcycles.'

Frankie stood up and gathered the dishes together. 'Jesus,' he said, 'I was only trying to make conversation. Anyway, if you were so concerned about Mrs Mac, why didn't you pop up there yourself?' He started on the dishes.

He heard Eileen taking off her pinafore, but didn't turn around.

She stopped in the doorway. 'Frank, I saw Mrs Regan today and I told her that you wouldn't mind popping up at the weekend and putting the door back on her hot press. I said that you'd organise the time with her.'

'Fine,' he said, but she was already heading for the lounge. The radio was playing 'Have You Seen Her' by the Chi-Lites. Frankie remembered Carmel in those days, when she worked in the cake shop on a Saturday. *Oh, I see her face everywhere I go.* Her face was lovely. Her front teeth crossed over a little and there was no hiding them, because she smiled all the time. He had sat with her in her back garden when the boys wouldn't let him join in. They both played with her dolls when her sisters wouldn't let her join in. She stuck red geranium petals on her fingernails with paper glue and made rings out of daisies threaded through their own stems. In school, she protected him. She stood with her hands on her hips and said: 'It's my elastic and Frankie Shaw can play if he wants.' He had stepped forward, happy to stretch tied-up knicker elastic around the backs of his knees, knowing that the knotty circle would bind him to her. Twanging and chafing them both as her friends jumped and twisted.

When they were teenagers, the atmosphere had stretched sometimes like elastic between them. He wanted to move closer, but he was afraid that it would ruin the game. It was Carmel who made all the rules. If he stood there long enough, she was bound to notice him.

Why, oh why, did she have to leave and go away? He had made a right fool of himself at her engagement party. They were all in the front room of the Macnamaras' cottage. Carmel was dancing with Billy and he had his hand on her backside. Even though it was dark, her ring kept glinting. It moved over Billy's cheek. It pressed into his shirtsleeve. It stroked the top of his leg. Frankie's girlfriend, Margaret, had tried to get him to dance with her, but he just stood and stared until he couldn't bear it any longer. 'Carmel!' he screamed as the record finished. 'You're not really going to marry him, are you?' Everybody looked at Frankie. Carmel came over to him, smiling, thinking it was all a joke. 'I mean it, Carmel!' His voice was shaky from holding back tears and his heart was breaking out of his eardrums. 'What about me?' Carmel's smile had gone and in its place was the look that had stayed with him ever since. 'What about you?' she said. 'Go home, Frankie. You're out of order.' She patted him on the shoulder and went back to Billy. Somebody put on another record and all the girls said 'Oh, I love this one' and Frankie went home.

He turned off the radio and picked up one of the last scones from the cooling rack. 'Mum,' he shouted, 'is it all right if I start on the new scones?' He heard the television from the lounge. 'Hell,' he said under his breath, 'I'm thirty-two!' and he bit into it.

Tumbling Tumbleweeds

There is a moment in all the best westerns which comes just before the posse rides into town. A moment of calm. Children are playing in the street, a dog is barking away in the distance, and behind the bar of the saloon the landlord is giving the sarsaparilla glasses a bit of spit and polish. Hank watched as his signet ring danced a sunbeam over the clutter of pictures and souvenirs on the wall. The Wild West hall of fame, from Gene Autry to John Wayne, was spotless, and Hank was the man behind the duster. He stroked his beard and daydreamed about being far away and free. About being held and kissed. About a posse riding into town.

It was time for a little steel guitar. The juke-box by the bar was serviced regularly by young men in heavy-metal T-shirts and no arses in their trousers, but Hank didn't let too many chart songs sneak into the repertoire. Just the odd Elvis Presley number for Frankie. He knew what people preferred. Country and western. A ballad and a waltz and, once in a while, a hoe-down. 'Swing partners. Change partners.' Hank didn't swing, not in Loughfergus anyway. He dreamed away the late afternoons until his annual holiday came around. There was a map of America by the door. A network of straight black lines crossed and stretched from the east coast to the west. Hank traced his finger over the route he had planned for the following month as a lone figure made his way down the street.

Frankie had left the garage early to please Michael with a new Elvis karaoke tape in his pocket. The rain had died out and the spring sun was stretching the fence posts right across the street. Davey Sheehan was behind the wheel of his tractor, holding up the traffic. Michael's son, Steven, and two of his friends were sitting on the wall next to the shop, passing a bag of crisps around. Frankie and Carmel and their friends Macca and Pauline used to sit on the same wall, waiting for something to happen. Nothing had happened yet. If anyone had owned a horse, Loughfergus would have been a one-horse town. A young girl at the top of the hill had a half-share of a pony called Muffin, but that didn't really count.

When he reached the Palace, Hank was crooning along to Patsy Cline. *I fa'hall to pa-hieces.* The karaoke machine was in the back room, tucked away in the corner so that the guys playing snooker wouldn't hit it. Frankie pushed the play button and kept his finger on the volume knob. In came the guitar. The deep twanging bass-line at the beginning of 'Baby I Don't Care'. His face was all pins and needles. His heart was racing. He knew the song backwards. He had lain on his bed time after time with his hands behind his head listening to it, jiggling his feet from left to right. He had sung a million duets, but this time it was different, because Elvis wasn't going to sing. The King was standing to the side and saying: 'Over to you, Frankie.'

He forgot the first line. 'Flick,' went the drums and in came the piano and he was still standing there saying, 'Who? Me?' He leaned over to turn the machine off, but the mike was too close and the room was filled with deafening, high-pitched outer-space noises. He wanted to jump out of the window and run across the fields. Run smack into a tree. Who was he kidding? The Irish Elvis. It sounded like a cue for a bad joke. Hank appeared at the door with his hands over his ears. Frankie swooped down and turned off the machine. 'I've got it! I've got it! Sorry about that.' Hank smiled and went back to slicing lemons.

Frankie sat on the makeshift stage and breathed deeply, his heart chugging a little more slowly. He leaned behind him and turned on the tape. The microphone was resting on the stage. He clicked his fingers along with the guitars and mouthed the first line. 'Flick,' went the drums, and this time he was ready. *You don't like crazy music,* he sang. *You don't like rocking bands.* It sounded good and he pulled the microphone nearer to his mouth. He added a little vibrato to his voice. The wobble that Elvis got at the end of a line. *You just want to go to a movie show and sit there holding hands.* Spot on. Hank heard and smiled from behind the bar. By the time the instrumental break came, Frankie was up and dancing. The empty cassette case jumped on the top of the machine as he bent and straightened his legs and nodded his head so his hair flopped forward. His fingers clicked and snapped by his side. 'Did you hear the one about the Irish Elvis? He was better than the American one.'

The doors opened for the evening and the first of the drinkers arrived. Michael came in with a pint for him as he started 'Return To Sender'. They filled the back room and applauded loudly and Frankie gulped it all in. By the door, he saw her hair. Long and dark. Tied with a purple silk scarf which shone out against the wood panelling. Carmel. He fought the urge to do something dramatic, like throw the microphone out of the window and leap off the stage into her arms. Dec moved forward and he saw her face. Her grey-green eyes and warm, freckled skin. She was smiling at him and he smiled back as he sang. He didn't sound like

Elvis when he smiled. His voice was softer, like it was when he spoke. 'Hi!' She mouthed the word and waved with one hand, fingers drumming the air. The song finished and the lads slapped him on the back and mussed his hair. Carmel put down her pint of lager as Frankie came towards her.

'Look who it is, Frankie,' said Hank. 'Our happy wanderer returns.'

'Well, well.' Frankie lifted her up by the waist. He was Elvis, so he could do anything.

'Frankie, I can't believe it! It's so mad to see you again.' She bounced up and down.

'Carmel Macnamarmel. You're looking great!'

'You too.' She leaned forward and took his left hand in hers, looking for a wedding ring. 'Are you still up the road at your mother's ?'

Hank pointed at Frankie over Carmel's shoulder. 'You know the first thing that the Birmingham Six said when they got out of jail?'

'No.'

'They said "Is Frankie Shaw married yet?"'

'Oh, shut up, Hank.' Frankie looked down at his shoes.

Carmel touched his arm. 'Hey, leave you alone for five minutes and you become a rock and roll star.' Frankie's heart did a backflip, even though he knew she was bullshitting him. She led him to an empty table. 'So, what's the scandal, then?' She fumbled in her bag for a pack of cigarettes. He felt that there really was so little to report. She had been in a spaceship, travelling from one galaxy to another, and returned to find that time had not moved on at all. She leaned back and put her feet on a spare chair. The room was full of Carmel. She was light and glitter and, when she laughed, Frankie was the world's greatest comedian. 'How is Billy, then?' Frankie had to ask.

'He's fine. Mad as ever.' She looked at the door.

'Is he still up in Dublin? I mean, he didn't come with you, did he?'

'No. He's pretty busy at the moment.' She looked up at Frankie and smiled. 'Well. I'm mega-busy. The pottery has really taken off. We had to move to a bigger workshop and take a few students on part time, did you know that?' She was talking so fast that Frankie was frozen to the spot listening to her. 'Myself and some friends are having an exhibition in London later on this year. Not bad for a country girl, eh?' She crossed her ankles and hit the table with her boots. The rest of her pint went flying all over the place, filling the grooves made by years of domino-tapping on the polished wood. She screeched and guided the beer on to the floor with her palm. 'Oh, God! Did you see that? I'm so cool aren't I?' She raised a wet finger to her cheeks and touched them, making a 'tsss' noise, like spit hitting hot coals. 'That was God paying me back for bragging.' She laughed and, for the first time, he saw the fine lines around her eyes.

An old man with a fuzz of white stubble on his chin leaned over to Frankie and mumbled something in his ear. Something about Joe Shaw and his beautiful voice. 'Gone but not forgotten, son. Gone but not forgotten.' His yellow-stained fingers tapped the back of Frankie's hand. Carmel looked bemused. 'I see they're still saying novenas to your father around here.' She blew a smoke ring and watched it hula away.

'It's quite a reputation to live up to.' Frankie raised his eyebrows. 'Tell me, did you ever hear from your father?'

Carmel's expression darkened like a cloud shadow on a field. 'No. Nothing. He's probably dead by now. I thought he might come for the funeral. Spent the whole day looking around for him, in case he was standing somewhere.' She got up from the table. 'Listen, Frankie, I'd better make tracks, but why don't you pop in. I'm doing some work there in Dad's old cooling room, so I'll be in most of the day.'

Frankie wanted the pub to sink. The vanishing of Mr Mac had had the whole village whispering in corners fifteen years earlier. Nobody had pointed a finger, but groups of women used to go quiet and smile politely when Mrs Mac went by. Frankie nudged Carmel as she climbed out of her seat. 'I might pop in on Saturday on my way down from Mrs Regan's. I'm doing some jobs for her.'

'You haven't changed a bit, have you? Still putting up shelves for your mother's friends.' She put her hands on his shoulders. All the times she had come down to visit her mother, she had hidden herself up at the cottage while Frankie had almost died of anticipation at the pub. He wanted to lean back against her breasts. He turned his head around and saw that she was still wearing the ring. It was still shining. He cleared his throat.

'Will I walk with you?'

'No. I have a car, thanks. See you Saturday, then.' Her hands lifted from his shoulders and his neck felt the draught from the door.

Walking on the Moon Days

Up the hill and into the village. Wave to Dec in the shop. Over the crossroads. 'Hello there, Mrs Dunphy.' Past the garage on the left. Past the pub on the right. Up a bit more. Turn left at the old social club. Third cottage on the right. Crunch-a-ta-crunch-a-ta on the gravel and up to the door. Grey gravel like moon rocks. They used to do a slidey, side-to-side dance and sang: *Giant steps are what we take.*

The cottage hadn't changed much. A picture postcard house with white walls and deep blue frames around the windows and a thatched roof that made it look like a man in a woolly hat. The years had taken their toll, cracked the paintwork and darned the hat with green moss. Inside, there was the landscape on the wall, the companion set by the grate and Mrs Mac's crocheted doilies all over the place. Frankie had wanted to live there when he was little. Wanted it so badly. He had imagined waking up to bakey smells and the sound of children arguing, instead of whispered conversations and the smell of cabbage.

Nobody answered when he knocked, so he wandered

through the hallway, checking in all the rooms. There was a large mixing bowl on the kitchen table with a wooden spoon in it. Daddy Bear's breakfast, he thought. He bent over and sniffed it. Carmel was at the back door, rubbing her boots on the mat. 'I didn't think much of the porridge,' he said. 'Not enough sugar.'

'What are you on about?'

'This. What in God's name is it?' He turned the wooden spoon in the grey mush.

'Papier-mâché. Come with me and see.'

The back room was damp and smelled of Calor gas. In the corner by a small window, a desk was covered in little white bowls, lined up on a sheet of newspaper. On a shelf beside them was another row of bowls painted in swirls of sea green and gold and deep blue seahorses with silver eyes. She picked one up and dabbed her index finger over the surface. 'Still a little sticky. Don't get it on your shirt.' She handed it to him. The inside of the bowl was painted in the same colours and there was a tiny gold starfish resting at the bottom. As he turned it in the light, he noticed that the smooth, glossy varnish was smudged on the side by a perfect oval fingerprint. He wanted to keep it for himself.

They sat at the kitchen table and aired all the old stories. Frankie struggled to think of anything daring he had done while they were at school. Only pranks that Carmel had orchestrated. He had often tried to work out why she had chosen him as her best friend. Perhaps because, next to him, she had always shone so brightly. She was still shining. Galloping over her words, pulling faces and cracking jokes. 'Remember when I died my hair pink?' she said.

'Talking of which.' He opened his wallet and pulled out half a photo-booth strip. Frankie and Carmel squashed into the frame with an orange curtain behind them. The picture was faded. Their complexions had a blue tinge to them. Frankie was sixteen and spotty, his hair flattened down

and parted in the middle. A striped blue shirt and the knot
of a thin black leather tie. He was holding up two fingers
like bunny ears behind Carmel's head. She glowed fuchsia
against the curtain, her hair crimped and hiding her eyes,
her face caked with pale foundation and heavy lipstick. She
was wearing a leather jacket with badges all over the collar.
Her head rested against his arm. In the second photo, she
was looking at him, but his eyes were screwed up with
laughing.

She held the picture up to the light, wanting to crawl
back into that photo booth and the boldness of it all. She
remembered the way everyone had looked at her that day,
as she sat with Frankie on the wall down by the river in
Enniscorthy, smoking cigarettes and watching the dog-ends
float downstream and catch in the weeds, blinded by the
sunshine coming through her luminous, fluffed-up fringe.
'Oh my God! Oh my God! Oh my God!' She put her face
right up against the picture. 'Look at your hair, Frankie!'

'My hair?' He smoothed his hands over the quiff he had
worked on for an hour before coming to the cottage.

'I know. I looked like a gonk, but yours was so neat. It's
how your mother used to do it.' She licked the palm of her
hand and ran it over the crown of her head. 'Made you
look like a small-town footballer. The ones they put on the
cigarette cards. Centre-forward for Cowpat United.'

Frankie bit into a biscuit. 'I'm in the local team, you know.
We are playing the Christian Brothers this afternoon. Bit of
a grudge match. You should come along.'

Carmel's heart sank. She had been too busy bragging
about what a rebel she used to be and what a high time
she was having up in Dublin. She had broken every promise
she had ever made to him. Promises about backpacking
around Europe and driving across America and thumbing
their noses at Loughfergus. It was 'next summer' and 'next
summer' and then came Billy.

Billy Stevens had really taken the town by storm. The tallest lad doing leaving cert. The image of Bryan Ferry, if you believed the girls at the bus stop. Nearly expelled four times and he had brilliant records. It was just like the song, 'Leader Of The Pack'. He rode into town on a motorbike and all the girls fell for him. They sidled up to him in the chip shop and passed him notes in class and did his homework for him, but it was Carmel he went for. *Hey! Is that Billy's ring you're wearing?* He was kissing with his mouth open when all the other lads were practising on their arms. From the moment she had clapped eyes on him, Carmel had got a dose of the shivers. Her voice was shaky when she talked to him. Her knees were trembly when he kissed her and, as for the motorbike, Billy's big, black, vibrating saddle-for-two, she was lucky she didn't faint away and topple off and end up in a ditch. What's more, her mother had loved him, and she was always scant in her praise of others. He was no mother's ideal candidate, but the moment he came shuffling through their door, Mary Macnamara was aglow. She thought he was something, with his high ideals and his wild looks. A bit of rough, maybe, which Paul the baker never was, and Paul was long gone by the time Billy showed up. Carmel thought about her mother dying on the bus, lying between the shopping bags. She thought about all the brown sweet sherry bottles she had left behind and all the secrets she had taken with her.

She leaned over to Frankie and touched his hair. 'It looks great like this,' she said. 'Just like Elvis. Are you excited about the contest?'

'Nervous. I don't even know what to sing.'

'Well, let's go through all the ones you like. The old team back together again. I bet you anything, you'll win.'

She owed it to him. Carmel tried to imagine what he would look like dressed up as Elvis Presley.

Frankie thought: If I were Elvis and this was a film, all I

would have to do is sing the right song and she'd know how I feel. The song would say that her eyes were a lovely colour and her hair was brilliant and that she made me laugh and that there's never been another girl for me, really.

'How long have you been making the pots?' he said.

A Daydream Believer and a Homecoming Queen

Half-time and Loughfergus were kicking the arses of the Christian Brothers. Hank lined up cans of beer, while a woman on the opposite side cut oranges into quarters for the school team. As the Loughfergus men jogged off the pitch, a crowd of boys ran up to Michael and slapped him on the back. He hadn't scored. He had done something far, far greater in their eyes. Something that would make him a legend for two whole terms. He had attempted an athletic header, but had misjudged and hit the slippery, filthy ball smack into the face of the P.E. teacher.

The men stooped in a circle, resting their hands on their kneecaps and breathing frosty breath at each other. 'You're doing good, lads,' said Hank, handing around the cans, 'but keep the concentration up.' The others looked at Frankie, but nobody said anything. He had missed a couple of easy crosses. They reckoned that it was because his mind was on greater things, such as his choice of songs for the contest. Michael leaned on Hank's shoulder while he picked a stone from between his shoe spikes. 'Just think,' he said. 'In a few weeks you'll be watching the baseball. Where is it this year?'

Hank took a swig from his can. 'L.A.,' he said as the Christian Brothers team jogged on the spot. 'I have a friend there. Haven't seen him since college.'

'Oh yeah?' said Christy, the goalie. 'That'll be nice.'

There was something about his tone that made Hank nervous and feeling like he had to explain. 'He was one of the lads I used to go drinking with,' he grinned. 'Mad fella. He's married to an American girl. Has been for a few years. They're taking some time off so that we can go to Monument Valley.'

'Excellent,' said Michael. 'Cowboy country!'

The referee blew his whistle and the boys jogged back on. Hank cleared away the beer cans. He shouldn't have lied. Damian wasn't some sports-mad macho man. He wasn't married, either.

As the second half got under way, Frankie's mind still wasn't on the ball. He kept looking over at the clubhouse, just in case she had turned up. It had been the same for Hank twenty years earlier. Sometimes he had looked over during a match and Damian had been there: a blond boy in a brown cardigan. He came again and again, even though the lads in the team gave him a hard time. Hank's had been the loudest, rudest voice of all, but the boy kept coming back.

It had been the last match of the football season and the sun had shone. Hank was standing by the bar with the P.E. students. They were chanting, drinking beer and feeling the chill from the rims of the glasses against their sun-reddened noses. Damian brushed past them carrying two lagers. He tripped over one of the players' kit bags and stumbled for a few steps, the handle wrapped around his ankle, spilling beer on table-tops. There was a cheer from the football team. All of them except Hank. Now he wanted to protect the boy, tell the others to lay off him. Into his mind came a dazzling image. He was carrying Damian in his arms, a bleeding fawn. It made him more terrified than he had ever been. The juke-box played: *Cheer up sleepy Jean. Oh what can it mean.* The boy looked up at him. Looked right into his Judas eyes and smiled.

Hank left the bar and walked slowly and jerkily to the bus stop. He never could tread on the cracks between paving stones. 'Wait!' said a voice behind him. He wished with all his heart that it wouldn't be Damian, but he turned and saw the blond head bobbing in and out of the streetlamp beams. He fell into step with Hank, swaying left to right, missing each of the black lines. Damian said: 'I had a dream about you the other night,' and shivering twinges made Hank lose his concentration and his measured stride. He couldn't think of anything to say. He didn't even know this boy. It wasn't what he wanted for himself. Not if he stepped back and took a general view, but standing there by the cluttered window of a shoe shop, he had never desired anything so much. Damian flicked his hair away from his face. Hank wanted to smooth the last few golden strands that caught the light. 'It's not so bad, you know,' he whispered to Hank. As he ran for his bus, Damian turned and shouted: 'I'm getting out of the city next week.' The words pounded out of him with every wide stride. 'Come along if you like.'

As the Christian Brothers scored a crafty equaliser, Hank remembered their journey to the west coast. At eight in the evening, they had sat in the car on the top of a hill above Dingle Bay and eaten sandwiches. Damian took his hand and held it. Hank didn't pull it back or pretend to scratch his nose. He had done that once in the pictures with a girl called Veronica. Damian's hand was not clammy like hers had been. His palm had a slight roughness to it, like the finest grain of glasspaper, but the back was soft and downy. Beneath the skin was the busy network that made their hands warm and real and gently pulsing. Hank felt the pulse come up his arm and head in a roundabout way to his heart. The two hands stayed together, moving now and then to cool between the palms. Two hearts were beating around two bodies. Chugging in the neck. Crunching in the ears like a passing parade on gravel. Theirs was an Indian blood-brother line. No need for a cut. Flowing from one to the other. That was all they needed for the day. Enough to be going along with. They silently watched a tangerine sun that peeled itself and spilled its juices into the pale sky.

Damian had kissed men before. He knew what to expect. Not Hank. He had memories of Yardley lips like a peach with a bite taken out of it. He wasn't one for peaches. The girl at the college party had been pissed on Pernod and tasted of aniseed all over. Hank had gone upstairs with her to a coat-covered bed. It had been nothing more than a release of pressure. All kinds of pressure, but mostly the kind that came from the lads at the bottom of the stairs. 'Did ya fuck her, then?' The girl didn't come down after him. Not even for 'Hi Ho Silver Lining'. Someone had found her later, asleep under a bomber jacket.

On the third morning, Damian had walked to the beach from the youth hostel. When Hank parked the car, he was wading out of the sea. Gasping and hugging a towel to his chest. 'Jesus, you're a brave man,' said Hank.

'I know. I'm scared of nothing, me.'

Hank didn't reply. He was scared of the heartbeat. Not even hand-holding now, their blood-line went through the thin, salty air. He sat with Damian and they buried their feet, patting down the sand on top. Breaking the surface with big toes. It was Hank who touched first. He caught a fly that was circling the blond hairs on Damian's knee. Damian's hand came to rest on his, with the captive fly buzzing against Hank's palm. Damian eclipsed the sun with his golden head. The fly was set free. He took Hank's head in his hands. He had not shaved that morning and Hank felt the softness and the jangle of the stubble on his mouth. Not like a peach at all. Like some other fruit. Something exotic, like lychee. Rough on the outside but the flesh beneath was sweeter and better than any other he had tasted. That kiss and the feeling of Damian's goose-pimpled skin warming and softening against his own. It was like all the things he tasted that summer, each one more potent than the last. For those few weeks, Hank was the first man on the moon. Bouncing around as light as air and feeling like a hero. All alone with his companion on the lunar surface of the Galway coast. Nobody to tell him he looked stupid or out of place. The world he feared was far away. A little blob in the sky full of people sitting watching men just like him on their television sets. They had discovered the West.

As they drove back east to Dublin, Hank's feet turned to lead again and the rest of his body to dough. Ugly and cumbersome. Damian slid back into city life. To his graphic design course and his friends who talked about films and politics. Hank was a man from the moon and he didn't speak the same language. He was doing business management and talked about football. It didn't matter when they touched, but the touching fitted less and less comfortably into the days and months that followed. Then Damian moved to London and bought a jeep with smoked windows. He joined a group who dressed up as nuns on Saturday nights. Damian was called Sister Concepta of the Drawing Boards. He sent Hank a photograph of himself in his habit. Now he was living in Los Angeles with his partner, Carl. Just a few days' drive from the desert and twenty years away from Galway.

As the final whistle blew, high above the football pitch, a plane cut through the sky like a silver bullet.

ʃ

That's All She Wrote

'A one, two, three, four!' Michael pressed the button and the saxophone played. Frankie had his legs parted and his head down. He swayed from side to side. The backing singers joined in. *Return to sender. Return to sender.* Frankie's movements became bolder, one leg bending and straightening like he was using a foot pump. His head slowly lifted, then his eyes, until he was looking straight ahead. He lifted the microphone up to his lips.

> *I gave a letter to the postman*
> *He put it in his sack.*

It went quiet. Frankie opened his mouth to sing the next line. Michael was waving his arms around. 'You stopped moving, Frankie. The audience will think you've forgotten what to do. You've got to get them going. You're not in the garage now, you know. You're on stage.'

'Well, I'm only in the pub. It's hard to get the feeling this early.' Frankie rolled his head round and clasped his right shoulder.

Hank got up from his chair in the corner. 'How about if I pour us all a pint?' he said.

'No way, Hank. He's in training now. Now Frankie, imagine you are in Vegas and get those hips moving.' He started the song again.

> *I gave a letter to the postman. He put it in his sack.*
> *Bright and early next morning he brought my letter back.*
> *She wrote upon it . . .*

'No, that's not your bit.' Michael stopped the tape again. 'It's the singers that do that bit. You just come in with "Return to sender" or it will sound silly.'

'Otherwise, it was magic, Frankie,' said Hank. He looked sideways at Michael, who was rewinding the tape. 'How about clicking your fingers there, you know, when they do "she wrote upon it".'

'Yeah?' Frankie mouthed the lyrics: '*He brought my letter back* . . .click! . . .That's good. I never know what to do with my hands. They tend to flap about a bit.'

'What did Elvis do with his hands?' said Michael, his finger hovering over the play button again.

'Well, his flapped about too, but it looked sharp when he did it.' Frankie clicked the mike into the stand. 'Mind you, Elvis did have a guitar with him most of the time. He kind of grabbed on to it while he sang.'

'Why don't you use the one on the wall up by Roy Rogers? Wait till I get it.' Hank went into the bar.

'I can't play.'

'Neither could Elvis,' said Michael. 'You know that video you lent me? Every time he sings a song, he just keeps holding on to the same bloody chord. Honest injun! I thought it stuck out a mile.'

'Here.' Hank came back in, running a bar towel over the top of the guitar. 'Try this for size.' Frankie held the guitar against his belt and swung his hips to one side. Michael stretched out his arms in front of him. 'Brilliant! That looks brilliant. Now, let's try a few moves. Don't worry about trying to play it. He sure as hell never did.' Frankie slid his left hand up and down the neck of the guitar. The strings squeaked. He pulled the neck forward and pointed it towards Hank and Michael, like a rifle, tucking his trigger hand under its curvy body. 'He sort of held it like this sometimes, like he was out to kill. In fact, in the song "King Creole" there's this line about him holding his guitar like a tommy-gun.' Michael walked up to the stage, so that he was level with Frankie's knees, and scratched his chin. 'Aggression,' he said under his breath, then out loud. 'Aggression, that's what made Elvis great.' He stared at a patch of dust on the guitar. 'To him, it was a gun. He was an outlaw. Yes. An outlaw! Try and focus on that, Frankie, and I think you'll really have something.' Michael nodded. He didn't notice that Frankie and Hank were having a laugh at him. 'Let's have another stab at it, shall we?' He pressed the button on the machine and the saxophones started up again. 'Don't forget the anger, now.'

Return to sender. Return to sender. The window of the back room was pulled open from the outside. Carmel was standing on tiptoe peeping in. She watched Frankie singing the opening lines, holding on to the neck of the guitar. Instead of clicking his fingers, he patted the body of the guitar, making a satisfying thud. Hank gave him the thumbs-up sign and turned to wave at Carmel. She put a finger to her lips. *Return to sender. Address unknown.*

Standing on a slimline tonic crate, Carmel remembered all the letters that she wrote to her father after he left. The first time she had gone against her mother's wishes. They were addressed to Mr Paul Macnamara (Baker) and care of a different post office. She had sent away for a leaflet about all the post offices in Ireland. The money she had saved from her Saturday job only got her as far as the G's. Gort, County Galway. Then all the letters started coming back to her, just like in the song. Wherever her father was, it sure as hell didn't begin with the letters A to G.

I write I'm sorry, but my letter keeps coming back.

Frankie was going great. He had that smouldering look in his eye. Carmel was excited. If she was the judge, she'd give him all nines. She liked the way he moved, the awkwardness of it. He was looking out for Michael's approval. He saw her at the window and grinned as the guitar bounced against his pelvis, flashing light up into her eyes. His whole body felt looser and he wasn't embarrassed by the way he moved around the stage. He lifted his right arm and brought it down against the strings. 'Thwaang!' One of the strings snapped and Hank sprung out of his chair. 'Jesus!' shouted Michael, switching off the tape. 'Nice one, Frankie!' They laughed hysterically. Frankie walked over to the window, wiping his eyes. 'Hiya, Carmel, shall I let you in the front?'

'No, I was only popping out to the shop. You sounded so good I thought I'd come over and tell you.'

'It's a bit of a mess, still, but I'm getting the hang of it.'

They could hear the birds in the field next door and the cars going by on the road. Michael soon wiped them out with his shuffling and finger-tapping. Carmel looked over Frankie's shoulder. 'He's all coiled up like a spring over there. He's turning into that fella who used to manage Elvis.'

'Colonel Tom?'

'Yeah! He's Colonel Mike. Aren't you, Michael?'

'What was that, love?' Michael was rewinding the tape again.

'You're a right little slave-driver, aren't you?'

'You've been talking to my kids, then? Come on, Frankie, from the top!'

Carmel mimed cracking a whip and winked at Frankie. 'See you later,' she said, then jumped down from her plastic perch. As she walked around the side of the pub, she could hear Michael saying: 'How about throwing the microphone from one hand to the other?' and Frankie saying: 'Nah, you wouldn't be able to hear me if I did that. Anyway, knowing me I'd drop it.'

The saxophones started again.

The Rottweiler

Frankie sang 'Return To Sender' more times than he could count. He was pissed off with Elvis for recording it. He was pissed off with the man who invented the postal service. Everyone was pissed off with Frankie, because the song had been coming at them from out of the pub window so often that none of them could get it out of their brains. Even Eileen found herself singing it once while she was peeling some potatoes. The whole village was counting down. 'Zero minus twelve,' said Michael in the mornings. 'Zero minus eleven.' Frankie felt like he was going to be shot out of a cannon. The heats in Kilkenny were for the two counties and were bound to be packed. Hank had booked a minibus so that the lads from the Palace could see his moment of glory. Frankie wished they weren't coming. He dreamed about forgetting his words and standing on stage in his underpants.

Carmel dreamed about country living. Dublin was a million miles away and full of busy people with no time to chat. She was walking up the hill, feeling the strain in her calf muscles, when she saw Betty's car stopping to let someone out. 'Christ, it's the Rottweiler,' she said as she recognised Eileen Shaw. Age had made Eileen thinner and she seemed taller. Other old ladies shrank. As Betty pulled away, she squeaked open the gate of the cemetery and disappeared silently around the side of the church. Carmel had always thought Eileen could have made money out of haunting places. Frankie's dad was so different. He made sweets come out of your ears.

The birds were screeching, fighting each other for branch space to watch the setting sun. Eileen came three times a week to stand in the cold and remember her Joe who never lost his broad shoulders or his rich voice or his good looks because he was not left to decay above the ground like so many of his contemporaries. They moved around the village now like little old men, and Eileen found a strange comfort in watching them and thinking that Joe had the last laugh. Her mother was buried a few yards away, as well as the three babies that she and Joe lost before Frankie was born. There were more of Eileen's loved ones on that mossy hill than there were in the village. She passed Joe and stopped for a while at the new grave which she knew to hold Mary Macnamara. All on its own in a corner. No husband to lie by her in life or in death. Eileen brushed away fallen leaves and stood with her hands clasped in front of her as the chill wind whipped around the side of the grey stone church and puffed up her hair. Mary Macnamara had been a good friend, once. The two of them had been as close as Frankie and Carmel were, but Joe disliked her when she started drinking a little too much. Didn't want her coming around. He never could stand a woman who drank. Joe could be intolerant at times.

Eileen noticed Carmel in her leather jacket and jeans, zigzagging up the steep hill. At her age, she could have walked all the way to Enniscorthy. She moved over to Joe's grave as Carmel came up to the gate and manipulated the rusting catch. Carmel was certainly the pick of the Macnamaras. Her two sisters were on the stout side. They took after their father. She had her mother's long limbs and dark hair, but those green eyes must have come from way back. The same place she got her loud mouth. Joe always said it was her mother's fault. She had no control. 'Hello, Mrs Shaw.' Carmel smiled as she stumbled over the long, wheaty grass by the gate. 'You're looking well.'

Carmel hadn't planned to visit the graveyard. Her mother's death had accentuated the gap between them. Eileen Shaw had seen her, though, and she couldn't walk by such a holy woman and have her thinking that she didn't love her mother. Carmel hated silences, even where they were expected. 'Isn't it exciting about the Elvis competition, Mrs Shaw?' she said. 'Frankie is only brilliant. Will you be going?'

Eileen shrugged her shoulders. 'He wouldn't want me there. He knows how I feel about that rock and roll stuff. The racket in our house over the last few days would wake the dead. I don't know how anyone could put up with it. He's never this loud usually. It's Michael and those men at the pub who are getting him all worked up.' She pressed her lips together so hard they disappeared completely.

Carmel silently counted to ten. 'It's just until the competition. You should hear him sing up at the pub some night.'

'A public house is no place for a lady.' She went cold as soon as she said it. How could she, standing next to the grave of Mary Macnamara, looking into the face of her little girl. Who in the world knew why that poor woman turned to drink for so many years and shut herself away up at that cottage? Eileen wanted to say she was sorry, but the silence continued. They turned away from each other and tidied their graves up with throbbing hearts. Eileen stood when she heard a car pass by the gate. 'I thought it was Betty,' she said. Carmel managed a flattened smile. 'I could walk home in five minutes, but it's little Liam. He's mad about his Auntie Eileen, bless him.' There was a genuine smile on her face. 'You know I look at him and I can see you and my Frank at his age. It seems like only yesterday that you were all over the lounge floor with your colouring books and what not.' Carmel leaned back on one hand. 'Look at you now. All grown up and living the life of Riley. How's that young man you married? He must be thinking you've gone to seed down here.'

'He's fine. Well, I'd better be going. I still have some work to do before it gets too late.' Carmel picked her way through the graves to the gate. She looked back at Eileen, then broke into a childish gallop down the hill, stretching her arms out to the side, dipping and weaving and shedding the smell of death.

'You'll learn, young lady,' mumbled Eileen as Carmel spun in the cider-coloured light. She felt older than her sixty-eight years. Years that had diluted her eyes from dark brown to the colour of puddle water and had taken the shine from her tight-permed hair. She looked down at the village, mapping the events of her lifetime against the same slowly changing backdrop. 'I had to learn,' she hissed. 'Learn the hard way.'

Frankie's mother had been on the back of a motorcycle. Lain half naked on the beach. Cut her hair and rouged her lips and didn't listen to her mother. She preferred to hear Joe say: 'My Eileen's a little live wire.' Loved the way he kissed the nape of her neck. She missed him now. Missed him in a way that old ladies aren't supposed to. Eileen had whistled in the chapel. Danced on the hard wooden floor and heard her steps crack around the statues and up against the duck-egg-blue paint. She and Joe were going to buy a tinker's cart and travel the land and let their children run wild. The priest gave them prayers to say together. Prayers that grew dusty in the bottoms of drawers while they sang and made love and thought of nice things. Prayers that stayed there until their first child was born dead. Joe carried on as normal, but with every little wooden coffin she tried to think less about the nice things in life. That way, they might just happen. Her reward was a son who lived. Remembering what she lost gave her acid indigestion. She was pulling a chalky tablet from her handbag when Betty's car drew up at the gate.

The Young Ones

Saturday came and the minibus gleamed on the forecourt of the garage. Frankie was in pieces. He was feeling guilty because he had told Michael to travel up with the rest of the crowd, rather than follow him around with last-minute suggestions. Carmel was taking him in her car. She had to be in Kilkenny anyway, to deliver some of her work. The sun sparkled the raindrops on the windscreen. Carmel was wearing petal-shaped sunglasses with tortoiseshell rims. She looked like a fifties film star. Frankie felt sick. He was shaking. The side of his face was frozen and the pain went right down his neck to where it joined his shoulders. He leaned back and flipped the sun visor down with his fingertips. Dried roses scattered all over the front of the car. 'God, sorry, I made such a mess.' He gathered the crisp stems together. Carmel smiled. 'Not to worry. Everyone does that.' He pressed the flowers back under the mirrored visor. 'Frankie, there are sunnies in the glove compartment. Help yourself to a pair.' They were round and small, like two old pennies on wire, but he put them on. She was playing a Cat Stevens tape.

'What do you reckon? From Elvis to John Lennon in one easy step.' He carried on in a Liverpool accent. 'So, like, why are there flowers all over the car?'

'Ah, you know me, dead camp. I put some aromatic oil on them and they drown out the smell of the fags. Be a sport, Frankie, and get one out of my bag, will you.' She pointed over her shoulder. He clipped open his seat belt and stretched over. The back of the car was littered with old chocolate-button wrappers, screwed up and torn. A few buttons had melted into the metal floor, dotting it with brown.

'Three guesses as to your favourite sweets.' He pulled a packet of Silk Cut from her bag.

'I know, I know. I keep meaning to clear them all out, but I hate littering up the roads, so they either go in my pockets or back there. You can tell when I've had a bad week.'

'Bloody awful, by the look of it.' He smiled at her as she lit a match. For a moment, there was a dark look on her face and the cigarette shook in her lips. His sick feeling returned. 'Sorry,' he said. 'I wasn't getting at you or anything. God, there are days when I could eat a thousand packets of chocolate buttons.'

'It's all right, I'm fine.' They passed a road sign. 'Well, only two and a half miles to Kilkenny. How do you feel, Elvis?'

'Like flying to the moon.'

There was a long silence between them as the tape finished. Frankie stared at the crescent of mist on each side of the windscreen. Carmel wound the window down and threw out the cigarette end. 'Hey, Frankie.' She beamed. 'Why don't you let me be your backing singer? I have a fabulous voice.'

'Ah, well now, you'd have to audition.' He turned towards her, smiling. 'How are you on Elvis numbers?'

'I can do "Your Teddy Bear". Billy's mates used to do it down the pub. They'd sing the verse and we'd have to sing "half a lager, half a lager" behind them.' She tutted. 'Second thoughts, let's not do that.'

'Carmel . . . thanks for taking me. I would have killed Michael by now.'

'Oh, do you think I'm not serious about the singing, then?' She pinched his arm. 'I see you as my big chance for stardom. Let's do "The Young Ones".'

'That was Cliff Richard.'

'Well, he was the English Elvis, wasn't he? Ah, go on.'

'All right.' He started to sing and she accompanied him. *The young ones . . . oooh . . . Darling we're the young ones . . . oooh.*

Behind the hall, there was a line of cars. They parked next to a pink one which had 'Love me tender. Dial for an Elvis-o-gram' on the side.

'Hey. You're up against professional Elvises. Or should it be Elvii?'

'What?'

'The plural of Elvis.'

At the side of the building, there was a sign saying 'Artists this way'. The rain had smudged the black lettering and dislodged some of the yellow sticky tape. People were milling about. Contestants from an earlier heat carrying suit bags and props. The sky was darkening again. They were met by a man in a striped blazer. 'How do you do. John Reed. And you are?' John Reed looked up from a clipboard. His glasses were thick and black-framed, and his eyes, magnified behind them, looked half-crazed. Frankie was reluctant to say who he was.

'Shaw. Frankie Shaw.'

Mr Reed's index finger moved up and down the list. 'Ah, there you are.' He looked up and smiled. Frankie stepped back a little. 'You're in dressing room number ten. It's through the door and on your right. Anything else you want to know, I'll be right here.'

'I'll see you later, then,' said Carmel. 'Now are you sure you don't want me to stay with you till the show?'

'Yes. Honestly, I'll be better off by myself.' They stood looking at each other. Soft rain frizzed her hair as she stood with her hands in her pockets. She stepped forward and slapped her hand on his shoulder. 'Good luck, Frankie, you'll be brilliant.' She kissed him on the cheek and walked back to her car. Coming towards her was an elderly man in a black teddy-boy suit with leopardskin lapels. His hair was neatly arranged to hide his baldness which glowed underneath. Behind him, a woman in a hairnet was shouting: 'Keep your trouser legs off the ground or you'll get dirt on them.' Carmel passed them, then turned and grinned, pointing at the couple and making a thumbs-up sign to Frankie. He waved back, his hand lifting his suit bag.

Dressing room ten smelled of cigarettes. It was small, but contained a mirror with lights around it that made Frankie's heart lift. 'Show business,' he said under his breath. There was a hook on the wall, taken up by a suit bag. Frankie gently unzipped the bag and peeked in. An ornate belt buckle studded with diamonds formed the letters of the name Elvis. The door opened and a young man walked in. He was very good-looking, with dark, glossy hair that fell perfectly into a Brylcreemed quiff. He wore no shirt and his chest was tanned, muscular and hairless. Frankie pushed the buckle back in the bag and zipped it up smartly. 'Sorry,' he stuttered, 'I was curious.'

'That's all right,' said the other man, smiling. He had perfect teeth. He stretched out his hand. 'Glad to know you,' he purred in a light American drawl.

'Frankie Shaw. I'm not sure what the hell I'm letting myself in for.' He gave a nervous laugh as his roommate pulled up a chair and sat on it backwards like they do in westerns. 'Have you ever done anything like this before, er . . .'

'Elvis,' the man said, lifting himself to pull a Zippo lighter from the pocket of his jeans.

'What? You mean you're actually called Elvis, or do you use it as a stage name? I mean, do you want me to call you Elvis?'

'Sure thing. That's my name. Official. ' He pulled a wallet from out of his back pocket and handed Frankie a pink calling card.

'Elvis O'Donovan,' Frankie read aloud. 'Parties. Singing telegrams . . . Oh, right, that's your car outside. The pink one.'

Elvis broke into a warm grin. 'My girlfriend painted it.'

Frankie lifted his suit bag and hung it on a water pipe running along the wall. He let out a big breath. 'I'm relieved, Elvis. I mean, I thought at first that you thought you were Elvis. I mean the real one.'

Elvis got up and stubbed out his cigarette. 'No, man. There was only one Elvis Aaron Presley . . . and he's supposed to be working in a kebab shop in Dublin.' Elvis opened a case and took out a big, shiny guitar with swirling mother-of-pearl inlays. He brushed his hand over the metal strings. It sounded like a tense moment in a horror film. He tried each string, one by one, teasing the keys at the top of the neck, until they all came together in a rich chord. It made Frankie shiver. 'What are you singing tonight?' he asked. He tried to put his feet up on the other chair, but his heel slipped and he sat bolt upright.

'"Devil In Disguise". Gets the ladies going, that one.' Elvis smiled at himself in the mirror as he spoke, then bent over his guitar again.

'Oh, I was going to do that one at first. Good thing I changed my mind.' Frankie looked at himself in the mirror and curled his lip. 'Funny if we had all turned up with the same song.'

'Do you want some make-up?' Elvis was emptying a

black sponge bag and laying out its contents in a neat
little row on the table. He took a circular sponge out of
a plastic wallet and dabbed it in a tin of beige pancake
make-up. When he rubbed the sponge around his face, it
left a thick line of brown, like a marker pen, over his cheeks.
He kept on until the colour was even and his eyebrows and
hairline were clogged. Frankie buttoned up the lumberjack
shirt halfway to show his white T-shirt underneath. Elvis
was drawing a line under his eyes with a kohl pencil. His
mouth contorted with each movement until he put the
pencil down and leaned back. He looked like an Indian
film star. 'Help yourself,' he said. 'You'll look awful pale
without it.'

He went out of the door as Frankie sat down. 'Good
evening, ladies and gentlemen, my name is Elvis Presley,'
he said as he smeared the brown sponge over his face. His
hands looked ghostly against the artificial tan on his cheeks
and his mouth was so dry that it was hard for him to talk
to himself, let alone sing a song. There was a jug of water
and a couple of glasses and he drank over half of it in one
go. Elvis came in, shaking his hands. 'No bloody towels,' he
said, and he wiped off the last of the moisture on the seat
of his jeans.

'Are there many others out there?' Frankie's voice sounded
like he was being strangled.

'Five or six.' Elvis unzipped the suit bag. 'But they look
awful sad. One is about sixty.'

'There must be more than that with ten dressing rooms.'

Elvis stepped into the white jump suit. 'Here's a little
lesson for you, Frankie. In places like this, things are
never that straightforward. I could only see four dressing
rooms and they were numbered one, six, ten and eleven.
God knows why. Lotto numbers or something.'

'Have you been doing the act for long, Elvis?'

'Couple of years.' His voice was more American with the

outfit on. He was getting into the part. His hips were slinkier. They swayed from side to side. Frankie was mesmerised.

'Do you make much money? I mean, if you don't mind me asking?'

'It isn't bad when I can get the work, but it's not something you can rely on. I'm a plumber, really. The Elvis stuff is just an extra. Comes in handy. I'm getting married next year and we're looking to get a house together.'

'Oh, that's nice.'

Elvis O'Donovan was a prince. Frankie wanted him to win. There was a knock on the door and John Reed put his head round. 'Only a few minutes to go, gentlemen. Do you have your backing tapes for me?'

Frankie dropped the tape twice before handing it to him. 'Side one. It's at the right place.'

'And you, Mr O'Donovan?'

'I have a guitar, thanks, and the stage hand is setting up the amp.' There was a click as Elvis fastened the diamond belt buckle.

'You are number four, Mr Shaw, and you are number five, Mr O'Donovan. There's a couple of bands on first. You will all be introduced and the lights will go up at the end for your bows, or boos maybe.' He chuckled. 'Just my little joke. Good luck, gentlemen.' The door closed again.

'Don't forget your lips, man.' Elvis presented Frankie with a coral lipstick.

'Jesus, I'm not wearing that. My mother doesn't approve of women who do.' He handed it back.

'Is she here, then?'

'No.'

'Well then . . .' Elvis patted the pale orange on to his lips, making them glow in the harsh lighting. Frankie followed suit, saying 'I am Elvis Presley' under his breath. He couldn't look at himself. The make-up was sitting on his face like a mask. Like an auntie at a wedding. He thought about

Elvis; the real Elvis. He was standing on a porch singing 'Love Me Tender', looking like he had just come out of the fields. A million miles away from all this cheesey diamante stuff. Michael was right, it had to come from the inside. Make-up would not help at all. The other Elvis had no problems with his reflection. He was giving himself those 'over-the-shoulder smoulder' looks. The kind of eye contact that was strongly discouraged by the nuns. He bit his lips again and again, pretty hard by the look of it, so he could get that soft, full mouth that Presley had. Frankie sat and gripped his stomach and watched as Elvis sang to the mirror, moving his hips from side to side as he went over the first verse of 'Devil In Disguise'. He shook his hands in front of him and breathed in and out very loudly. Frankie felt his bowels lurch and he ran out into the cold corridor.

A Hot Night in Memphis

'This is hell.' His voice boomed around the thin walls of the toilet cubicle. There was nothing left in him. Nothing at all, but he couldn't get up, just in case. He could hear the thudding of the band and the audience clapping. They weren't quite in time with the music. It sounded spooky. Frankie leaned forward and rested his elbows on his shuddering knees. His face was damp with brown pancake perspiration. His T-shirt was sticking to his back. He had never felt less like Elvis Presley in his life. He closed his eyes tightly and tried to imagine that he was in some great theatre in America and the warm-up artist was playing cool blues. It was the late fifties. A hot, sticky summer's night. He was the greatest star the world had ever seen and every member of that audience knew it. They were hanging out for him, eager to catch sight of him through the curtains at the side of the stage. He stood and did up his jeans, walking on jelly legs to the hand-basin.

Backstage, they could hear the whispers and creaks of the audience and the crackle of packets and wrappers. The band were putting their instruments into cases. His stomach was still bubbling and the cheeks of his bottom were clenched tightly together. An Enya tape was playing. The other Elvises were standing by, coughing and shuffling. There were six in all, including a boy of about twelve whose hair had been gelled and smoothed so perfectly it looked like record vinyl. Something slipped out, silent but deadly. Frankie stepped to the side and tucked himself into a dark corner. A muscle was pulling in his cheek, twitching. He gingerly placed his palm on the seat of his jeans. They were warm but dry. The fat man from the carpark let out a smoker's cough. He was wearing a purple jacket now, with black lapels. I bet he sings 'Hound Dog', thought Frankie. Out came another one. A blowtorch, scalding the pile of lights and cables behind him. Frankie stayed where he was. Another move would have made it obvious. John Reed shuffled past, smiling at the contestants. There was a half-hearted ripple of applause as he reached the centre of the stage and blew into the microphone.

'Hello there, ladies and gentlemen. I hope you are all enjoying the entertainment we have for you tonight.' Frankie could see only his right arm. It was gripping the microphone stand. The stripes on his blazer strobed under the lights. The audience were hidden by blackness. Lurking in a cave. 'Let's have an extra round of applause for Talisman.' The stripy arm pointed to the off-stage area. 'Thanks, boys.' John Reed's voice was drowned by clapping. 'Arsehole!' said the last of the musicians as he pushed his way past Elvis O'Donovan. Frankie laughed and farted again.

'And now, ladies and gentlemen. It's time to put on those blue suede shoes. The moment you've all been waiting for. A tribute to the King of Rock and Roll. Now, as you know, we have a fine panel of judges here tonight, but they all have ears . . .'

'Bleedin' hope so,' said a large Elvis in black leather.

'. . . and they will be listening out for your reaction.' There was a spontaneous round of applause, peppered with cheers and whistles. Frankie thought about Michael and the lads from the Palace. What if he finished his song and nobody clapped? What if he never made it through the song? What if he had to stop halfway and run to the toilet again? John Reed introduced the first Elvis as 'The Carpet King of Kilkenny' and the music began. Frankie closed his eyes, but thought he might faint, so he opened them and held on to a rope. Sure enough, the big guy was singing 'Hound Dog'. His voice had a gravelly, Lieutenant Columbo sound to it. Not at all like Elvis, but the audience were clapping away to it. Frankie's jeans felt tight. His stomach was swollen and the belt was cutting into him. He was like a bloated sheep. He wanted to puncture himself and let out all the gas before it was too late. He had to go out on that stage and dance. He couldn't just stand there with a rock-solid backside. God help the fella on after him. He looked on to the stage. It was the instrumental break and the singers on the backing tape were going 'aaaaahh'. The Carpet King was doing the twist and his leather tie was swinging like a pendulum in the opposite direction to his hips, bouncing every now and then off his stomach. Above him, the lights were shining blue and orange.

Frankie looked at the door which led to the dressing rooms. The exit sign was glowing; drawing him to it as another Elvis started his act, shining in a gold jacket. He was so tired, he could have lain down and slept on the wooden floorboards. He closed his eyes and tried to think of Elvis, but he couldn't picture him. He was a blob in his mind. A sad, fat blob. The little boy was on now, singing 'Heartbreak Hotel', leaning the microphone to one side and spreading his legs. Frankie was next. He couldn't remember the first line of 'Return To Sender' and his throat was closing up again.

Suddenly, a voice said, 'Frankie Shaw.' He felt a hand on his shoulder. It was Elvis O'Donovan. 'Good luck, man,' he said, and pushed him between the shoulder blades. A freezing plunge-pool of sweat rose up his body, then evaporated. He stepped into the light and moved to the centre of the stage. Blue, orange, blue, orange, farting with each step. He stopped by the microphone and went into his opening position, his head down and his whole body buzzing like the stage was electric. Just before the music started, something fluttered down from the rafters and landed between his feet. A spray of sequins. They shot tiny beams of coloured light up into his face. None of the other contestants had worn sequins and yet there they were. As the saxophones started and Frankie's leg began to move in time with it, he imagined that the sequins had come down from rock and roll heaven and fallen through the roof.

Return to sender.
Return to sender.

Frankie opened his mouth and looked up. The light hit him in the face. The hot lemon light of sunbathing, pouring like syrup all over him. He sang the first line and the voice he heard was thin and shaky. It was better by the second line and his face felt warm. By the second verse, he had got that Elvis feeling, the one he got standing in the back room of the pub with Carmel smiling through the window. He shuffled his feet and pulled the microphone stand from side to side, kicking the magic sequins all over the stage. The audience were with him now, clapping on the beat, boxing his ears and clattering around his ribcage as he stood there and swayed. His stomach felt fine. For four whole minutes, Frankie Shaw stood on a stage in Memphis, Tennessee and it felt like home.

It was over and the shock was overwhelming. Frankie retched into a sand-filled bucket backstage as a man with a ponytail set up the amplifier for Elvis O'Donovan's act. He was sure he could still hear Michael and Hank yelling their approval at him. The other Elvises were very complimentary, all asking him how long he had been performing. Elvis O'Donovan had been the first to congratulate him, shaking him by the shoulders and saying, 'Deadly. God! that was deadly, man!' His face was dry and powdery and there was not a hint of nerves in the air that surrounded him. Frankie still wanted him to win. The finals would be for those who took it seriously. He could go home to the Palace and be the local hero and tell his mother it was nothing and know that he would never, ever have to feel that scared again.

Elvis O'Donovan cracked his knuckles as John Reed started his announcements. The amplifier was humming and the mother-of-pearl guitar gleamed centre stage. 'Well,' grinned Frankie. 'This is it, Elvis. All the best.' They turned and looked into the corridor of light as John Reed raised his hands in theatrical applause and came towards them. In the ten seconds or so that followed, Elvis O'Donovan underwent a change that only Frankie could see. His upper lip beaded with moisture, lifting the thick make-up into beige globules. His face went slightly green. The colour that faces go on knackered old tellies. He walked on to the stage and was met by a tidal wave of applause. At that distance, he must have looked devastating. Slim in the figure-hugging suit. He stepped up to the microphone and grasped his guitar, flipping the strap over his head. It hung straight, the neck following the line of his belt. He closed his hand around it and tilted his pelvis, then hit the first chord. They screamed; all the women and a couple of the men. Out came a voice like Elvis, though a little flat around the edges. The guitar's bass strings bounced out of the amplifier, round and heavy as medicine balls. The tinny top notes tangled like coiled wire in all directions. In between, Elvis sang the first verse, then the chorus . . . then the first verse again. An easy enough mistake, but one that made Frankie's stomach turn over. The crowd didn't notice, but Elvis did. He should have been singing: *I thought that I was in heaven,* and he was singing: *You fooled me with your kisses* for the second time. The power fizzled out of him as he tried to find a way out of the mess. His voice trembled and the guitar produced a few chords that didn't quite fit and Frankie's heart broke for him. When he came off-stage, still gripping his guitar, the lead dangling like a dog's tail behind him, he patted Frankie on the shoulder and said: 'Ah, shite!' Frankie knew what was next and didn't know whether to laugh or cry. When he was called on for his winner's encore, he did a bit of both.

In a hot little room to the side of the hall, a girl handed round glasses of warm white wine. They had photographs taken and Frankie was presented with a certificate and an enormous bottle of champagne. Carmel stood next to him and he held on to the sleeve of her jumper. Michael and Hank waited by the door like expectant fathers, grinning all over their faces. Frankie and Elvis shook hands. 'Sorry you didn't win, Elvis. You've a great act.'

'When he remembers it,' said his girlfriend. She held a single red rose in her hand, its stem wrapped in kitchen foil. Her other hand rubbed the back of his shirt.

'Fair play to you, Frankie.' Elvis gave her a squeeze. 'You were fantastic. I'll be putting a bet on you in the finals. We'll be watching.' Even with the trophy in his hand, Frankie was jealous of Elvis O'Donovan. He was jealous of the love he saw between him and his girlfriend. If only.

Frankie waved as the pink car pulled away.

Moonlight and Champagne

They were silent after the excitement. Frankie bought chips and ate them from a greaseproof envelope as Carmel flicked cigarette ash out of the little triangular window by the steering wheel. He reached for the bottle of champagne they gave him, undid the wire cap, opened the window and aimed the cork out. Carmel turned a corner just as he eased it from the bottle-neck. It hit the interior light and flew into the back seat, landing among the chocolate-button wrappers.

'Frankie, what the hell are you doing?'

'Celebrating.'

'I thought that was for your mother.' Carmel turned and looked at Frankie's face, blotched with the shadows of rain on the windscreen. He swigged the champagne, choking on the gas. She took the bottle. 'Congratulations,' she said. They passed it to and fro.

Frankie pulled the backing tape out of his jacket pocket and put it in the cassette player. 'Viva Las Vegas' was just starting and they sang, although Carmel only knew the chorus. She looked out through the windscreen and listened to Frankie and the fields and hedgerows melted away. They were driving through the desert and the moonlight was dusting the rocks and cacti with silver. He sang about the *neon flashing and the one-armed bandits crashing all those hopes down the drain*. Carmel wanted to drive for ever, until the horizon was lit by the glow of Sunset Strip. With Frankie, she believed that it was possible. She could even believe that he was Elvis Presley. That's why he had won the competition. He had them all fooled. Everyone but himself. He was singing about Las Vegas and heading back to the other Caesar's Palace where he felt safe. It was a good night for driving, though, and for believing in things. He sang: *Gonna keep on running, gonna have me some fun if it costs me my very last dime*, and Carmel leaned out of the window and shouted 'Yahoo' into the night. The world was wonderful. They drove into a ditch.

It was no good, even when Frankie put his shoulder right up against the back of the car and pushed until his shoes dug deep into the mud. Carmel was sitting half on, half off the bonnet. She wrapped her coat around her, a hand in each pocket. 'Forget it,' she said, 'you'll only wear yourself out.'

'What do you want to do, then?' Frankie sat down beside her. The headlamp warmed one of his legs. 'It's a bugger of a walk from here.' He looked ahead. It was completely dark. The sky had gone from blue-black to nothingness. He felt her hair brush his cheek and then her arm leaning against his. He didn't move. It was the stuff that dreams were made of and he was King of the Dreamers. A perfect setting for an Elvis Presley seduction, for slipping an arm around her shoulder and leaning forward, not quite by accident. He knew a few moves. He was no boy scout. (His mother wouldn't let him join.) He could hear the bubbles fizzing in her mouth and the noise as she pulled the bottle away from her lips. He leaned his head over. The sides of their temples touched. A chill wind came across the fields and bent the blades of grass lit by the headlamps. Frankie sat up straight and said: 'I bet you wish you were with Billy on the motorbike. Does he still have the bike?'

'I don't know.' She gulped down several mouthfuls of champagne, then passed him the bottle. 'I haven't seen Billy Stevens in a year.'

'What? What happened?' Frankie tried not to show the flush of excitement. The loud 'Yes!' that was drowning out all other thoughts. He knew it. Billy was all wrong for her.

'Oh, nothing, and I mean nothing,' she said. 'It just got to a point when we had nothing to say to each other. One night, we were watching some game show and Billy answered one of the questions wrong. Do you know, I just sat there and I thought, "God, he's ignorant. What a stupid thing to say." I realised I didn't even like him any more. He wasn't that interested either. Spent more time looking in the mirror than he did looking at me. I tell you, it's a big mistake to marry a man with better legs than you.' Frankie wanted to put his arms around her. He wanted her to cry so that he could comfort her, but it would have been a cheap trick. 'God knows where he is now.' She gulped down several mouthfuls of champagne, gasping for breath when she pulled the bottle from her lips.

'Why didn't you come home?'

'Oh, for God's sake, Frankie, can you honestly see me coming to see my sick mother who doted on Billy and telling her I'd made a mess of it?'

'Carmel, I'm sorry.'

'And also, can you imagine what the village would be like?' She was shaking. Frankie could feel the vibrations on the car bonnet. 'I know what they used to say: "Ah, your Carmel's a scream. Wired to the moon, that one." Being a dreamer is great here. Standing in the cake shop talking about art, I was a credit, but running off to Dublin and leaving Mum was just selfish.'

'You're wrong, Carmel. Look at me, for Christ's sake. I'm thirty-two and I can honestly say that this is the most exciting night of my life. I'm not complaining or anything, but staying here is a big price to pay for loyalty.'

'Thanks, Frankie.' She found his hand and held it tightly. He hadn't said 'I told you so'. On the day she had married Billy, she knew it was a big mistake. Her Uncle Balbo gave her away. Everyone turned around to look at her in her short puffball wedding dress. Billy had his hair down and it was gleaming far away in the coloured light through the window. The pews were a mass of bright hats jumbled together like jellybeans. The music started and Uncle Balbo gripped her by the elbow and Siobhan's baby started crying and none of it seemed real. She felt like Dorothy in *The Wizard of Oz* as she is running over the field of poppies and daisies, heading for the Emerald City. The witch has poisoned the flowers and all she wants to do is lie down and sleep. If only she had stopped and curled herself up in a ball, waking when the church was empty and everyone had gone home and forgotten that it had ever happened.

There was a faint rumble in the distance. Frankie got up from the car bonnet and felt his way along the hedge until he came to an iron gate. Davey Sheehan was driving home from the Palace. He usually took the tractor at weekends. No Garda would think of breathalysing a man in the middle of a field. He knew how to cover the whole six miles between the pub and his farm without crossing a single road, though he had been obliged to fork out a few pounds over the years for damaged hedges. Frankie ran across the field as the lights wobbled towards him. He stood in front of the tractor and waved his arms over his head shouting, 'Stop! Stop!'

'What in the name of God do you think you are playing at, you little hooligan.' Davey's voice was slurred.

'Davey. It's me. Frankie Shaw. Our car's gone off into a ditch. Have you a rope?'

'Be the holy. Frankie. What have you got on your face?' Frankie wiped his kohl-lined eyes with the back of his hand. Davey backed the tractor up and climbed down. 'Hello,' said Carmel, shuffling her feet. 'Sorry about this.'

'Not at all.' Davey winked at her.

Frankie said: 'This is Carmel, Paul Macnamara's daughter.'

'Never.' Davey grabbed her hand. 'Ah sure, you're a fine-looking girl. I'm sorry about your mother, love.'

'Thanks.'

'There y'are, now.' Frankie took her arm. 'You'll be home in no time.'

Carmel looked at his smudged eyes. 'Do you think your mammy will be waiting up?'

'Ah, shut up. She's not so bad.'

'All the same, I'd give your face a wipe.'

What a Night it Was. It Really Was Such a Night

The Palace was busy when Frankie arrived. Stars-and-stripes bunting criss-crossed the ceiling and a couple of the guys were in waistcoats with knotted kerchiefs at their necks. Hank's Friday night line dances always drew a good crowd. Palace regulars and line dance junkies who travelled in packs and practised at home with their sofas pushed back against the lounge wall. 'The Trailblazers', otherwise known as Denny, Mick and Eamon from Waterford, were set up in the back room; shining in their red gingham shirts. They were playing 'Gentle On My Mind' and Hank was dancing with his sister, Brede. He pointed to the wall behind the juke-box. There was a sheet of paper pinned up. A clipping from the local newspaper with a picture of Frankie and Carmel. The headline said: 'LOUGHFERGUS ELVIS ALL SHOOK UP.' Hank had underlined the part that said: 'Frankie performs at the Caesar's Palace pub.' Michael jogged across the floor, punching the air like a boxer in training. He always did that when he was excited. He slapped Frankie on the shoulder, looking at the newspaper clipping as if it were the greatest thing he had ever seen. Apart from pictures of the football team, Michael had only made the local paper once. That was when he was ten and got a wasp's nest stuck on his foot at scout camp.

Hank had pulled the tables back and they danced. Betty and Michael swung round and round until Betty shouted, 'Stop, you idiot, or I'll be sick!' Carmel collided with them as she walked towards the tables at the back. Frankie was sitting with Christy and some of the lads from the football team. Their voices rose and fell and laughed. 'Hiya, everyone,' she said. 'Thought I'd come for the party.'

Hank put a bottle of Budweiser beer in her hand and said, 'The first one's on me.' Dec's wife Margaret had been on the Bacardi and Coke. 'My Declan . . .' She waved a long bony finger at her husband as the others looked on. 'My Declan is not a strong man. No, he's not, God bless him.' Declan was trying to lift her coat from under her. 'Come on, love. Will you get up now.' His face was scarlet.

'Ah, leave her be, Dec,' said Christy, grinning. 'We're very interested in what you're telling us, aren't we, lads?'

Margaret laughed. 'Now Frankie Shaw,' she said, 'is a very strong man. Strong and handsome.' Frankie was looking at Carmel, but turned at the mention of his name to see Margaret, pointing and staring at him with blurry, blue-shadowed eyes. 'If I had married Frankie Shaw, I'd never have to lift them boxes of ketchup . . .'

'Come on, love.' Dec was pulling on her arm now, trying to lift her out of her seat.

'Are we going to dance, Dec?' she asked.

'That's right, love, let's show them how it's done.'

She staggered to the dance-floor. Dec draped her coat over her shoulders and took her handbag from Betty. There was a scuffle as she was led towards the door.

'Oooh!' the lads chorused. 'There's going to be trouble!' Frankie was mortified by the attention and was red around the ears. Carmel moved to the seat next to him and whispered: 'I'd say you had a lucky escape there. Do you want to dance, you strong, handsome man?'

They stepped on to the dance-floor and started to loosen up, but within seconds the song had finished and they were both standing with their hands behind their backs, looking around. Hank plugged the microphone into the karaoke machine, using it as an extra amp. He looked splendid in his blue jeans, fringed western shirt and cowboy boots. People were gathering around Carmel and Frankie, forming lines, as Hank welcomed everyone to the evening's entertainment and introduced the members of the band. 'Our first dances this evening will be a Tush Push, a Vancouver Boogie and a Duchess Hustle.' The couples in western gear lined up, radiating confidence. 'Damn,' said Carmel. 'The only dance I know is the one from *Saturday Night Fever*.' She and Frankie silently shared another memory. 'If you know it,' Hank's voice boomed over the crowd, 'then get on the floor and show it!' The first few bars of the song sounded and they stood together in a middle line and stepped from side to side. 'What do I do?' Carmel shouted.

'Follow that cowboy!' Frankie pointed to the man in front of them. The dancers cut a strange pattern across the wooden floor, turning left and right, screeching at every sharp turn, narrowly missing chairs and sliding on beer slops. 'Did you see the picture from the paper?' He leaned forward and cracked his forehead off hers. He felt her hair against his lips and smelled the shampoo. 'Two, three, four,' she said, nodding, then turned and found herself facing the wrong way. Frankie grabbed her by the shoulders and turned her back into line. Michael was horsing around, deliberately crashing into Betty and pretending he was a soldier with a gun on his shoulder. 'Right turn!' he growled. The dancers were into their third rotation of the sequence, finding their way through the backward and forward movements, the cha-cha shuffles and the twisting grapevine steps. The buzz that came from dancing together like something out of a Gene Kelly musical was tangible. The hunched shoulders slackened and the movements became more fluid. Carmel bit her lip, her eyes glued to the feet of the tall man in front of them. Then she turned the wrong way again and they were face to face. For a moment, Carmel was staring into Frankie's eyes and Frankie's kneecaps were starting to dance all by themselves. Carmel screamed with laughter and pounded her fists on Frankie's chest. 'I can't get it. I'm so crap!' she shouted. Frankie stepped out of line and stood behind her. He put his arms around her waist and pushed himself up close against her, spurred on by the beer. She relaxed, letting him steer her through the dance, like a little girl riding on her father's shoe-tops.

'Hey, hey,' said Christy. 'Frankie has his hands full. Look at him go. He *is* Elvis Presley.'

The evening rolled on with empty American beer bottles filling the crates in the back alley. Everyone had hysterics when some old woman started asking the band for requests. 'Do you have that beautiful song by Glenn Campbell?' she said. 'The one about the nine-stone cowboy.' Later on, Carmel and Frankie were dancing close. 'Are they looking at us?' She pressed her lips to his ear and felt him shiver. His mind was in a mess, trying to block out the thoughts he was having about her. He looked into her eyes, but was too close and felt his own eyes crossing. She laughed. 'Remember, we used to do that when we were little?' She put the tip of her nose against his and they both looked into each other's eyes, then rocked their heads from side to side, giddy with beer. That's when the Elvis song came in. Denny of the Trailblazers nodded at Hank, stepped up to the microphone and sang: *Wise men say, only fools rush in*. Frankie rushed in and it was the warmest, softest, most never-ending kiss in the entire history of the world.

'Frankie!' It was Hank calling him from behind the bar. 'Frankie. Sorry to break it up, but there's a call for you.' As he walked towards the bar, the others cheered and Christy called out: 'It's your mammy, Frankie, she's checking up on you.'

It was a man's voice. 'Is that Frankie Shaw?'

'Yes, that's me.'

'I'm calling in reference to the Elvis competition.' His voice was businesslike. 'We need some more information for the TV station and I was wondering if we could meet up over the next couple of weeks.'

'Sure. No problem.' Frankie spoke slowly. 'Um, where do you want to meet?' He put his palm over his ear so he could hear the man's voice over Hank and Michael who were singing *I'm a nine-stone cowboy!*

Carmel had gone to the ladies' room. Betty squeezed Michael's arm. 'You're delighted with yourself, aren't you?' he said. 'Don't forget that the girl is married. Frankie might get hurt, you know.'

There was a strong wind blowing outside the pub, turning the fan in the toilet window like a propeller. Carmel rubbed the tops of her arms. Her head was fuzzy and her stomach was still tingling from the kiss. There was someone in the cubicle. The sign on the door-bolt was stuck halfway between VACANT and ENGAGED. It read: AGED VAC. She imagined an old Hoover sitting on the toilet. She put her hand on the side of the sink and turned to look at herself. 'Whoops!' Her heavy forehead rested against the mirror. 'Oh God!' she groaned, fogging up the glass under her nostrils. 'What are you doing, Carmel? Here you go again.' Oh, for a clear head, for a sensible voice to tell her what to do about Frankie now that she had snogged him in front of the whole town, practically. The door clicked open behind her and she lifted her chilly forehead from the glass. A woman came out of the cubicle and nudged past her, reaching for the soap. Carmel recognised her as one of those who used to stand, scrum-like, outside the post office and watch her mother through the window of the bread shop. All sanctimonious, they were, with their arms tight-folded across their breasts. Carmel used to stick her tongue out at them and her mother used to say: 'Pay no mind to the noddy-dogs, love.' She called them that after the brown plastic Alsatian in the back window of their Uncle Balbo's Vauxhall Viva. When the car went over a pothole, the dog went 'yes, yes, yes' for about a minute, thanks to the spring that held its head to its body.

Carmel sat and waited for the shuffle and the creak of the woman leaving the ladies' room. She leaned to one side, resting her head on the paper dispenser, and sobbed until her nose ran, holding her mother's image in her mind. Mary Macnamara, striding with her head held high, a holier-than-thou look on her face and Carmel trailing after her, pink-haired and angry. That anger was replaced now by a void inside of her that needed to be filled right away. Filled with comfort and cuddles and cotton-wool wrapping.

Back in the bar, Hank and Brede were having a disagreement. He was trying to pull himself another pint, and Brede was holding the pump handle up. 'No, love. You've got a plane to catch tomorrow and I'm not having a repeat of last year.'

'Bye, Hank,' said Frankie. 'Send us a postcard.' He felt Carmel's arm slip through his.

Hank winked at them. 'Be good children, now.'

As they went out of the door, Carmel looked back. 'I hope he finds himself a nice cowboy and they just ride off into the sunset.'

'Yes.' Frankie put his arm around her waist. 'I love happy endings.'

It was quiet apart from the clop of Carmel's shoes on the road. She held on to him tightly, bunching up his jumper at the back. He kissed her some more in the doorway, then turned to start the walk home. 'Where do you think you're going?' she said, taking off her jacket. 'Aren't you going to come in for a coffee?' Frankie stood in the light coming from the hall with his mouth open. 'Tea?' she smiled, but he didn't move. 'Um, Ovaltine?'

'Well, if you're sure.' He stepped forward. She put her hands on the seat of his trousers and had a bit of a feel around. A bit of a squeeze. Frankie smiled stupidly, hiding a bit of a panic. 'Yeah, Ovaltine would be lovely.'

'The last of the great romantics, aren't you,' she said, patting him on the shoulder. 'Make yourself comfortable, I'll be with you in a moment.' Frankie flopped in one of the armchairs in the lounge. All around him, Mrs Mac's things were lying in boxes, wrapped in newspaper. The light in the corner had no shade and flashed like fireworks in his eyes as he looked at it. He and Carmel were waltzing through the marble ballrooms of his mind. Prince Charming and his Princess. The Princess was standing at the cooker. She raised her voice so that he could hear her in the lounge. 'It's a funny tradition, isn't it, Frankie? Asking someone in for a coffee.' She lit a match and whoosh went one of the burners. 'Wouldn't it be great to say: "Would you like to come in for a screw?"'

There he was in his rose-covered fairytale, and she was talking dirty. He walked around the lounge, playing little drum-rolls on his stomach, and looked out of the window. It was pitch black out there and all he could see was his own reflection. Perhaps he should leave. It had been a great night and he could apologise in the morning for not drinking his Ovaltine. Carmel held the smoking match still for a moment as he headed for the door. 'Well, I suppose there's not much romance in that,' she said. She poured a pint of milk into a small pan and Frankie clung for a moment to the door frame. 'Yes, I suppose it's the not quite knowing whether it is coffee or a screw.'

'Coffee would be fine.'

'I've started on Ovaltine now.'

'No, that's great.'

'Sorry, Frankie, I'm a bit pissed actually.'

Frankie laughed. 'No, you're fine.' He went back into the lounge. 'What's my problem?' he said to the pale bit on the wallpaper where a picture used to be. 'This is so un-rock and roll.' He looked at his reflection in the window. Cool as a cucumber, like those fellas in fifties films who went around with a pack of cigarettes folded up in the sleeves of their T-shirts. Big hits with the women. 'There will be no more jokes about my track record,' he mumbled. 'Carmel is a grown woman. She knows what she wants and she wants me. Yeah.' He leaned on the mantelpiece, trying to look all nonchalant. She appeared at the door, carrying a tray, and Frankie started to panic again. He sat down and crossed his legs. 'Oh, lovely,' he said, and took one of the cups. It was awfully quiet. She slopped a little of her drink down the front of her top. It left a mark like a hot-air balloon. Frankie stared at it for ages until he realised how it must have looked from her end of the room.

'This is cosy,' she said as he swilled the last of the drink around in his mug. 'Would you like the sports pages to read, Grandpa?' Frankie looked up. Carmel was getting up from her chair and coming towards him. She took the mug out of his hand and tried to put it on the floor. It tumbled on to its side. Frankie lunged forward, fishing a tissue from his pocket, but Carmel said, 'Leave it. It's good for the carpet.' He made a motion to get up, like it was time to say his thank yous and leave. He didn't get a chance. Carmel sat in his lap, sat side-saddle so that her legs dangled over the arm of the chair. Frankie was punch drunk with the taste of her milky mouth and the feel of her fingertips on the back of his neck and was feeling a little uncomfortable in his trousers. They had not yet danced in the marble ballroom or walked along the beach or gone shopping together in a covered market. The kind of things that were in 'falling in love' sequences in the movies. But those kinds of things hardly ever happen and there is usually the wrong song playing in the background. This was his big romance. Late in coming, too fast-moving, but good enough for rock and roll.

She pulled him by the wrists towards her parents' bed-room. They weren't allowed in there as children. Once, they had both got a telling-off for trying on grown-up clothes and poking their noses in where they didn't belong. Mrs Mac had gone berserk when she had found the two of them pulling things out of drawers. Mr Mac's Y-fronts were enormous and they both had runny noses from laughing. They had sat together at the back of the garden and watched the hand marks change colour on the backs of their legs. Frankie got a flash-frame of Mrs Mac with her bright coral lipstick and another wave of panic hit him as they reached the door.

'Wouldn't you like to talk for a while?' he said.

'What about?' She was right. She had just fast-forwarded through the talking bit. She slowed down a little, though, remembering his gentleness and how different he had always been to Billy and the other boys she had hung around with. She ran her fingertips along his jaw. The silence was crushed by a loud crackling, like the sound of a needle on a record. He pushed the hair back from her face and the needle found the groove. 'Surrender.' The piano and the cymbals and the bongo drums hit him like a tidal wave. Frankie felt the nervousness flowing out of him in a spiral. Swirling and swirling as he took Carmel in his arms and the Latin rhythm pounded in his head. The room was bathed in pink light as the brass section kicked in and a little fella at the back clapped sticks together. Frankie was singing, or was it Elvis, or was it just his imagination? *When we kiss, my heart's on fire. Burning with a strange desire.*

The cold cottage was ripped from its foundations by a whirlwind and dropped on a tropical island. The warm breeze from the sea was blowing in the window and fanning the net curtains out so that they glowed silver in the moonlight. The band was standing a little way down the beach, with a heavenly chorus floating in with the fishing boats. *So, my darling, please surrender . . . surrender . . . All your love so warm and tender.* Ever dreamed you could just sit at a piano and play, even though you had never had a lesson in your life, or stand up on some table and dance like Fred Astaire? Frankie was there in Technicolor. The bed opened up its arms and wrapped them in a white cloud and they turned and twisted like the beads in the maracas which were shaking and shaking in Frankie's ears. Like Elvis, the ending was almost operatic.

The curtains were unfamiliar when he opened his eyes, although the window was in roughly the same position as it was at home. It was the first time Frankie had woken up with someone. Waking up when you didn't have to get up was a brilliant feeling. This was ten times better. Carmel was facing the other way and there was a channel of warm air between their two bodies. He had wanted her to fall asleep in his arms, her head resting on his chest, but it was hot and clammy and her hair kept getting caught up under his elbow. Now it was all fanned out behind her on the pillow. The cows over the road were back from milking. They were having their usual gloomy conversations with each other. To Frankie it was a serenade. They were singing. Big, cartoon cows with huge eyes and smiling mouths. Woodland creatures were going to come over and stare in the window any moment. Deer and squirrels and chirrupy bluebirds nudging each other and looking at the happy, sleepy couple.

Frankie wriggled forward so that his chest brushed against Carmel's back. She slid down the pillow a little and tucked her legs up. She kicked Frankie in the shin, but she didn't wake up. There was a little whistle coming from her nose with every breath. He could smell the cigarette smoke from the pub on her hair. Half of his clothes were still hanging off the end of the bed, caught up on the candlewick spread. They probably smelled the same. His mouth was sticky and there was an ache behind his eyeballs. A real Sunday morning feeling. If he was at home, his mother would come in and mutter something about missing Mass and him lying and stinkin' in bed all morning. He put his hand up to his mouth and breathed on it. Useless. It was always useless doing that. You could never smell anything. He tried to remember what he had eaten the night before. Stew. His mother had been chopping onions, pushing the flashing blade of the knife through layers of little white rainbows. There was all the beer as well. Pint after pint of it. The pub smelled dreadful in the morning. His breath was probably twice as bad.

He needed to sneak out and clean his teeth. Carmel had a green toothbrush and she used sensitive toothpaste. If he went and gave them a rub now, she wouldn't notice. Some people are funny, though, about toothbrushes, he thought. And hairbrushes and wearing other people's shoes. Perhaps a quick rub around with toothpaste on the end of the finger will be better.

Frankie slid backwards until his bum was poking out from under the duvet. He stopped, thinking that Carmel might smell the toothpaste. Men should not be ashamed to smell like men. He couldn't see Sylvester Stallone smelling his hand. He'd probably turn over and fart right in the girl's face and she would think he was a real hunk. Anyway, if he was all minty, he might make Carmel feel self-conscious. She had drunk as much as he had last night. Frankie was starting to lose his balance and slide backwards out of the bed, so he put down a foot to steady himself. It was freezing. The tops of his legs were killing him and when he tried to put on his trousers quietly, he hopped forward and hit his head off the door. Carmel was certainly a sound sleeper.

'Breakfast.' He went into the kitchen, hugging his arm tops and putting one foot on the other when he stood still. The linoleum was like a sheet of ice. Mrs Mac's kettle was the old type that went on the stove top and she didn't have a toaster. Lighting the old eye-level grill nearly took all the hairs off his arm. He found the teapot in the cupboard with the cleaning stuff and gave it a rinse out. Frankie did a commentary like a TV cookery programme. He swooped around with the tray and the teacups. He even remembered a spoon for the honey. His mother would have given him a round of applause. Carmel's cupboards were a mess. All of her painting stuff was mixed in with the food. He got out a jar that he thought was runny honey and found that it was the glue she used on her pots. 'That would have taken the romance out of it,' he said. 'I hope you don't do that at home, ladies and gentlemen.'

The toast wasn't brown yet and the tea was just starting to brew, so he sneaked to the bathroom to freshen up. He peeped in the bedroom door on the way. She was still sleeping, her hand curled against her chin. She hadn't changed much over the years. The Ribena smile was replaced by the ghost of last night's lipstick. 'Jesus, the toast!' The kitchen was all smoky. It wasn't the toast at all. It was the tea towel. Carmel had put it on the top of the grill the day before and now it was slowly being eaten by orange flames. Frankie grabbed a fork and lifted it up. Bits of black flew up in the air and fluttered like feathers all over the kitchen. It fell off the fork and on to the floor. He couldn't stamp on it with bare feet. There were loads of newspapers around, waiting to be shredded for papier-mâché. He crouched over the remains of the cloth, swatting frantically. The smoke made his eyes water. It occurred to him that a newspaper was a poor choice. The end of it was already smouldering. The Ovaltine pan was still in the sink from the night before. He filled it up with water and poured it over the towel and the paper. What a mess! He found a coal shovel under the sink and managed to get most of the soggy black cloth off the floor. He headed for the back door, holding his arm out to the side. It was locked and there was no key in it. There was a window over the dinner table, so he climbed up and managed to open it with his free hand. He was just leaning out, emptying the shovel into the flowerbed, when Carmel arrived.

'What?' he heard her say. She was wearing the big pink dressing gown that had been hanging on the back of the bedroom door. 'Well, Frankie,' she said, leaning against the cooker. 'I've had men try and run out on me before, but never through the kitchen window with the coal shovel.'

'Oh,' he stuttered. 'Father Tom says it's good to set fire to a tea cloth first thing in the morning. Penance for sins of the flesh.' There was black stuff all over his face and chest. Carmel stepped over the remains of the campfire on the floor. Her eyes were streaming. The smoke was still thick, but they were tears of laughter. Now the toast really was burned and the tea was going to be like treacle, but everything was all right. She said, 'Well, that certainly got rid of the morning after bit, you know, when you panic about whether to clean your teeth or not.'

'Yeah,' said Frankie. They laughed, and every corny sixties song about sunshine and buttercups and daisies was playing in the background.

Beach Glass

A gull flew over the beach, cutting bold diagonals in the pale grey sky. He wasn't aware that it was Tuesday or that the two people on the sand had taken a day off work. Bold as brass. They didn't see him. They were walking with their heads down. 'There's one,' said Carmel. She picked up a small, triangular piece of beach glass. Once sharp and glossy, it had been scoured by the suck and blow of the sea until it was smooth and opaque. She put it in the pocket of her anorak with the others. She had decided to make a picture frame out of them, press them into plaster like a mosaic. 'My hands are freezing!' She blew on her red fingers.

'Here.' Frankie took her hands in his and rubbed them together. 'Mine are warm.' They sat on a bench out of the wind. The sun on the wet sand made them squint. Carmel put the fragments of glass in her lap, brushing them with her damp jumper sleeve to make them shine. 'I had a spaghetti jar full of these once,' she said. 'I used to think they were valuable, like real jewels.'

'They are pretty.' Frankie picked up a large green piece

and held it to one eye. He remembered Sunday afternoons in the summer with his parents. Driving to the sea with the car seat sticking to his hot legs, Joe singing and everyone betting who would be first to see the white-crested waves over the hedgerows. Eileen used to sit on the sand and look out to sea. Always. She tutted if a child or a dog ruined her perfect view of the horizon. 'Waiting for her sailor boy's return, that's what she's doing, aren't you, Eileen?' Joe tanned so quickly. Looked dark and brawny, a cigarette glowing whiter than white against his face. Played footie with bucket goalposts. 'Don't get the ball too near Mammy, now. She's enjoying the peace and quiet. She gets precious little of that at home.'

Carmel's stomach was turning over. She had to talk to Frankie and get herself out of the mess she was in before it got any worse. It had started with a few beers too many and a lot of feeling sorry for herself, but when the fog of alcohol cleared, there he was, all cow-eyed. Sleeping with Frankie Shaw was way up in the top ten of all-time stupid things she had ever done. She had dumped all over every man she had ever loved. They all ended up hating her, so what does she do? She sleeps with probably the best friend she's ever had. Stupid, stupid, stupid! It was time for the old steamroller. A horrible job at the best of times, but this time it would be unbearable. She would start off by telling him how great the last few days had been, and they had been great. That's the point when the old steamroller would be heard rumbling in the distance. Then she would tell him how important their friendship had always been to her. Steamroller getting a little louder now, belching behind Frankie as she mentioned how different their two lives had become and how she should get back to Dublin and how he'd forget her soon enough, then crunch, there he'd go under the relentless roller and her voice would be drowned out by the chugging of the engine. Nothing left. No love, no friendship, no Frankie, apart from his squished remains. She felt sick. It was such a lovely day. Not steamrollering weather. She felt the sun on her eyelids and mulled over the possibility that she could be wrong. She could be throwing away the greatest thing that ever happened to her. She wasn't in love with him, although she was very near to the edge of the precipice. What harm would it do her to dangle there a little longer? She turned to him and shaded her eyes with her hand. 'What are you going to do, Frankie?'

'It's like the earth is breathing, isn't it? The way the waves go. Big breath in. See. Now big breath out.'

'Earth to Frankie! I was asking you a question.'

'I know. I was avoiding it very poetically.'

'So you're going to sit on a beach for the rest of your life, are you? I'm going back to Dublin.' There now, she had said it.

Frankie stared out to sea. Grey clouds getting lower. 'Maybe I'll come up for a while,' he said. 'Do a bit of singing. Get a job.'

'I'll believe that when I see it.' Carmel grinned.

'What was that supposed to mean?' He tried to sound offended.

She slid down on the bench and stretched her legs out. She felt calm and dreamy, as if she were being given anaesthetic. 'It would be like a revolution, Frankie,' she said. 'It would be in all the papers.' She traced the headline over the sky with her finger. 'Frankie Shaw leaves home.'

He poked her in the ribs. 'Shut up, will you.'

She held an imaginary microphone under her chin. 'I'm standing outside the house of Mrs Eileen Shaw. Mrs Shaw, I believe that Frankie isn't usually late for his dinner.' Frankie grabbed Carmel by the waist and tickled her. She squirmed and the little glass pebbles spilled out of her pockets. 'Stop. Ow!' They didn't notice the man walking the dog or the seagulls that fought over the remains of a sandwich. 'Sing to me, Frankie.' She stood up and pulled him up by the hands. The wind caught her hair and blew it back from her face.

'Here?'

'What, you mean in front of all these people? Come on.'

'What do you want?'

'Nothing by Elvis.'

'Don't you like Elvis?'

'I like you. Now sing.' Carmel walked backwards facing him, holding her arms out to the side.

Frankie sang: *Let there be you. Let there be me. Let there be oysters under the sea.*

Carmel closed her eyes and smiled as the wind blew Frankie's voice and his love over her face and her body. It was warm like the winds that blow over tropical beaches. Frankie looked at her as he sang. At the way her fingers stretched towards him like a mother teaching her child to walk. Pretty soon he would be running. Two elderly women were coming down the beach towards him. 'Look at that fella shapin' over there,' said one. 'It's only lunchtime.'

'I think it's lovely. He's singing to the girl. I wish someone would sing to me.' Frankie sang to both of them: *Let there be cuckoos, a lark and a dove. But first of all please. Let there be love.* 'Very nice,' they said, and Frankie bowed.

∫

Um Kisses

Watching videos of Elvis impersonators, Frankie discovered that there were three things they had and he did not. The first was a weight problem. They may not have sounded like Elvis, but they were every bit as bloated; huge thighs and stomachs and round, sweaty faces. Avocados in nylon. The second was a worrying personality disorder. Over-polite and grinning one moment then, for a flash, there was a look in their eyes which told you that they may flip at any time and shoot holes in their own television sets. The third (and the only one that Michael agreed with) was a white jump suit. Frankie never liked dressing up. He was the kind of man to go to a fancy dress party as the guy next door, so the idea of walking around in sequins was not a popular one with him. He would far rather have remained in Elvis's denim period. That was the Elvis he admired; the young, handsome man with floppy hair and close-shaved cheeks and bags of energy. The older Elvis was sad and disillusioned and someone Frankie didn't want to be. Besides, the shops weren't exactly overflowing with cabaret outfits. The assistants just laughed and pointed him towards the karate wear. But Michael would not be talked out of it. Nothing would dim his image of the theatre with the audience clapping and dropping their Maltesers all over the floor and Frankie, all in white, singing his heart out over the nation's television sets.

Betty was enlisted as their seamstress. Her only success in the past had been Liam's sailor suit for the school pageant, but Michael managed to convince her that the same pattern would work if it was a few sizes larger and the join was hidden by a big belt. Frankie was under the sink, emptying a load of old tea leaves into a bucket as Michael and Betty argued about his act and how the suit would focus his mind and give him confidence. He was used to the way they cajoled and outsmarted each other. He had been an attendant at their wedding. All red in the face because he had to sing a solo. He went croaky halfway through and his father laughed at him. Betty never forgave Joe Shaw for that. She was the only person in Loughfergus who didn't think Joe was the greatest thing since sliced bread. Frankie loved her for it.

While they watched an Elvis video in the lounge, he lay there and dreamed that he was in a pink Cadillac, driving home. The sun was bouncing off the polished chrome which covered every dial on the dashboard. Ahead of him lay the ornate, curving gates of Graceland. The two wrought-iron Elvises parted as the gates swung open and he drove through. He was wearing sunglasses. They took the glare off his white suit. His perfect white suit with tassels and beads and little mirrors which beamed a thousand images of his square, tanned jaw to the security cameras. Frankie heard a creak. He saw Elizabeth's sneakers and socks as she came through the door. She was doing a waltz and singing to herself as she made her way to the fridge: *You know we belong together.* The shoes stopped as she noticed Frankie's lower half poking out from the press that usually held the detergent. She cleared her throat. 'Hiya, Frankie,' she said, her voice wobbling with the embarrassment of singing in public. 'What are you doing down there?' He wiggled out and sat up against the units. Elizabeth sat down beside him and picked at some pink nail polish on her fingers. She was ten, but big for her age – that's why she was the class champion at basketball.

'Oh, the usual,' he said. 'I was thinking about Elvis.'

'Elvis who?' Her thoughts were far away, at the surf club in her favourite Australian soap opera. Frankie looked astonished.

'Elvis Presley. The King of Rock and Roll. The fella I impersonated at the contest. God! I thought you'd have had enough of him with your father droning on night and day.'

'Oh, him. The one on the video. Sorry. I thought you were thinking about Carmel Stevens.' Elizabeth cracked open a can of cola. She had a big grin on her face. An 'I know something you don't know' grin.

'Macnamara,' he said. 'Her name is Carmel Macnamara.'

'Auntie Eileen says it's Stevens.'

Oh no, thought Frankie. His mother had been showing her disapproval at mealtimes. Plates met the table with more gusto than usual and she had stopped asking direct questions. It was all 'I suppose' and a lot of heavy sighs. 'Well, I suppose you're off to the pub again . . . I suppose I won't need to leave the snib up this evening.'

'She's your girlfriend, isn't she?' Elizabeth rocked her heel on the floor, so her sneaker nudged Frankie's leg.

'I thought you were my girlfriend,' he said. She was when she was six.

'Liam told Mammy he saw you up the road and you were giving her one of those Um kisses.'

'One of those what?' Frankie was enjoying the scandal, even though it was about him. Elizabeth rolled her eyes upwards.

'You know, like Uuuhhmm.' She opened her mouth, then closed it again as if she were taking a spoonful of medicine. 'Janie! That Liam's so stupid sometimes. He says you're going to marry her, but Auntie Eileen says . . .' She stopped when Frankie put his hand on her leg.

'Don't pay any attention to what Auntie Eileen says. She's got a very vivid imagination. I put odd socks on and she thinks I'm running off to Dublin with a group of devil-worshippers.' For a flash, Frankie was in the Cadillac again, but this time he was driving through Dublin, snaking in and out of housing estates and shopping centres and Carmel was at his side, passing him chocolate buttons. The streets of Memphis were paved with Elvis impersonators, but in Dublin there was only one. Well, two or three probably, but there was nobody who gave two hoots if Carmel was still married to Billy. In Dublin, Frankie could give her Um kisses all day without the fear of his mother's carpet slippers creeping up behind him. It was a fear that had been driving him crazy over the last week. One night, up at the Macnamaras' cottage, Frankie had heard a car stopping outside and he lay there for twenty minutes, frozen solid, convincing himself that it was Eileen in one of those vans that spies have. He could see her as clear as day with her orange cardigan and her reading glasses, wearing earphones and twiddling knobs and gazing at a wall of TV screens. Well, pretty soon he would be where she couldn't see him. Out of sight and dressed in white.

. . . A Long, Long Time Ago

The pub chosen by the man from the television station was a real poky little place. All kinds of junk was hanging out of the ceiling – jugs and saucepans and tractor seats. They were playing the Saw Doctors. Two women in big leather jackets were singing *I useta lover, I useta lover once* and swinging their pints from side to side. One looked up at Frankie and gave him a big smile and a wink. 'Lamped by a woman,' he thought. 'The first of my many groupies.' He had spent the bumpy bus journey rehearsing his interview to his reflection in the window, trying to look like a pop star in the making. His hair had gone just right for once and he was wearing the new denim jacket he had bought for the occasion. It had been sandblasted from indigo to a powder blue veined with white, giving it the look of something Jimmy Dean would have worn under the scorching California sun.

There was a young man at the bar. He stood out a mile. He was wearing a sharp suit in a chocolate-brown colour and his shiny, dark hair was tied back in a ponytail. He was having a conversation with a girl in a long, bright jumper and leggings. Frankie stood at the bar and tried to earwig him while he waited for his stout to pour. 'Well, I see it like this,' the man was saying in a Dublin accent. 'You don't have to have had a traumatic childhood. We all have problems with relationships. The thing is to forgive yourself, start liking yourself. Very few women do.' Frankie's hand groped around the bar, trying to find his pint without looking. The girl was lapping it up. Frankie shuddered to think what was on the man's mind apart from her soft, fluffy jumper draped over his suit on a bedroom chair. He looked down at the briefcase. It was one of those metal ones. For a tape recorder or a camera, he thought. This had to be the guy from the television station. Frankie cleared his throat, but the man didn't notice, so he leaned forward and tapped him on the shoulder. When he turned round, Frankie held up his pint and gestured towards an empty table. 'I'll go and sit over there. I'll see you later.' He smiled widely at the man and nodded to the girl. As he made his way to the table, he heard her say: 'Who is he?'

'I dunno,' said the man. 'They are all a bit interbred round here, I think.' He looked around the pub, nodding and smiling. She straightened her back. 'What do you mean by that?' she screeched. 'My family are all from New Ross!' Frankie was scarlet. He had to pick the night when there were two out-of-towners in the pub. As the conversation at the bar grew louder, Frankie heard his name being called.

'Frankie? Frankie, lad!' An old man was sitting behind a table. He was wearing a faded pin-striped suit with a green sweater underneath. The sweater was frayed and straining a little over his stomach. His face was as red and round as a beetroot and topped with a shock of white hair like a dollop of cream. It was a familiar face.

'Jesus. Mr Macnamara! I was just talking about you the other day. Where have you been? We thought you must have died. God! I can't believe it!' Frankie ran to the table.

'It's good to see you.' The old man gripped his hand. Frankie felt the fatness of his fingers. 'Two pound of bangers,' they used to call them at school. He looked up at Frankie, studying his face, his eyes dusting over every feature, then nodded his approval. 'Do you live round here then, Mr Mac?' Frankie released his hand and looked around him. 'Is this your local?'

'No. No. I live up the North-West now, have done for many years. I just came down for a day or so. I wanted to see you.'

'God, you were lucky. I'm never usually around here. I came in to meet a fellow from the TV station. Did you know I was going to be on the telly?' Frankie grinned.

'That was me, Frankie. I'm sorry about the lie, but I had to see you.' He reached into the breast pocket of his jacket and pulled out a creased piece of paper. He opened it carefully and spread it out on the damp table. It was the photograph from the local newspaper. He looked down at it, studying the face of his daughter, running his finger gently over her smile. Frankie thought that he must ration it. Only take it out once an hour or twice a day in order to retain the thrill of seeing it anew. His little darling was a series of inky dots in the shape of a face. Frankie glazed over. Everything was happening so fast. First Carmel walks back into his life, now her father. The way things were going, pretty soon Joe Shaw would come back home from the cemetery and start singing in the bathroom. The horror of that brought him back to his senses. Mr Mac was still looking at the clipping. 'You want to know about Carmel? Now?' said Frankie. 'Did you know she married?'

'Oh, good Lord, yes. I have my spies. I know Mary died. I imagine that Carmel came down to see to things. She's a good girl.'

Frankie had trouble swallowing his beer. This was the man who broke her heart. The person she loved most in the whole world, who walked out of her life with no explanation. But it was Mr Mac who was always kind and had time to mend broken kites and wipe grazed knees. He let Carmel blow on the tops of his fat arms to make fart noises. He swung them round by the wrists until their feet left the grass. His face was still kind, although the red veins on his nose had spread over his cheeks and his big voice sounded tired. 'This is really difficult, Mr Mac. Why don't you get in touch with her?' Frankie tried to stop his leg from jittering under the table.

'I can't talk to her. It would be too difficult for me. I just need to know one thing. Is Carmel still with that fella in Dublin? I want the truth, now.'

'Didn't work.' Frankie was dying to tell him all about himself and Carmel. He felt nervous like maybe he should ask Mr Mac for his permission. He decided to build up to it.

Mr Mac sighed and the green wool stretched a little more over his stomach. 'Is she with you?'

Frankie couldn't help smiling. So much for building up to it. 'Yes,' he said. 'She's with me, now.'

Mr Mac's arm shot across the table and his whole face changed. There was a hard side to him that Frankie had never seen before. The huge fingers bit into his flesh. 'You'll have to put a stop to it right now, young man.' Frankie sat bolt upright, pulling his arm away. A cold trickle of fear ran down his spine and his mouth dried up. Mr Mac's older, softer expression returned and he bowed his head. 'Sorry,' he said. 'You must believe me, Frankie. It's the only thing you can do.' He looked down at Carmel's grinning face again.

Frankie grunted and swallowed and pulled his hands up inside the sleeves of his jacket. 'Look,' he said, trying to keep his voice down. 'I don't want to know why you and your wife split up and I don't want to hear why I am not suitable. Why don't you go and have tea with my mother?

The two of you can discuss it until the cows come home.' As he spoke, little bubbles of spit flew from his mouth and landed on the dark table-top. 'Nothing in the world is going to change my mind.'

'Listen to me.' Mr Mac raised his voice again and the room went quiet.

'No, I will not listen to you! I'll flatten you if I have to.' He got up from the table and his half-empty glass rocked from side to side.

Mr Mac caught up with him by the door of the gents' toilet. 'Look, Frankie, it isn't you. Things went on that you didn't know about.'

'What kind of things?' Frankie pulled away from Mr Mac's hand. He didn't want to hear about a stupid family feud.

Mr Mac steadied himself on the side of the phone booth. His eyes were glassy. 'Carmel was the best thing in my life,' he said as Frankie stared at a load of numbers scratched into the wallpaper with Biros and pencils. 'The other girls were lovely, but I missed a lot of their growing up because of work. Carmel came at just the right time. You remember what she was like, Frankie?' He stretched out his hand to Frankie. 'Mary wanted her to work in the shop, but I knew that she could do anything.' Frankie was moved. He could see Mr Mac jumping in puddles of pride every time Carmel brought him home something she did at school. It was her father's love that showed in her work. That's why she painted things that were unusual and bold.

'So what's the problem?' said Frankie. 'I don't intend to hold her back.' He moved to the side to let a man into the gents'. The smell of piss wafted out of the door.

'She's not mine.' Frankie looked back and saw Mr Mac filling up with tears. 'I'm sorry,' he said, and wiped his eyes with his thumb and forefinger. Frankie felt like he was trapped inside a hideous soap opera. 'We had a disagreement, myself and Mary, one Saturday night,' said Mr Mac. 'She just came out with it. Told me that Carmel was another man's child.'

'Put that in your pipe and smoke it!' she had said, kicking off one of her shoes and steadying herself on the shade of the bedside lamp. She tried to say more but couldn't hear herself for the sound of the giant steamroller which was belching across the room and crushing her husband to a bloody mess on the carpet. *'Who?'* he had said as the great wheel came down on him.

'Who?' said Frankie to the remains of Mr Macnamara, although he knew already. His stomach was taking a nosedive. Suddenly it was as clear as day, just as other things had been clear in the past. He knew when he had failed French at school, he knew when Elvis Presley had died, just as he knew what the next words would be to come out of Paul Macnamara's quivering lips.

'It was your father and that's why . . .' Frankie's mouth hung open. From the bar came the sound of Bryan Adams singing and a woman laughing. Frankie felt the whole pub landing on his head. It must have been how Mr Mac felt all those years ago. 'Sorry,' said Mr Mac.

'Sorry,' said Frankie. 'Jesus, why are we both apologising?'

'Force of habit, I suppose.' He managed a half-smile.

'Is that why you left, Mr Mac? My dad should have been the one, not you.'

Mr Mac looked down at his big, clumsy hands. 'No, I left because I am a coward, I suppose. It's hard to explain, but she wasn't mine any more. I looked at her and I saw him. All her prettiness came from him. That's how it seemed.' He stared at the leaf shadows dancing on the windows. 'I saw your mother the day after Mary told me. She was going off to do her shopping and she had that faraway look on her face. "Lucky woman," I thought. "What she doesn't know won't hurt her." Then I saw yourself and Carmel a little later on, dangling your legs on that wall by the post office with your friends. I couldn't do it to you. Couldn't carry the lies around either. God knows how your father and Mary found a way of living with it all those years. She must have been delighted when Carmel married that lad. Saved you all a bit of grief, that did.' A lot of grief. More grief than Frankie imagined he could ever feel.

The gap of time had been a long one, but still Mr Mac was haunted at night by the laughter of his girls. Their childish voices crying: 'Daddy! Daddy, look!' He had drifted from town to town like an outlaw, travelling from alcoholism to respectability and back again. Then one day, he found a strange quiet inside his head as he lay on a boarding-house bed, staring at the dust motes. He was in Donegal, surrounded by black hills that were ridged by the turf-cutters and fractured by violent, white streams. The village was grey and tightly shuttered. At its heart was a large church with ornate masonry and a steeple that stabbed at the low, dark clouds. The people seemed as buttoned up to the world as he was, but like the church, there was light within.

His new life had been centred on the care of two people: Mrs Maura Corcoran and her son, Brendan. She was a quiet and devout woman of fifty-five who had spent her middle years in almost total dedication to Brendan, who was twenty-four and viewed the world from within the confines of severe cerebral palsy. His father had been elderly and had died before Brendan reached ten. Every evening, Paul could be seen tending to him, tucking blankets around his legs and chatting away as they toured the village while his mother cleaned the church and dusted the dried flowers that made do in the absence of a local florist. Paul wiped Brendan's chin and the thin-fingered hand that always nestled under his jaw, catching the spitty bubbles. Paul told him all the craic from the pub until his head arched back with pleasure. He took him and his mother to a hotel by the coast every Sunday for lunch and played long games of Monopoly in the afternoons with tea and cakes and Mr Brendan Moneybags.

So that was Paul the Baker's lot, and he was happy with it. Now that he was a widower, he could marry Maura and develop their chaste relationship if she would have him, and live out his days in windblown contentment. Seeing his daughter's photograph in the Wexford papers sent all the old ghosts rushing back in. It worried Maura to see him like that and she urged him to go back and find out the truth. Brendan was off for the weekend with the lads from the community centre, watching the football in Dublin, so here he was, talking away, trying to ease the pain poor Frankie was feeling. Matching it with his own instead.

They parted with touches to the shoulder and promises to sort things out without despairing, believing neither themselves nor each other.

When Frankie left the pub, the fresh air made him feel light-headed. He walked past the bus stop and along the dark, winding road to Enniscorthy. It felt as if his father were there under the tarmac. He was reaching out and pulling at Frankie's ankles. Trying to slow him down and trip him up. He was in the trees that blocked out the light. He had always been around when Frankie stepped out of line, like the day Joe was hiding under the mud by the lake.

Poor little Captain Scarlet. He was the best present that Frankie ever had and it wasn't even his birthday. 'Mum, can I have a dog? I'll look after it and walk it every day and get a job after school so I can feed it. I promise.' His mother was having none of it. Dogs were smelly objects that left hair on the furniture and paw prints on the linoleum and did their business behind the long curtains in the lounge. He was taken out from his father's coat and put on Frankie's lap one night at dinner. 'The lad should have a dog,' he said. His parents looked at each other like they were having a secret argument and it was very quiet. It was so quiet, in fact, that Frankie could hear all the little noises that Captain Scarlet's stomach was making. Captain Scarlet was a pipsqueak. A bit of terrier and a bit of dachshund. 'A Heinz 57,' Uncle Con called him when he was paraded in front of the family. He was reddy-brown with a bit of grey, like Mrs Ryan's hair, and his eyes were lots of colours, but green mainly. Carmel's sister Siobhan gave him some of her doughnut. 'You're all skin and bone, aren't you, little fella? Can I pick him up, Frankie? Does he bite?'

'Only doughnuts.'

'You'd better watch out then, you big doughnut,' said Carmel.

Siobhan scooped Captain Scarlet up and held him like a baby, so that his creamy stomach could be stroked and tickled and his fluffy genitals looked at closely. 'God, I can feel his ribs. It's like playing the accordion.'

'Yes,' said Frankie. 'You can feel him working, you know, his insides. It's brilliant! Put him down now, I'm not sure if he likes it.'

Captain Scarlet slept in a Tayto crisp box and wasn't allowed in any further than the kitchen. Frankie lay in his bed and talked to him because he knew that dogs had super-hearing that went through walls and up stairs. He ran so quickly that Frankie got red in the face every morning. When he reached the park there was a kind of explosion as the chain was taken from round his neck. 'I wish you were a dog,' Captain Scarlet said to Frankie in their secret language, and bounded off into the bushes and ran in twirly-whirly patterns over the grass. 'I am a dog. Inside I am,' said Frankie, because his heart was beating loudly and he loved the sun on his face and the springy grass under his feet.

'Don't take him down by the lake or you'll never get the dirt off him,' said his father.

'I can wash him, Dad.'

'Do as I say, now!'

The banks were brown and smooth as glass. Melted chocolate with the green fields on one side and the misty water on the other. From the gate, Frankie imagined their two sets of tracks on the mud, trailing up towards the factory. Captain Scarlet sniffed the air and turned to look at Frankie. 'Why not?' he said. 'It's a special day today.' Frankie had been his best friend for two weeks. They ran over the field so quickly that the tops of Frankie's wellingtons made his legs sting. Captain Scarlet was so happy on the mud. He ran over its surface with nothing to get in his way. Frankie threw sticks and he soon caught on to the game and brought them back. The mud caught in his eyebrows and the long hairs on his stomach and made Frankie's feet feel heavy when he walked.

A long, knobbly stick was thrown for the fifth time. This time it landed a little nearer to the water where the mud shone. Captain Scarlet raced right past it and had to circle back. The stick had started to sink, so his little paws worked fast. Frankie watched as his stubby back legs disappeared and his stomach rested on the mud. He looked up at Frankie, asking for his help. He had taken on too much and the stick was still out of reach. 'Don't worry, I'm coming.' Frankie smiled and started to walk towards Captain Scarlet whose struggling paws served only to dig him in deeper. Frankie's feet grew heavier and heavier as he moved towards the water, so he lent over and grabbed the tops of his boots. 'Help!' cried the dog as one of the wellies stuck fast. The mud was halfway up it. He pulled, but felt like he was going to fall over. As he looked up he heard a whimper. Captain Scarlet's body was under the mud and only his little head was poking through. 'No!' Frankie shouted, leaving his boot in the mud and running in one fawn-coloured sock. The little head disappeared just before he got to it. Frankie clawed at the mud with both hands, his trouser legs sinking. 'Captain Scarlet. Please! Please don't die! I'm sorry, Dad. I'll not do it again!'

Everybody looked at him and several people came up and asked if he was all right. He sat with Carmel on her back step and Mrs Mac made him some tea. Carmel cried a lot and wiped the mud off Frankie's white face with a spitty tissue. 'I can't go home,' he said through chattering teeth. 'I can't.' His mother came to get him that evening and he hid in the shed. She didn't shout. She looked like she had been crying. Much later, Frankie realised that they were tears of sympathy and he understood a little of the horror that she lived through three times before he was born. He didn't want another dog because he knew he could never love it as much and that he would probably never be happy like that again. His father never said a word.

A loud hoot shook the memory from Frankie's head. A lorry was coming up behind him. Its headlights lit the heavy rain which had been falling for over an hour. 'Where are you going?' said a voice from the driver's seat. It was a woman's voice.

'Nowhere, really.' Rain trickled down the back of Frankie's neck as he looked up. 'Well, Enniscorthy way?'

'Come on up.'

'Thanks.' Frankie climbed on to the step under the door.

'Do you want to drive, then?' The woman laughed. 'Come around the other side, you fool.'

'Sorry!' Frankie pulled himself into the front seat which was the size of an armchair. 'I was miles away.' Her name was Christine and she was blonde and thirty-five and only

five foot three. She had cushions on her seat and wooden
blocks tied on to the bottom of her shoes so that her feet
reached the pedals. 'Isn't that dangerous?' asked Frankie as
he watched her change gear.

'Nah!' She smiled. 'I normally drive a van, but I keep them
in the back of the wardrobe for when I have to stand in.'

'Stand in for who?' Frankie took off his wet jacket and
hung it over the side of the seat so it dripped on the floor.
Christine's curly blond hair was fastened back with a pink
plastic bulldog clip and her long earrings rattled with the
vibration of the engine. 'My brother,' she said. 'It's his rig.
Fuckin' idiot got pissed out of his mind at lunchtime, so
here I am. Fed up. I was supposed to be at a party tonight.'
Christine made him feel far away from his problems for a
while. He didn't envy her brother, but he liked her a lot. In
a film, she would be the one who got all the funny lines and
ended up marrying the best friend of the hero. 'Where are
you going?' he asked, letting his head bounce on the side
window.

'Dublin. Shouldn't take too long.' The lorry brushed an
overhanging tree and streams of water came down the
windscreen. 'By the time I get this lot unloaded I will
be past my prime.' She pointed to a compartment in the
dashboard. 'Open the brown envelope in there and take
one. You never know when you might need something
shifting.' Frankie pulled out a plastic key ring. White with
red writing. 'Owen Brothers Haulage and Delivery.' On the
back was a phone number. 'It's just me and my brother,
really, but Pat said that it would look stupid putting Owen
Brother and Sister on the side of the lorry.'

Frankie's heart gave a lurch. He closed his eyes and tried
to think of something else. America. The open road. The
bright blue skies and the low horizons of Arizona and
Montana and Virginia. Colours changing like a chameleon
from state to state. Vivid green to dusty brown to vivid green

again. The trucks are comfy like a living room on wheels and there is always music, exactly the right music because you are king of the tape deck, king of the road, king of all you survey.

'Do you like Prince?' Christine opened a cassette case and pulled out a tape. 'I think he's wonderful. Saw him in concert in London a couple of years ago. Amazing dancer.'

'I don't know his stuff very well. I'm more rock and roll myself. A bit of country.'

Christine turned her nose up. 'I'm afraid country music gives me the vomits. All those songs like "I scraped my dog off the bumper last night".' She smiled at him and winked. Frankie leaned his head on the window and said: 'How about "My lover is my sister and my mother doesn't know!"' Christine threw her head back and laughed. Frankie started to cry.

Just outside Enniscorthy, the lorry shuddered. The passenger door was half open and the cabin light was on. 'Bye, Frankie,' she said. 'Are you sure that you don't want to come to Dublin with me? I could probably do with another driver. I think I'm a fair judge of character.'

'No. I'd better sort myself out before I do anything. Thanks, Christine. Thanks.' He squeezed her shoulder. 'You should have "Mobile Confessional" added to your key ring.'

'Some priest I'd make!'

She had been better than a priest. Frankie had told her everything. He hadn't felt bad about his anger or the dreams he had had about Carmel. The hard lines around Christine's mouth in the light of an oncoming car told Frankie that she had been there, that she understood. Anyway, Father Tom had never said 'The bastard!' or 'Too fuckin' right!' through the confessional screen. Christine opened a green tin and hid something in her fist. 'Come here, Frankie,' she said, and took his hand. She leaned over and kissed him gently on the lips, transferring the present from her palm to his. It was a tiny crêpe bandage. 'It's for your heart,' she said. 'Just in case.' As the lorry pulled away, she shouted at him from the window. 'Don't try and be too much like Elvis, will you? Remember, he died on the toilet!'

A Scene from a Movie

He stood outside the cottage. It was past six and there was still blue light in the air. His shivering had been replaced by an aching all over his body. There was nowhere to sit down. He knew that the sensible thing would be to go home and shower and change into fresh clothes and face Carmel when she was up and about, but his mind was too busy. The story was going over and over, time after time until the words tumbled and jumbled together like clothes in a dryer. Carmel was in a dressing gown and the left side of her face was lined from the pillow. She frowned. 'Frankie. What's wrong? What's happened?' The kitchen was cold. His hands shook as he took the cup of tea she made. 'Jesus, you're freezing.' Her voice was croaky. She came towards him and put her arms around his shoulders. He smelled her bed and felt her warmth and her hair on his face but he stayed frozen still. He wanted to push her away, to fling her back against the cooker and clear a space around him. She slowly pulled away, blowing hair from her mouth.

'I saw your father last night,' he said through his chattering teeth. She didn't move. Frankie looked down at the swirling bubbles on the surface of the tea turning jolly circles like a couple waltzing. Carmel asked too many questions. She fired them at him. One after another. Bang! Bang! Bang! It wasn't how he planned it on the road. She was walking all over his big speech. He wanted to hit her. Throw his tea at her. Say 'Listen, woman!' like his father used to. 'Frankie? What is it? Is he dying or something? Please tell me, for God's sake.'

His speech untangled in front of her. When the room went quiet, his jaw was stiff and his arms and legs were crossed and folded. She cried. Big ugly sobs and big fat tears. They jangled his nerves. 'He just clears off out of my life and now he, he, he . . .' Her words were squeezing and blurting out of her throat. She talked and talked. Frankie picked up a felt-tip pen from the table and pressed it into the leg of his jeans, making little dotty patterns.

Just before he left, he hit her. One moment sooner and he would have made it out of the door. He was standing in the hallway, putting on a coat she gave him. 'Are you all right? Will you get home OK?'

'Yes. I'm fine, thanks.' He shivered.

'No, you're not.' She came towards him again. He stepped back.

'Leave it. Please leave it.' He waved his hand in front of his face.

'Don't, Frankie. All this strong and silent stuff doesn't work with me. It's stupid because you think you're always in the wrong and you're terrified to ask. I haven't done anything. Neither of us have.' He leaned against the door frame and put his hands in his pockets. His fingers closed around the bandage that Christine had given him in the lorry. The paper wrapper popped open and he felt the soft fabric inside. He wanted it to be big enough to wrap him up completely so he could lie down somewhere like an Egyptian mummy and forget about the world. Carmel's breathing was nearly back to normal after all the tears. She wiped her nose on the cuff of her dressing gown. 'What do you want me to do, then? Should we talk to your mother?' Her voice got louder. 'Look, I know you! You'll just run away and hide! You'll just use this as an excuse!' She was looking at him so intensely, the way she had looked at him at her engagement party; the way she had looked at him when she had said 'What about you?' and cut his heart out and walked around with it on a spear.

'Oh, you know me, do you?' Frankie pulled his hands out of his pockets and the bandage came with them, unrolling like a yo-yo and running over the hall carpet. Carmel moved forward to pick it up, but changed her mind. Frankie swooped at it, winding it around his hands in big, white loops. 'I'll do what I damn well want,' he said. 'I'll be fine.'

'Yeah. You look fine,' she said, and started to laugh as Frankie chased the end of the bandage through the living-room door. The laughing got hysterical. He hit her on the shoulder with his open palm. On the way home he hit himself. Repeatedly. On the head with his fists.

He lay in the hospital bed, bandaged and swollen. He was unable to talk and his face had a serenity to it like a sleeping child. He watched her as she moved around the room. He had been praying that she would come. She had every right not to come. He had treated her so badly the last time he saw her, couldn't control his temper and his love. She stood over him and smiled. 'Hi,' she said, and held her hand out to him. He took it and kissed it. He turned his face away, unable to look at her. He was so ashamed of what he had become. 'Don't be afraid to love,' she whispered, 'because I love you.' So he reached out and touched her soft cheek which was moistened by a single tear. She kissed his bruised face, then rested her head on his chest. Her dark, shiny hair nestled under his chin and brushed against his lips and he closed his eyes and knew that he was safe at last.

Frankie rewound the hospital scene and watched it again. *Jailhouse Rock* was his favourite because it was honest about Elvis. He was rough and crude and came from the backwoods and that's why the kids liked him and their parents didn't. For the last hour and a half, Elvis couldn't have been any nastier. He was violent and conceited. He insulted people for no reason and he put his dirty shoes on a white sofa. But she had loved him, the girl with the dark hair. Carmel had never said it. Never said 'I love you'. Not once.

'It's nine fifteen. Are you not going out to the pub?' Eileen stood in the doorway. 'I never see you normally and now you're under my feet every evening. What's the matter with you?'

'Oh, nothing. I just feel a bit low, that's all. A bit depressed.'

'Depressed! Every time I turn on the television and the radio, I hear people saying that they are depressed. We never got depressed in my day. Too much work to do. Turn that blessed thing off now. *The Late Late* will be on in a minute.' She sat down on the warm armchair as the kettle clicked in the kitchen. She watched Frankie eject the cassette from the machine and put it back in its case. She saw him as a child on the same carpet, tidying away his toys. He had never once complained in all the hundreds of times. Her sister's children had thrown their blocks and pulled faces and said 'Mum, please' and 'It's not fair' until their cheeks were hot. Frankie just stopped playing and tidied up. She knew that he cried when he was hurt and laughed out loud when he was happy just like she did, but they both hid it and stayed even, like the bubble on a spirit level. She didn't know why. He was sad now and she felt it between her ribs. A little kick like the ones he gave her before he was born. 'The kettle has boiled,' she said. 'Will you have a cup of tea with me and watch the show? It sounds like a good one.'

∫

Wanted

'OK, you can try it now.' Michael had his head under the bonnet of a blue estate car. 'Um, when you're ready.' He looked at Frankie, who was sitting in the driver's seat. 'For Christ's sake wake up! What's the matter with you?' Frankie was gazing over the road to the side wall of the pub. He thought he had seen someone at one of the windows. 'First you tell me you're thinking about dropping out of the contest, then you stand around all week with a face on you like a dog chewing razor blades. If you're not going to tell me what's wrong, would you mind getting on with your work?' Frankie turned the key in the ignition, still looking over the road. He wanted it to be Hank. Michael was the last person he could tell. He was lousy at keeping secrets. Hank was OK, though. He would be back from America, fresh and full of energy, and he would know what to do.

Later, Frankie wandered over. The bar area was dark, but he could hear music playing. A woman's voice singing: *Don't let the stars get in your eyes, Don't let the moon break your heart.* He walked around the pub and looked in through the back window. Hank was standing there in the dark, throwing darts into the board. 'Hey, Hank!' Frankie shouted, and Hank dropped a dart on the floor. 'Good to have you back.' He smiled and Hank beckoned him around to the front door.

'Hiya, Frankie.'

'Hiya, Hank. Did you have a good time?'

'First class. How's the rock and roll shaping up?' Hank smiled and slapped him on the shoulder.

'Oh, not so good, really.'

'We can't be having that, can we?' Hank headed towards the bar. He took a beer glass from the shelf, but Frankie said he would rather have an orange juice. 'I got you a present,' Hank said. Before Frankie could say anything, Hank was heading upstairs. Frankie looked around him. There was a large brown paper package propped up against one of the chairs. It looked like a painting. He was kneeling down by it when Hank returned. He was carrying a paper bag with 'Pop Shop' on the side. 'Here you are. Oh, I must show you that.' He pointed to the brown paper package.

'In a minute, Hank. You're running around like a blue-arsed fly. I was hoping we could have a chat.' They both sat down and Frankie looked into the paper bag. Inside a roll of white tissue paper, he found a small plaster bust of Elvis. 'Oh, thanks. It's great.' Frankie looked at it, turned it over in his hands. He felt like he was in a relay race and he had just dropped the baton. Everybody wanted him to win the contest, but how could he sing feeling the way he did? 'Actually, Hank, things have changed,' he said, but his words were drowned out by a rustling. Hank was tearing away the brown paper from the parcel on the floor. 'Look at this,' he said. 'Some friends in L.A. gave me a present of it.' It was an old wanted poster. 'Hank Green. Dead or alive.' A sepia picture of Hank in the middle, made up to look like an outlaw. He went to the bar and lifted the barometer from its nail.

Frankie smiled. 'Yeah, it'll look great there. Come back over here, Hank.'

'Would you look at this! Frankie, come over here and look at this!' Hank was kneeling down behind the bar, looking into the glass-washer and yelling. 'Look! She's gone and put the empty coffee jugs in with the glasses and the filter is all clogged up. Look at all that black stuff down there. I'm surprised the machine is working at all. I knew I shouldn't have left her in charge. That's why I can't go off for as long as I like. Now imagine if this had been left to gather for another week or so.' Hank stuck his hands into the filter, pulling out coffee grains and throwing them on to the floor at his feet. Frankie stood over him.

'Calm down, Hank. It's not the end of the world. Brede didn't realise. She's been great, really. It's your jet-lag.'

Hank poured himself a tall glass of lemonade from the little soda shotgun. 'So, what's on your mind?' he said.

'Let me clear up this mess on the floor and I'll tell you.' Frankie took a dishcloth and gathered together the sloppy coffee grains on the floor. 'I don't know what to do, Hank,' he squeaked. He could feel a sore throat starting. The one you get when you are trying to say something and be brave at the same time. For years he had been learning how to control it by coughing and laughing and saying 'sorry' and pretending that a breadcrumb had gone down the wrong way. He did a combination of all of them and Hank slapped him between the shoulder blades. 'Are you all right down there?' he said.

'Yeah.' Frankie went to the sink and watched the coffee grains swirl out of the cloth. 'Hank,' he said at last. His heart was beating up in his neck somewhere. 'I don't want to be Elvis Presley any more. I'm not sure if I ever did want to . . .' Hank didn't look over. Frankie felt unable to say what he wanted to say and paced up and down, gesticulating to the air. 'Remember when you left for your holidays, Hank? Well, that was the most perfect week of my life.' He paused. The air was still in the Caesar's Palace. Hank was leaning on the bar, running his finger through a beer slop on the polished wood, pulling out a daisy-petal pattern from the circle of liquid. 'Then this . . . this thing happened. I'm going to tell you what it is now and you'll just die, Hank.' Frankie twisted the dishcloth so that it looked like a length of rope.

When he finished his tragic tale, Frankie waited for Hank to say something. Say 'wow!' and fall over. He walked towards him, his sneakers squeaking on the newly mopped floor. 'Hank,' he said quietly. He stopped because the sore throat was coming back again. A tear snaked through Hank's beard and dropped from the end of his chin. His finger swirled, blending it with the others that came patting down on top of it. Frankie touched his shoulder and Hank came tumbling down. He twisted at the waist and buried his face in Frankie's neck, one fist pulling on Frankie's sleeve and bringing the collar in tight against his windpipe. He sobbed so hard and cried so much that Frankie could feel the little bubbles of snot soaking through the fabric and on to his shoulder. Frankie cried too, but his tears were silent and sneaky and ran straight like raindrops down a window. He patted Hank on the shoulder and moved one leg back so that they didn't both topple over. Hank was a hell of a weight with the cares of the world on top of him.

There is only so much you can fit on the back of a postcard. You just say that you are in one piece and that the weather is good and that it would be nice if the person reading the card could just jump into the picture and join you for a while. Michael, Frankie and Brede had all received views of Monument Valley, the desert full of big orange sandcastles where John Wayne and his friends had played under cloudless skies. They had all imagined Hank in the middle, riding tall in the saddle, holding his stetson high and shouting 'yee-ha!'.

Sitting astride a horse called Chucky, Damian had looked like a film star. Standing by was his partner, Carl, with a camera in his hand. Their Malibu flat was full of long-term love. Goofy pictures of the two of them at parties, furniture carefully chosen, notes on the fridge and one bottle of everything in the bathroom. Wherever he went, Damian was cocooned in Carl's love. Real love turned Monument Valley into a bunch of rocks.

Sitting astride a fat piebald called Myrtle, Hank managed a smile for Carl's snapshots. He was finally in his western, but he didn't feel like a hero. He was vulture food. A parched, crawling, raggedy man. Lost, lonely and longing. Consumed by jealousy. Aware of himself. Of the low-down, scum-suckin', yeller-bellied, home-lovin' coward he always would be. He was sick of holiday romances. Guys who picked him up in western theme bars where the cowboys slow-danced, their belt buckles clicking together. Some of them were rough. Some of them were married. None of them were John Wayne. The guy Hank really wanted didn't go to clubs and watch drag shows. He stayed at home and dined with friends and usually married the girl next door. Hank was in a needle-and-haystack situation. He went to America every year, brimming with hope. All he found was a bigger haystack.

Eileen rang Michael. 'Where has he got to?' she said. Michael didn't know, but they soon had a pretty good idea because the pub was locked. Frankie and Hank sat behind the bar and ignored the knocking on the door. 'You knew!' said Hank. 'You didn't say anything.'

'Like what? "So, Hank, what's it like being homosexual?" We all knew. Well, most of us. My mother refers to you as a "confirmed bachelor", whatever that means. You don't want to be worrying about what she thinks, though, or Mrs

Dunphy. They were off praying for you when you started wearing the Stetson.'

Hank laughed through the last of his sobs. 'Christ,' he said. 'I thought that if I told everyone, they would stop coming to the pub.'

'Don't flatter yourself! People around here are much too fond of drinking for that. Anyway, we've known you all our lives. It's not like you're going to leap on top of us all and say, "Give us a kiss." Feckin' flatten you if you did!' Frankie nudged him playfully.

'You wouldn't be the first.' Hank stroked his beard. The beard he grew in order to hide a large scar along his jaw. Poor Frankie was wrong if he thought that nobody batted an eyelid at two men together. He had never wanted to hide, but being big and being brave don't always go together. 'Secrets,' he said, staring at a shelf of bottles. 'Do you think that your mother knew about Carmel?'

'No. She would have put a stop to it.'

'I wonder if anyone around here isn't feeling guilty about something or other.' Hank was grasping at straws but Frankie appreciated it. Their faces were close. Hank patted him on the leg. 'Come on, Frankie. We've been good boys all our lives. But incest and sodomy? Can you imagine? Nine hundred thousand Our Fathers and sixteen million Hail Marys.'

Frankie finally cracked a smile. 'So, you reckon I should go on with the Elvis thing, do you?'

'If I can be John Wayne, you can be Elvis. At least you won't be doing it for your father. He was a bigger bastard than either of us.'

'And that's saying something.' Hank and Frankie hugged each other among the last of the coffee grains.

The Pot Plant

'Oil, yes. Tyres, yes. Petrol, yes.' Carmel did a circuit of the car. The back seat was filled up to the roof and there was a pot plant spreading all over the front. Michael brought out her change from the office. 'Right, then, Carmel. Go easy, will you. That car looks fit to bust.'

'Don't worry. I'm in no desperate hurry. I'll probably stop off for lunch along the way. Anyway . . .' She kissed him on the cheek. 'It's been really brilliant to see you all again. Betty has my address, so why don't you come up for a weekend in the city? See a show or something?'

'That would be lovely. I'm sure we'll be seeing you soon, though. Won't you be coming down to see Frankie, or are you waiting for him to break the habit of a lifetime and move his backside out of here?' She jangled her car keys around in her hand. 'Do you want me to call Frankie for you?' Michael gestured towards the office. 'He's only down the road.'

'No. Don't worry.' Carmel wanted to run to the car and drive off like a bank-robber. To get Loughfergus well and truly in her rear-view mirror. When she had closed the door of the cottage for the last time, she had decided that she was ending a chapter. Now, fifteen minutes later, she was feeling lost and starting to panic. As she was getting into the car, Hank came running across the road. 'Are you off, then?' he said, and scooped her up into a big hug. 'Don't leave it so long next time, girl.'

'See you, Hank. Look after yourself. Come up and see me. Promise?'

'Sure will. Take care. Keep in touch.'

Michael chuckled. 'She's only off up to Dublin, not the North Pole. I was just saying that we'll see her at the finals of Frankie's Elvis competition.' Hank put his hand on Michael's shoulder and let Carmel get into the car. 'Bye, Mike. Bye, Hank,' she said, and drove away.

They waved at her until the car was out of sight. 'You know,' said Michael, 'I reckon Frankie has to be the biggest eejit on the face of the earth. He's letting her get away. Anybody can see that he's mad about that Carmel, but one word from the blessed Eileen and she's leaving for Dublin without him. A few weeks back, he was planning to go with her. Did you know that? Betty says that she's seen so many young people waste their lives out of guilt. Staying at home with an ageing parent instead of going out and getting a life for themselves.'

'That's rich, coming from you, Mike.'

'It's different with my parents. We choose to live around here.'

Carmel stopped for a moment outside Frankie's house. She could see Eileen in the garden, hanging out the sheets, sliding the peg-bag along the line. Frankie came out of the back door. Carmel watched him, standing half in and half out of the flowerbed, handing pegs over to her as she fastened the flapping tea towels. She drove on, not looking again in case Frankie heard the car and let his eyes stray from his mother's floral pinafore and the first of the busy Lizzies.

She had a late lunch at a coffee shop in Wicklow. The woman behind the counter recommended the toasted sandwiches. Carmel played with hers, even though it was very good. The menu was smudged and someone had been to a lot of trouble writing it in italics. The woman behind the counter moved to one of the tables. She had turned up the radio, as there was only herself and Carmel in the place. The news came on and it floated in and out of Carmel's head. After that, there was an advert for Boland's biscuits and the woman flicked through a magazine which she had taken out of her handbag. Carmel had just got out her purse, ready to pay for the half-eaten sandwich, when they put an Elvis song on the radio. The woman put the magazine down and slid out from behind the table. Carmel was weeping, pulling a handful of serviettes from the little dispenser. 'What on earth has happened?' The woman was holding out her arms but not touching. 'Oh, you poor girl. Would you like another cup of tea?' Carmel shook her head. The woman was about fifty. She died her hair. Orange over white. It was luminous and didn't go with her pink uniform. She sat down in a chair next to Carmel and stroked her hair. 'Lovely hair. Such lovely hair,' she said gently, as if she were saying, 'There there.' Carmel slid over and cried into her arms. The warm, rounded arms of a perfect stranger. A woman who smelled of bread soda and Youth Dew and cigarettes.

The woman let her stay on a while in the café and give her face a wash. She didn't ask any questions. Carmel thanked her and got back into her loaded car. She drove off in silence, afraid that if she put on the radio, she would start crying again. Anything would set her off. She wasn't sure what she had been crying about. Whether it was saying goodbye to the place where she grew up or to a mother she had never really known that well. Was she crying for Frankie and what might have been? Was she just needing to get rid of some water she had been retaining? The pot plant in the front seat was starting to annoy her. She was hoping that she could get rid of it, but nobody in the village had a corner of a room big enough to take the sprawling lime-green plant with its spidery children dangling from its sides. Her mother had tolerated it for years as it sat quietly in the corner. Carmel had wanted to throw it away. She had put it out on the back step on a cold night, hoping it would be all brown and shrivelled the next day. She couldn't sleep. She had felt so guilty about letting it die that she had got up and rescued it. Apologised to it when she brought it in. It had been witness to so many things. It must have learned to live with tension and loneliness. Nobody had thought enough of it to bite their tongues and say, 'Shh. Not in front of the P.L.A.N.T.'

As Carmel's car left the greens of the country behind and started to make its way through the suburbs, the plant began to panic. As she reached down to change gear, a few tendrils, rough as kitten's tongues, scratched her on the back of her hand. She leaned over to the side and pushed the pot away from her. 'Bugger off, will you,' she said. It didn't like that at all and next time it got her on the shoulder. A ghostly tap with skeleton fingers. Carmel flinched and pushed it away, but the leaves sprung back to where they were, scratched and tickled, poked and prodded until she swerved the car all over the road. 'What?' She tried again to move the pot over on the seat cover, but the leaves on the opposite side were pressing against the window. 'Stupid bloody thing,' she yelled, tucking handfuls of leaves behind the seat belt. She started to cry again. 'Now look what you've done!' Three leaves broke free and slapped her on the cheek. She pulled the car over. The street was quiet apart from a far-off car alarm. Carmel got out and opened the passenger door. There was a litter bin a few yards down on the left. She lifted the plant, showering the front seat with dried-up soil. She turned and shut the car door with her backside, looking at the bin. A cylinder of criss-crossed wire, half empty. She started towards it, but was jerked back. The leaves had caught in the door. The plant was clinging on. Carmel's nose was running and she couldn't wipe it. She rested the plant on the roof, feeling a trickle of sweat running from her armpit down to her bra. She stood there for over a minute, crying, with her head resting against the plant and the door half open. She let go to wipe her nose on the back of her hand. The pot slid down the windscreen, tipping dirt over the bonnet. Carmel caught it by the leaves and reached across the car until the wing mirror stuck into her stomach. She grabbed hold of the pot and pulled it back towards her. The dirt was scraped off the bonnet and returned to the pot, patted down with muddy, tear- and snot-covered fingers. Gulping and sobbing, Carmel put it back in the front seat and slammed the door.

It was still light when she got back to Loughfergus. The orange light that comes at the end of long, fine days. The garage was closed and the pub was open. Kids were playing on the grass outside, sucking Cidona and Coke through flattened drinking straws. Carmel drove past and up towards the church. Her mother's grave was clean. Little green pebbles, untouched by weeds. She put the plant down at the head of the grave and then backed away. 'Happy now?' she said. She smiled, thinking that it was a pretty groovy thing to do. To drive for over two hours just to put a pot plant on a grave.

She sat on a headstone. Some other old woman. It was softened with moss. There was hardly any breeze, but the trees all around were whispering. They were graveyard trees, so spooky noises came naturally to them, whatever the weather. On the way back from Dublin, she had planned a little scene. She was going to sit by the graveside and talk to her mother. She leaned forward. 'Mummy,' she said, but it sounded so loud, like she was using a megaphone and all the people way over in the village could hear it. Talking out loud in a graveyard was really embarrassing and she couldn't find anything to say. She had messed things up with Billy. Her mother had messed things up with her father. It happens. She looked around and saw Joe Shaw's stone, still clean and shiny, and there were flowers in the jar. She waited for a while, but nothing came to her. He was Frankie's dad, really. She had nothing to say to him, either. She thought about giving him the pot plant, but reckoned he didn't deserve it.

Outside Frankie's house, the tyres of her car fitted perfectly into the marks they had left earlier that day. She sat for a while and cried some more, enjoying the drama of her own sobbing. She touched up her make-up and smiled at Eileen when she opened the door. The house smelled of cabbage. 'Hello, Mrs Shaw. Is Frankie in?'

'He's in his room. He can't talk to you for long because his dinner's almost on the table. Frank!' she shouted, resting her arm on the banister. 'There's someone to see you.' She turned back and gestured for Carmel to go into the front room. It was dark and Carmel didn't feel like she could turn on the light. She wanted to, because there was a picture on the mantelpiece. A wedding photograph of Eileen and Joe. Carmel had never seen Eileen smile like that before. So warmly, like she didn't have a care in the whole world. It was almost identical to the photograph that used to be on the side table in her house. Taken at the same studio in Enniscorthy by the same photographer. If she had cut out the heads with nail scissors, she could have swapped them over. She heard Frankie coming down the stairs and was suddenly terribly nervous. She needed to use the toilet.

He stood in the hall for a few seconds, looking in at her. The atmosphere would have killed the pot plant for sure, if she hadn't left it in the graveyard. Carmel's face

was prickling all over. Hot little needles making two pin-
cushions out of her cheeks. 'I thought you left,' he said.

'I did, but I came back. Is it all right if I use the toilet?'
She walked towards him, not looking at him at all.

'You came back to use the toilet?' They stood together in
the doorway. She looked up at him. They both burst out
laughing. Nervous, silly laughter that didn't know when to
stop. She patted him on the shoulder and crossed the hall
to the bathroom. Frankie walked around the lounge, still
laughing. He looked at the wedding photograph.

She couldn't go, now that the ice had been broken with
Frankie. She sat there for a few minutes just to show willing,
then washed her hands and went back to the lounge. 'I
couldn't go after all that,' she said. 'It's always happening.
I go to the theatre and I'm busting all the way through the
first half, then I join a queue a mile long during the interval
and I know full well that as soon as I get in there, nothing
is going to happen. I start worrying about the people in
the queue behind me and then I can't go myself. Stupid,
isn't it?'

'Just a nervous thing, I guess.' Frankie's heart was racing.
He was glad that they were only talking about toilets. He
could hear his mother breathing in the doorway of the
kitchen. She was having a listen to their conversation.
Carmel was quiet. She had turned on the light and was
staring at the photograph. 'You are like him, you know.'
Frankie said it quietly. Carmel went over to the window
and looked out. 'I got all the way home nearly,' she said.
'But it was no good.'

'What made you come back?'

'Don't ask.' She paced around the room with her arms
folded across her chest. 'This is horrid, isn't it? I don't
know what to do with myself. Whether I want to touch
you or run away or . . . I don't know . . . You didn't tell
her, did you?'

'Who? Mum? No.' He pressed himself back against the door, as if Eileen were going to come through it with a battering ram. 'I couldn't do it to her. It's tempting, sometimes, but I couldn't. What would be the point?'

'Yeah. I know. It's the same with Katie and Siobhan. I've picked up the phone about a hundred times, but I can't work it out. What to say, I mean. Did Daddy say where he was?'

'Donegal somewhere.'

'God love him. Well, that's what I think half of the time, then I think that he was such a chicken, you know, running off like he did. Oh, I don't know what I think.' There was a knock on the lounge door.

'Frank. Your dinner is on the table. Don't let it go cold.'

'Right, Mum. I'll be along in just a minute.' Carmel put her hands in the pockets of her jeans, looking for her car keys. Frankie opened the door. 'Sorry. Look, will you be in the pub later on?'

'No. I had better get back. It's a long drive and I've already done it twice.'

Frankie opened the front door and they stood, less than a foot apart. There was something that felt very safe about being together. Something that took them both off the terrifying, runaway train of emotions that they had been riding. 'Look,' he said. 'Talk to me now, then. I couldn't eat if you paid me.' He walked down the path with her. The last of the light was still in the sky.

'Frank!' Eileen's voice came from the kitchen. Carmel raised her eyebrows and smiled at Frankie.

'I'll warm it up later, Mum.'

'Oh, you will, will you?' Frankie didn't answer. Didn't flinch, even. 'Well, will you at least shut the door. It's letting in a draught.'

They sat in the garden for over an hour until it was pitch black and Carmel was shivering. 'You're still going ahead with the singing, aren't you?' She reached out and put her hand on his arm.

'Yes. Definitely.'

'Good. Look, if you need to get away, you can always come up and stay with me. As long as you like. I mean it.' She tried to stop her teeth chattering as she was speaking. 'In fact, I think it would be a brilliant idea.' They both knew they couldn't bear the thought of not seeing each other again. They leaned together, so their shoulders touched.

'I don't know, Carmel. It would be weird, knowing what we know and what we've been up to lately, and anyway, I'd drive you mad. I'm hopeless. Can't boil an egg.'

She patted his leg. 'I'll teach you. It's easy. Just remember not to break it before you put it in the water or you get egg soup.'

Eileen drew the curtains in the lounge, chasing the last bit of light from their faces. They found their way to Carmel's car and she stood by the open driver's door. The light inside was on. She gave him a card with her address on it. He had about six of them in his room already, but he took it and tucked it into the back pocket of his jeans.

'Bye,' he said. He leaned forward and put his arms around her. She hugged him back and neither of them saw the little triangle of light coming from the lounge window. 'I'll call you, Carmel. They'll be organising some rehearsals for the show, so I'll be up in Dublin no matter what.'

'Yeah.' That was all she could say. She was exhausted, but a lot happier. Having Frankie to stay was a strange suggestion, but late at night when you're sitting on wet grass with your best friend in the whole world, all ideas are good ideas. Even swimming the Atlantic or flying to the moon or driving through Memphis in a pink Cadillac.

The Visible Man

'Hold still, will you.' Betty was hard to understand. There were several pins sandwiched between her lips. Frankie stood on the coffee table in the lounge. He could see that the picture rail needed dusting. Betty's plump fingers squeezed the layers of white fabric together. She leaned back on one arm every so often to check the line of the trousers against his shoes. His hands were oily from the garage, so she had made him wear a pair of washing-up gloves. They glowed rose pink in the mirror above the fireplace. From where he was standing, Frankie could see himself from just below his knees to the middle of his chest. A bright white torso against the yellow of the wallpaper and the brown of the sofa. The suit fabric was dappled by the daylight through the slowly shifting net curtains. All around the room there were reflections, coming at him from the glass of the children's communion photographs and from the cabinet that held Steven's football trophies and Elizabeth's basketball cup and Liam's clay models.

Frankie felt strange. It happened every time he put on the suit, even though it was half finished. As a child, he had wanted to be the Invisible Man. Take some magic medicine and wander around the town and do whatever he wanted and nobody could touch him or shout at him. They would just go 'Ooh! Aah!' at all the amazing things that were happening. In his white costume, he was the most visible person alive. He was sure that if he stepped down from the coffee table and walked through the main street, cars would stop and people would all point and say: 'Who *is* that man by the door of the post office?' Slush thrown up by car wheels would just bounce off him, leaving no mark on the fabric, and the children would all ask: 'Is that Jesus, Mammy?' Their mothers would pat them on their little heads and say: 'No, love, it's the second coming of Elvis.' There was a sudden bright flash like lightning which made Frankie dizzy. He nearly fell off the table. 'Classic!' said Michael from the doorway. He was holding up his camera. 'Jesus, Frankie, you look a right half-eejit.'

'Don't, love, you'll make him all self-conscious.' Betty knelt up and squeezed Frankie's ankle. She was scared that any comment might send him back to the glum little world he went into just before Carmel left.

'Are these what you're looking for, Mum?' Elizabeth stood next to Michael in her school uniform. She was holding a brown paper bag in front of her.

Betty nodded and she tossed it over. 'Where were they, love? I had the house upside down yesterday looking for them.'

'You don't want to know.' Elizabeth was smiling and twisting one foot inwards.

'Where?' Betty was smiling too. 'In the fridge?'

'Nah. They were in the bag with the bread.'

'Your usual filing system, love.' Michael went back into the hall. 'Do you want some tea?'

Betty opened the paper bag and took out a thick braid of silver sequins. 'We haven't the money for diamonds, so I'm afraid these will have to do. You won't be able to see the difference when you're up on stage and the light is shining on them.' She draped the sequins across his collar. 'I'll put them here and a few round the bottom of your trousers. What do you think?'

'Brilliant,' he said. 'I might as well go over the top.'

Betty looked up at him. He was making faces at Elizabeth. There were moments when Betty had thought she would be returning the white fabric to the shop. He had put off the first fitting time after time. Paced around the village for hours in the evenings, and once she had noticed him hiding from her in a shop doorway in Enniscorthy. But all of a sudden, things changed and he was a man possessed. He brought in picture after picture of Elvis, all done out in white with Hawaiian leis around his neck and sweat dripping off his face. His belt buckles were the size of picture postcards. Studded and embroidered with American eagles and silver starbursts. Large round stones like flat strawberry lollies on either side of his zip which was half open, revealing his chest hair and a heavy golden crucifix. In some of the pictures, Elvis wore a cape, fanning up from his waist to his pointed cuffs like satin bat wings.

'Jay . . . sus!' Steven breezed into the room. He was eating a Marmite sandwich. 'Are you doing that for a bet, Frankie? You'll look like something out of bleedin' *Star Trek*. Everyone will piss themselves.'

'Enough, Steven! You're not too old yet for a good hiding.' Betty turned around and made a swipe which sent the sandwich flying over the lounge floor. 'Frankie will look absolutely . . . What was it your granny used to say?'

'Maga-nificent,' said Frankie. He winked at Steven, who was propped up against the sideboard, laughing.

Chocolate Biscuits

Well, I quit my job down at the car wash.
I left my mamma a goodbye note.

It was amazing how all the lyrics came true at one time in his life. Right now, it was quitting time. Yes, and not a moment too soon. Time to shake the dust of Loughfergus from his shoes and head north. Frankie lay on his bed with the record turned up to six on the volume knob. Late teenage rebellion, that's what it was. When he came in from work, Eileen was watching children's television and Liam was sitting on her lap. The puppets in the show looked like ducks with long legs and they were playing banjos with their purple wings. Liam and Eileen were singing along. Each time he clapped his little hands, she brought hers together on either side of them. A hand sandwich with Liam in the middle. *La-de-da-de-da*, they sang, her knees twitching him up and down. They didn't notice Frankie for ages.

'Hello, there.' Liam heard him and wiggled off Eileen's lap. She looked up at Frankie like he was a real spoilsport.

He crouched down, holding his arms out to Michael's little lad. Stroked his hair when he came close enough. 'Well, young fella? Have you been having a nice time here with Auntie Eileen? Has she been spoiling you rotten?'

Liam nodded and hopped up and down. 'We made chocolate biscuits,' he said, then turned on his heels and ran back to Eileen, who stretched out her hand, resting her palm on his cheek as he stood beside her chair.

Frankie came towards her as the ducks took their bows and the adverts came on. 'Chocolate biscuits, eh? Did you leave any for me?'

'No!' they both said, pushing their two faces close together. Frankie gulped and folded his arms. His heart was still patched up with sticking plaster and he wasn't sure if it could take any more. He was so jealous of the child, he wanted to kick him from here to next Tuesday. Eileen's dearest friend. She had never shown Frankie how to make biscuits. She had never played 'one step, two step and tickle me under there' with Frankie. He would have remembered. It was clear to him where he must have stood in her estimation back then. Her only son. What was he still doing around here when he wasn't even offered a lousy biscuit when he came home?

After he had played 'Guitar Man' three times, good and loud, Eileen opened his door. 'For the love of God!' she said. He nudged the volume button with his toe and stared over at Elvis, who was stuck to his wall, standing in front of giant red lights spelling out his name. Eileen looked at him too. A withering look, like it was all his fault. 'Has Liam gone home?' Frankie said, pushing the rage back down inside him.

'Yes. Betty just came and got him. She had to go to a parents' day for Elizabeth, so I said I'd take him. He's no trouble. No trouble at all.' She smiled, the smell of the child's hair still clinging to her blouse.

'And I am, I suppose?' He looked up at her. 'No!' he wanted her to say. 'No, you are not. You are kind and gentle, Frankie, and I know how hard you try and, by the way, I thought all your projects at school were wonderful and I hope more than anything that you go out and win that contest.'

Eileen raised her eyebrows. No! she thought. You were never any trouble. The kindest little boy. The finest young man. She didn't say those things because she had stopped talking like that long ago. It was too late now. It would be unfair to start getting clingy now he was all grown up. 'Dinner won't be too long,' she said. 'Did you pick up that cream for me like I asked you to?'

'It's in the fridge . . . Mum?' Eileen came back around the door frame. Frankie was leaning up on his elbows. Before he said anything, she knew. 'Mum, I think I might move up to Dublin for a while and stay with some friends. I'll come back at weekends so I can practise with Michael and come and see you. I think it would be good, you know, with the contest coming up in a few weeks.' He looked over at the poster and wished he was Elvis, all smooth and sophisticated. Eileen looked at the poster too and thought that it would be so much better if the big red letters said 'Frankie' instead. Elvis looked at both of them. It was a few years before he died, and there was still a glimmer of hope in his eyes. Hope that somebody, somewhere would remember him as something really special.

PART TWO

Bright Light City

At the beginning of several Elvis movies, the hero turns up in a new town. Sometimes he is on foot or on horseback, or he is waving goodbye to someone who has given him a lift. He has a guitar and a small bag, and his denim jacket is draped over his shoulder. He has come to make a new start, find a job with a band and a girl from among the bouffanted, gingham-skirted locals. A girl who will hold his hand and sing duets and ride beside him in an open-topped car. And it is hot. It is always hot.

Frankie dragged his suitcase along the banks of the Liffey with perspiration running down his face. He looked at the houses and the mouldy little shops, faded like an old watercolour. Plaster cracking under the windows like crows' feet. Buses buffeted him and filled the warm air with fumes and there wasn't a soul around that he recognised. When he wanted directions to Temple Bar, he had to ask three sets of people before he found some that either understood English or knew the city well enough. Frankie was buzzing with it all. By the time he reached the address that Carmel had given him, he felt as if he had arms like a gorilla, stretched to twice their length from passing the case from one red hand to another. The sign outside the door was a mosaic set into concrete: 'The Works'. Frankie knocked but there was no reply. The door gave when he pushed it and released the smell that had taken over the kitchen and the back room at the Macnamara cottage. It closed behind him and the heat of the day was switched off like a light. As he hauled his suitcase along the dark corridor, a young man came out of a doorway. He was holding a roll of copper wire under one arm and had a baby cuddled in the other. 'Can I help you?' he said.

'I'm looking for Carmel.' Frankie dropped the suitcase and held out a prickling hand. Seeing that there was no way the man could shake it, what with the baby and the wire, Frankie used it to brush his hair out of his eyes.

The man nodded instead. 'Follow me. She's up the way. You can leave that case over there and pick it up later.' He smiled and his mousey little face was suddenly warm. He shifted the baby on his hip. 'You must be Frankie,' he said. 'I'm Mickey and this little fella is Jacko.'

Frankie grinned at the baby. 'After Jack Charlton?' He hadn't planned for this. He had this silly idea that Carmel would be all by herself as she was in her mother's cottage. But there were others and he wondered what Carmel had told them. He had no idea who he was all of a sudden. Was he her brother, class-mate or flatmate? He followed Mickey up the stairs to a large airy room divided into different areas by paint-splattered screens. Every centimetre of the wall was ringed with shelving. Slap-dash wooden shelving, covered in layers of paper and cluttered with paint cans and labelled boxes and row upon row of finished and unfinished goods. In between the shelving units, posters were stuck up for exhibitions and concerts. Reminders too, painted on scraps of paper. One by the door said: 'Turn the lights out!' Another said 'Clean the sinks!', but it looked as if nobody paid any attention to it. Mickey slapped the copper wire down on a workbench. His trade was clocks. Ornate, spidery clocks made from beaten metal. Hands of wire curling out from their faces and pointing back to the numerals with shining silver arrow-heads. Jacko was poppered under the top cover of his pram, his little bald head lolling out of Mickey's elbow crease as he was lowered. By the large, open window on the left-hand side, a radio played hissy music.

As Frankie walked towards the partition in front of him, he heard Carmel's laughter. Her corner was stacked with bright-coloured articles that made Mickey's clocks look like grey, everyday things. She was standing with a mug in her hand, talking to a young man with blond Shirley Temple ringlets and a pretty face. He was wearing a short Lycra jogging suit. Carmel was feeling his flexed arm muscle when she spotted Frankie, red-faced and grinning by the sink. 'Hiya, Frankie. Welcome to sunny Dublin.' She skipped up to him and hugged him. She still felt good in his arms. 'Isn't it warm today? We were just saying . . .'

Her words were cut off by the young man, who was walking over to what Frankie assumed was his corner of the room. 'Yes. I was just suggesting that we all worked naked for the afternoon. Rather liberating, don't you think?' He had the kind of voice that you heard on television adverts for expensive ice cream. Right away, Frankie didn't like him. Didn't like the way he smirked and pivoted from left to right on a wooden stool with his arms folded. Had she told him the whole story? Is that what they were laughing at when he came in? He looked at Carmel. She laughed and said, 'Oh, ignore Charlie. He's mad. He can strip off if he likes. It would give us all a laugh, wouldn't it, Mickey?' Frankie's shoulders dropped down a couple of notches.

Carmel's flat was nothing from the outside, just a faded blue door at the top of a set of stone steps. Once you were through the door and up a set of stairs, the magic began. In every corner of every room, there was something out of the ordinary. The kitchen was done out like a fifties American diner with a great big fridge and chrome bar stools and advertisements all over the wall for Coca-Cola and Doris Day movies.

She opened the bathroom door as if there were a surprise party waiting inside. 'Ta-dum!' She flicked the light on. It was like an underwater city. The walls all painted with murals of mermaids and seashells and Greek pillars. The colours were soothing greens and blues, blending seamlessly into each other, rippling over the walls like waves. Each little fish and each stone on the seabed was painted in detail. Carmel loved the bathroom, but for a reason Frankie would never understand. It was her therapy. Something that started when Billy walked out of her life. The day after he walked out, to be exact. She had been sitting on the toilet, weeping and picking at a corner of wallpaper that had come loose. Strip after strip was torn from the walls until she was knee deep in her old life. She was waiting outside the paint shop the following morning. The room was created over a hundred sleepless, lonely nights. Painted through tears and black moods in eye-crossing close-up and in big, numb, mechanical brush-strokes. Painted in time with a thousand made-up conversations in her head. A few mornings, she had woken up, slumped against the toilet, or curled in the corner by the door of the hot press. Seeing all the details, a team of psychiatrists would have had a field day. Some of the fishes looked like Billy, others like the Macnamaras. Angry fishes gnawing away on lobster legs. Sad fishes, twirling in circular patterns around the light switch and chasing after seahorses and mermaids that had a look of Carmel about them. On a table by the bath, a basket held five bars of soap. Each was delicately carved into a shell shape. Frankie picked one up and smelled it. Nice. Fruity. Carmel picked up another and stroked it. 'Use the one on the side of the bath, will you. These are more for decoration.'

'Well nuh!' As if he would just plunge in and wear down her special soap. She was looking at it with affection. 'A friend made them for me. An art student. Charlie. You met him today.' She smiled. Her voice was a bit too breezy for Frankie's liking. 'Wasn't it sweet of him?'

Frankie turned the soap over in his hand. Funny how Charlie's name kept cropping up. Funny how he had stared at Carmel when she was showing Frankie around the studio. Funny kind of fella who goes around carving five bars of soap for a girl, just for decoration. It wasn't funny at all. Frankie had been in Dublin for under four hours and already he was eaten up by jealousy. He knew he had to snap out of it or he would be back with Eileen and the boiled cabbage before he could say 'Jack Robinson'.

He sat in the spare bedroom for nearly an hour with his case open in front of him, listening to the traffic below. His room was the plainest in the flat. Pale green walls and polka-dot curtains. There was a picture in a frame next to the bed made out of beach glass. The picture inside was an old, square Instamatic shot of himself and Carmel holding Captain Scarlet in her back garden. Carmel knocked on the door. 'Frankie, do you want some dinner?' She had a towel under her arm. She put it on the end of his bed and sat down next to him. 'I thought we could go to a club tonight. If you're not too tired, of course.'

'Yeah. That sounds good.' A club? How long had it been since Frankie was in a club? Not since the days of 'Scratchy's' in Kilkenny after the football. Not since the days of 'Ride On Time' and *Pump up the volume, pump up the volume. Dance! Dance!*

'We normally meet up for a drink first, so we should be going in about an hour and a half. I'll put some pasta on, so why don't you have a bath or something.' She pushed the towel down the duvet cover towards him. Her eyes flicked over to the window, like she was uncomfortable with him being there. Her fingers stroked the towel and the moment of silence gripped Frankie's heart like icy fingers. He tapped the back of her hand, which was decorated with silver rings. 'That's some bathroom you have. Can you imagine my mother in there?' He gave out a breathy laugh.

'I'd rather not.' She patted him on the head. 'In fact, I suggest you put her out of your mind whenever you can.'

Frankie agreed, but knew he also had to put the mermaid out of his mind. The mermaid above the bath who looked like Carmel. Who had Carmel's hair and Carmel's face and Carmel's breasts. The mermaid who was gazing smugly at herself in a hand mirror as the funny-faced fishes danced around her head. The mermaid that Charlie must have seen at one time. Perhaps he had helped to paint it? Perhaps she modelled for him in the bath without her clothes? 'Rather liberating, don't you think?'

'Shut up. Shut up. Shut up!' said Frankie to the mirror.

∫

So Lonely

They went for a drink first, at a hotel with a big brass rail around the marble bar-top and enormous lights hanging above them that looked like spaceships coming in to land. It was an after-work meeting place for well-heeled youngsters. All around them, boys with spiky hair and stripy shirts and big, bold cartoon ties were twirling beer bottles around in their hands. The girls had little boxy handbags slung over one shoulder and workday creases in their linen skirts. Charlie was dressed like a docker, boiling himself alive in the name of fashion. Big steel-capped boots and ripped jeans and a frayed sweater and a black woollen hat. His golden curls twirled out from beneath the wool, so even and glossy Frankie figured he must have used rollers. He ordered a cappuccino which arrived with a tubular biscuit with chocolate in the middle. Frankie's pint cost nearly three quid and they were playing Michael Bolton very loudly over the speakers. 'Who's idea was it to come here?' Frankie said to Carmel.

'Oh, shush! It's all right,' she hissed at him. 'Nancy works in the restaurant next door. She's coming with us. You'll like Nancy.'

'Are you setting me up?' The thought of a double date made him feel sick.

'No, just getting a bit of a posse together for the club.' Carmel pushed her hair back over a dangly turquoise-and-silver earring. 'It's really good. A lot of the kids from the college go. Charlie said he saw that girl singer out of the Cranberries there one night.'

'I wouldn't know her if I fell over her. Will they let him in looking like that?' Frankie nodded towards Charlie, who was seeing if he could suck the coffee up through the biscuit. Frankie wished he had a camera.

'Yeah. You can wear what you like,' she said. 'Everyone will be in jeans.'

Frankie pulled at his cream-coloured trousers to make sure that they weren't creasing up around the crotch. Charlie leaned back in his chair and waved at somebody over on the other side of the room. A red-haired girl made her way through the crowd towards them. Charlie shouted out to her. 'Oh, diaphanous Diana! Pale huntress of the night!'

'Fuck off, will you,' said the girl. She was wearing a black-and-white uniform with a little white hat and her freckled face glowed. 'Bloody boil the arse off you in that kitchen.' She blew upwards to lift a lock of damp hair out of her eyes, then clamped her hands down on Carmel's shoulders. 'Listen. I'll be off at about half ten if I can manage. I think Becka is coming too. That OK?'

'Yeah. Fine,' said Carmel, tapping her hand. 'This is Frankie, Nance.'

'Hiya.' Frankie nodded, loving the sound of Nancy's voice. As Dublin as Dublin gets.

'See you later, then,' she said. 'I'd better get back.' She left with a final slap to Carmel's shoulders and a nod to Frankie which sent her hair back into her eyes again. 'Bye, sexy,' said Charlie, and blew a kiss at her.

Frankie scowled at him. 'Bloody idiot,' he said under his breath.

Nancy and Becka joined them before last orders. By then, Frankie was pretty drunk. He wasn't knocked out with watching Carmel watching Charlie drinking three coffees and a mineral water and talking about Robert de Niro. Nancy's head was shaved at the back. She asked Frankie if he wanted to touch the stubble, but he declined, blushing like a beacon. She lived upstairs from Carmel. Becka, her flatmate, was an Australian girl who talked in question marks. She had been in Ireland for nine months and showed no signs of moving on. 'Where are you from?' Frankie asked her as she pushed her fingers deep into the roots of her straight, yellowy-blond hair.

'Queensland. A place called Cairns?' Frankie wished he had thought of a more original question. 'It's like a big holiday resort? All sun, surf and sex, you know the sort of thing.'

'No. I'm afraid we don't have those in Ireland. Over here, we have, um, rain, rheumatism and . . .' He trailed off, trying to think of a third. 'Rosaries,' said Carmel, nudging his arm. Becka leaned back and laughed, cigarette smoke coming from deep in her lungs. 'You're funny,' she said.

'Funny ha ha, or funny peculiar?' He was getting the collywobbles, wishing so much for them all to like him. For everyone in the pub to like him, even the boys with the loud ties and the girls with the boxy handbags. Carmel put her hand on his leg. He saw the way she was smiling at him. Of course she hadn't told them about what went on in Loughfergus. She had never mentioned Nancy or the people at the workshop when she was down at the Caesar's Palace. She was a keeper of boxes. One who divided her life up into a filing system and hated it when it got all messed up. Frankie's box was being relabelled at the moment. He was being moved to subsection D for Dublin, cross-referenced

B for brother. Charlie (A for Arsehole in Frankie's filing system) was talking to Becka and Nancy about some survey: 'Women choose a sense of humour over good looks every time.' The girls nodded. 'Oh, I don't know, though,' said Nancy, pulling on one of Charlie's ringlets with her chubby, freckly fingers. 'Only kiddin', Carmel.' She wiggled her eyebrows and grinned over at Carmel, and Frankie felt a javelin going through his chest.

Even though Frankie was wearing his best shirt, the others had to persuade the doorman to let him in. Charlie, in his paramilitary gear, didn't get a second look. It was hot and dark inside. They were dancing in sheepskin jackets and layers and layers of T-shirts. The music was pushing so loudly through the felt fronts of the speakers it was distorting. Frankie sat on a bench and watched the others jumping in and out of the strobing light like a silent movie. He didn't feel up to dancing. Nancy and Becka were soaking wet within seconds, their hair flapping and sticking on their faces. They came over and pulled him by both hands. 'Come on, Frankie. Give us a bit of the old Elvis the Pelvis.'

'In a minute.' He stayed where he was and grinned at them until his face hurt. He was older than anyone else there, older than the bouncer on the pavement. He was only a year older than Carmel and yet there she was, leaping around like a teenager. Charlie had kept his hat on and the sweat was running down his face. He was a good dancer, and opposite him Carmel's hips were following every movement. Her jacket was tied around her waist. Her hand kept touching his shoulder, brushing against the soft, damp fabric of his T-shirt. Other women were watching Charlie with his beautiful face and his beautiful hair. It was the way they used to look at Billy Stevens all those years ago when Billy Stevens looked only at Carmel. Looked at her the way Charlie did now. Frankie closed his eyes and felt the beat pounding in his chest. They put on 'Groove

Is In The Heart' by Deee Lite. The three other people who
were sitting on the bench jumped up so quickly that it
flipped up and Frankie fell off the end. He lay there with
a flattened cigarette end staring him in the face on the dirty
floor. Carmel ran towards him but was lost for a moment
in a puff of dry ice which whooshed out of a tube just above
his ear.

'What are you doing down there, you eejit?' she screamed.
'Come on and dance. They're playing some oldies now.' She
reached out and took his hand. It felt safe. Right on cue, they
played 'So Lonely' by the Police. The kids didn't know it,
acted like it was some new indie band. Frankie said 'What
the hell' to himself and allowed her to lead him through a
load of moon-faced teenagers. He tried to copy what the
others were doing, but felt sure he was dancing with his
bum sticking out. Nancy and Becka were singing along. *So
lonely, so lonely, so lonely.* It was a good feeling. They linked
their arms around each other's shoulders and twirled like
Greek dancers, kicking their feet up, jumping higher with
each crack from the drums. Leaning back, Frankie watched
the spinning coloured lights above his head zooming in and
out of his vision. It was a brilliant feeling. Later on, standing
in the cold carpark, their ears ringing from the hours of
loud music, Frankie was sick all over Charlie's steel-capped
boots. That was an even better feeling.

Owen Brothers

Christine had a new landmark to look out for. It crept up on her the first few times, the turning in the road where she had dropped him off. She was past it before she realised. After a while she started looking for it, watching the hedgerows getting a little greener as the weeks passed by. The fact that they only met once made him important. Those are the people who can really affect your lives. The woman in the bus queue who tells you to forget whatever guy has made you cry because he's not worth it. That's why she had kissed him. Because she knew that she would never see him again. Theirs was a perfect relationship.

It was a darn sight more perfect than her relationship with her brother, Pat. He was around her all the time. It was OK when he walked her home from work or fixed the shelves in her living room, but Pat always turned up at the wrong time. Moments when she was crying at a mini series on the telly or dancing around the living room with the Hoover and he was there in the doorway with a concerned look on his face. They didn't need to say anything. Christine knew that however many times she said that she was fine, Pat would read something into it and spend the next couple of hours staring at her over the newspaper until she felt like she had just carried two buckets of coal across town. He just couldn't put the past behind him.

Pat Owen had made his name in the boxing ring. You could tell it by looking at him. He was short, but muscular with thinning ginger hair cropped to peach fuzz and a squashed-in nose. It looked like someone had managed to cram a much larger man into his taut, freckled skin. Faded posters for Pat the Rat were tacked to the office wall. His mates called him Pat the fish because his drinking had made him more famous across Dublin than his fists ever did.

Pat answered the phone when Frankie rang. 'Wha'?' he said when he heard about the trip from New Ross. 'Who the fuck is Frankie, then?' he said as Christine came in about an hour later. She swallowed hard and looked out of the window. 'Well? You picked this fella up by the road, didn't you? In the middle of the night. After all I told you. Are you out of your bloody mind?'

He was waving his arms around like a windmill, she could tell without turning around. 'So what did Frankie want, then?' she said.

'A job. The cheek of him. I told him we were fully staffed.'

'What on earth did you say that for? He would be perfect. He could do the local journeys for us in the van.' Pat got up and came towards her. 'And don't tell me that the others can do them. They are hopeless, the lot of them.' She looked over at the map on the wall. Stabbed so often with so many pins that some of the larger towns had disintegrated and there was just the creamy paint showing through. Pat was biting the black plastic plug out of the end of his Biro. 'We don't even know this Frankie guy,' he said. 'He might be the worst driver in the world.' The Biro clattered against his teeth.

'Impossible. It would be too much of a fucking coincidence. Anyway, how are you going to know unless you meet him? Hand me over that number.' She beckoned to him with her red-painted fingernails. 'This fella is a dote, anyway. He does an Elvis act in his spare time.'

'Oh well, that makes it all right. An Elvis act! Why didn't you say!' Pat was trying to be sarcastic, but it wasn't working because the pen had leaked all over his lower lip. Eventually, he tasted the bitterness of the ink. He handed the message over to her and picked up the keys to his rig. He stormed out, spitting into his hand.

After he left, Christine paced around the office. She was wearing the big jumper that always took the door handles with it. It was comfy for driving. She hadn't expected Frankie to call and she couldn't work out whether she was pleased or not. Usually, when she met a man, she would start building a wall around her. Slapping mortar on to a few bricks during the first bits of small talk. Throwing his jokes back at him and gradually building it up until she had to stand on tiptoe to see over. It took her half an hour to phone the number on the message pad. It was answered by a woman.

'Er, hello. Sorry, is Frankie there?'

'Yeah. Just a second.' Clunk went the phone and Christine started to get nervous all over again.

'Hello?'

'Hiya, Frankie? Yeah, hi! I don't know whether you remember me. Oh, of course you do. I'm returning your call, aren't I? So, how are things? What brings you to Dublin? Is it the singing contest?'

Frankie was silent for a few seconds. Christine sounded different from the way he remembered. He had thought she was so tough that night you could have bounced rocks off her. It must have been the lorry. He was standing in Carmel's living room with a Crazy Prices shopping bag over his head. He had decided to cover up the grey patch of hair over his ear and warm little dribbles of black were coming out from under the plastic and patting down on the top of the receiver. 'I was wondering if you still needed a driver, but your brother told me . . .'

'Pat. Oh, he's useless. You might as well ask the cat.'

'Have you got one, then?'

'What? A cat?'

'No, a job.'

'Yes. What I meant was . . .' She turned her head away from the receiver. 'Oh, for fuck's sake!' She turned her head back. 'Sorry. I meant there is a job going here. I mean, we'd have to give you a bit of a test first. See if you can drive the van all right. Why don't you come in?'

'Fine. How about Thursday? I still have the bandage you gave me. I washed it.'

Oh God. Oh God! thought Christine. I gave him that stupid bandage, didn't I? Thought I was Michael Landon there for a minute. She tried to sound more businesslike. 'Ten o'clock would be good. Bring your driving licence and don't be late.' She hung up the phone quickly, but kept her hand on it for ages.

ʃ

Cher and Cheralike

Frankie had a letter. His mother had pressed so hard when she redirected the envelope that her handwriting had left indentations all over the TV station notepaper. It started 'Dear finalist' and told Frankie that he was being given the opportunity to look around the theatre and discuss his programme with the organisers. As it was to be such a big event, they were looking forward to meeting as many of the 'would-be celebritics' as possible.

He met Nancy first for a coffee. He waited outside the café because everyone stared at him when he went in. He spotted her hair weaving in and out of the crowds. 'Hiya,' she said, and kissed him on both cheeks. He wasn't used to such displays of affection and made a right mess of it. He nearly got her lips. They went in the door of the café and everyone looked again. A man waved at them from a table at the back. Frankie waved back to be polite. When he turned to ask Nancy where she wanted to sit, she was disappearing out of the door.

'What's wrong?' he said. Nancy was squashed into a doorway and she had her left palm pressed against her lips. She took her hand away and Frankie saw that she was laughing. 'See that fella who waved at me?'

'Yeah?'

'I shagged him at a party last month. Did you see the state of him? I must have been really drunk. You know, it's like the end of the school dance when they put the lights up and you get your first really good look at the fella you've been snogging all night. It's always, like, your worst nightmare. Like "Oh my God! The parish priest!"'

'Away with you,' said Frankie as they walked up the street to another café. 'I never got to snog anyone at the school dances. Even if I got some girl to agree to a slow dance, she'd spend the whole feckin' song making faces over my shoulder at some friend of hers. Comparing notes or something.'

Nancy laughed out loud. 'I used to do that. Pretending to be sick down his back and stuff.'

'It's very cruel and, as my mother would say, most unbecoming of a lady.' They came to another café and Frankie opened the door for her.

Nancy looked over at one of the waiters. He was good-looking and winked at her. 'You know what they say in the Bible,' she said. 'When the working day is done. Oh, girls just want to have fun.'

Frankie was still laughing when he got to the theatre. Nancy had written her phone number on a serviette for the waiter. Neither of them had a pen, so she wrote it in coffee, using the end of her teaspoon as a quill, and popped the serviette in the front pocket of his apron as they left.

The front of the theatre was covered with pictures from the play that was showing there. It was a costume drama with soldiers in tall hats and women in long skirts. Frankie stared for a long time at their faces, but he didn't recognise anyone from off the telly. The letter told him to go around the back to the stage door. There was a woman in the alley, puffing away on a cigarette and blowing the smoke upwards. She gave him a dirty look when he passed her. Inside the stage door, there was nothing but a dark corridor. The woman from the alleyway was silhouetted in the doorway. She was slim and wore a skin-tight black jump suit with a big leather belt and high-heeled boots. She was putting on red lipstick.

'Excuse me.' Frankie inched forward. 'Do you know anything about the talent competition? They said to be here at eleven thirty but there's nobody around.'

She moved towards him, her stiletto heels making her hips sway. 'They're all in here,' she said, pointing down the passageway. She had the quietest voice. It was barely more than a whisper. 'I've been here over an hour,' she said. 'And they haven't got to me yet. That's why I went out for a fag.' She had a lisp. Frankie followed her down the dark corridor, straining to hear what she was saying. Her name was Angelina. She was twenty-two and she worked in a shoe shop in Trim. She was Cher.

The stage was set for the play. A vast Napoleonic drawing room with chandeliers hanging from the ceiling and ornate chairs with curly gold backs. There were three sets of French windows opening on to a balcony and manicured gardens stretching off to the horizon. In the middle of this stood Gerard Burke in cut-off jeans and a James Brown Sex Machine T-shirt. On either side of him was an identical man dressed from head to toe in black. There was a stopwatch around his neck and a clipboard in his left hand. He spotted Frankie and Angelina as they sneaked in and sat down in the second row of the auditorium. He shaded his eyes with his right hand. 'Are you a new arrival?' he said. Frankie nodded. 'Oh right,' continued Gerard. 'Well, I've just been showing our Michael Jacksons the kind of lighting we have on offer.' He looked down at his clipboard. 'Oh, you're not our gentleman with the candles, are you? Our Phantom of the Opera?'

'No. I'm Frankie Shaw. The Wexford Elvis.'

'Elvis. Oh, yes. That's the second half of the show. I'll be talking to you a little later.' He smiled, then shouted out: 'Let's try number four, then, David,' and the stage lights went blue.

Frankie looked around him. There were about thirty people in the audience. Thirty very ordinary-looking people. All ages, shapes and sizes. Men in jeans and sweatshirts. Women with their handbags on their laps and their children fidgeting in the seats next to them. He had no idea who they were going to sound like when they opened their mouths. Frank Sinatra? Doris Day? Julio Iglesias? One was a dead giveaway, though. He was sitting right at the back, far away from the reflected light from the stage. Frankie looked over when he heard the crack of his knuckles during a lull in the proceedings. He could only see the glint from his sunglasses at first, but they were silver-framed and thick-stemmed. Elvis glasses. A style that never caught on, apart from in Elvis impersonation circles. When his eyes adjusted, Frankie could see that the man had Elvis hair, too, in the longer seventies cut. He was all in black and had his legs up on the seat in front of him. He was looking straight ahead with his fists tucked under his chin. Gerard introduced the leader of the band and the producer, whose name was Patricia.

The five Elvis impersonators were called up on to the stage just over an hour later. Apart from the man Frankie had seen earlier, they were a fairly ordinary bunch. They shook hands and sized each other up. A couple were in their fifties with greying sideburns (one of them had no other hair on his head to speak of). Frankie stood next to an Elvis of about his own age. A large man in a dark business suit. The sovereign rings on his knuckles made him look like a bouncer or a gangster, but he turned out to be a photocopier salesman. He was called Jerry and was from Sligo. The man in the glasses stood apart from the others. He seemed nervous and kept his hands in the pockets of his jacket. Gerard pointed out where the band would be and how they would know when to start. The stopwatch around his neck was on and the digital figures were counting up and up. Frankie looked down at the rows of red seats in front of him and up to the brass rail around the balcony. He felt weak at the knees and wanted to sit down in one of the golden chairs in the living-room set. Up close, the scenery didn't look at all realistic. He could see where the shadows had been painted on the balustrades outside the French windows to make it look like the sun was hitting them. Gerard pointed to the corner of the stage. 'That's where camera number one is going to be and the other one will be on a "long lead", if you will.' He tweaked his fingers to indicate the speech marks around 'long lead'. Gerard continued. 'He may be running around all over the place, so don't get distracted. Try not to look straight at him. Concentrate on the audience.' Frankie tried to take it in. The reality of being on television was a scary one. What if he won? What if women threw their underwear on stage at him? What would Eileen say?

Another Elvis asked: 'How many of us will there be in the final?' Gerard looked at his clipboard and turned over a couple of pages. 'Nine altogether,' he said. 'And, believe it or not, you've all picked different songs. I was afraid we'd have a fight on our hands like we did with the Madonnas.' They all smiled politely. *Nine Elvis Presleys standing on a stage*, sang Frankie to himself. Which one of them would be left when the other eight had fallen? What would they do with the broken ones?

Very Barbara Stanwyck

Trussed up in his Sunday best, Frankie rounded a corner, turning the street map in his hand. Owen Brothers was in East Wall, tucked between two building sites and backing on to the docks. The air was loud with electric saws and jackhammers and the distant clatter of trains. Christine was only a few feet away from him. He could see her through the plate-glass window of the office, her hair neatly tied back and the phone nestling between her chin and her shoulder. Frankie was crawling with embarrassment. The last time he had seen her, he had cried all over her. It felt like she was his only chance. There were plenty of unemployed mechanics in Dublin and very few jobs and he was running out of money.

He smoothed his hair with his fingers and ducked into the shadow thrown by a large container. It was his first-ever job interview. He had gone straight from school to the Lone Star and had stayed there, year in and year out. His hands were sweating so much he had smudged the page on the street map. 'Calm down,' he whispered, breathing in as slowly as he could, holding it for ten seconds and then breathing out.

Something Elvis O'Donovan had taught him that night in Kilkenny. He was nearing a state of meditation when there was a deafening noise directly behind his head. It came from within the container and was followed by several more, every bit as loud. Frankie leapt forward and made his way to the back of the container, thinking that someone was trapped inside. The doors were open and belching out icy air. Inside, he saw a man in a grey tracksuit and boxing gloves, using a frozen beef carcass as a punchbag, swinging it back against the metal wall. In between punches he sprang from side to side and shadow-boxed. When he spotted Frankie, he stopped and clung on to the carcass like it was a dancing partner. 'All right?' he grunted. Frankie smiled and nodded. The man came towards the door, pulling off his gloves. 'Rocky,' he said. 'Or Raging Bull. I got the idea from one of them films. Something to do, eh?' Frankie started to creep away towards the office, but the man called him back. 'Give us a hand, then. Can't have it defrosting.' Frankie helped him to close the heavy doors and seal the back of the container, then walked with him towards the office. He guessed this was Christine's brother, who had been rude to him on the phone. He didn't seem so bad up close.

'Are you from the bank, then?' said Pat as they went through the main door.

'No, I'm Frankie.' He stretched out his hand. 'I'm here to see Christine.'

Pat snorted a laugh. 'The Elvis guy? Jesus Christ!' Frankie's smile turned to cement. Pat was laughing in a showy way. The way the whole family used to laugh at the end of *The Brady Bunch* and you knew that they had rehearsed it a million times. Pat slapped Frankie on the shoulder. 'You've got to be kidding,' he grinned. 'You? Work for us?'

'Look. What's wrong? Give us a chance.' Now Frankie was really nervous. Pat was squishing him into a corner just outside the door of the office. Near enough for him to cry out, but they both knew it wouldn't look good. Christine finished her telephone conversation and there was a ringing and a high-pitched whine as a fax came through. Frankie tried to pull himself out of Pat's grip, but it just made his shirt cut even tighter into his neck.

'I don't trust you,' growled Pat. 'Any of you.' Frankie hadn't a clue what he meant. Men? Elvis impersonators? Pat relaxed his grip and Frankie slithered down the wall. 'Just one thing,' he growled, pointing his finger at Frankie. 'You watch yourself with her, because I'll be watching you.' With that, he turned and disappeared down the hallway. Frankie tried to compose himself. Christine was reading the fax and he stood in the doorway waiting for her to notice him. Eventually, he felt too much of a lemon not to say something, so he shuffled and cleared his throat. Christine looked up. 'Hello,' she said. 'You're early.'

'Yeah. I'm always early.'

'Very unusual for a man.'

'Not for a man in need of a job.' His heart was going mad. He was nearly as nervous as he was the night of the contest.

'I suppose not. So, em, nice to see you again, Frankie. How's things?' Her mouth was a non-committal thin, straight line. On her desk was a service manual. It was open at the problem-solving page. Christine put the kettle on and opened a packet of biscuits. 'Do you want me to look at this van for you?' he said, lifting up the manual.

'No. I'm fine, thanks. It's only a squeak.'

'Yeah? What kind of a squeak?'

She snatched the manual from him and put it on the worktop by the kettle. 'I said I was fine, thanks. It's just typical of a man to walk in here and think that he's a mechanic and that I'm some sort of cocktail waitress.'

'Er, I am a mechanic, remember? I didn't mean to offend

you or anything. Fair play to you if you can fix the squeak. I mean, I'm sure you can.' He couldn't fathom her. One minute she was one thing; the next, she was another. He had the bandage in his pocket, but somehow knew that it should never be mentioned.

Christine was staring at the biscuits. All of the ones on the top of the packet were broken. Pat must have dropped them in the supermarket. 'God. Sorry,' she said. 'Mega-rude of me. I'd be a terrible cocktail waitress, wouldn't I? Probably throw the bloody drinks all over the first man who looked at me sideways.' She squashed the teabags around in the mugs. 'Talking of drinks. I didn't even bother to ask if you wanted a cup of tea. I just went ahead and made it. Is it OK?'

'Brilliant. So, how's business?' Frankie sat down gingerly.

'Well, we survived another year and that's something, I suppose.' Christine handed Frankie a mug and sat down, putting her feet up on the desk. She stared past him, out of the window. 'Could have been better, though, if Pat had got his act together. He's the only one I trust. When he's sober, I mean. It sounds mad, I know, but it's true.' She sighed. Frankie thought she looked tired. 'Anyway, we're the only two insured on the rig,' she said. 'The rest of the people we employ either have their own transportation or run about in one of the vans.' This was Elvis movie-plot stuff. A woman in distress, in need of a strong worker, like Barbara Stanwyck in *Roustabout*. Tough on the outside because she had to be, but inside, she'd be OK.

'Funnily enough,' he said, 'Elvis used to be a delivery driver for an electrical company.' Frankie could see him, bouncing around in an old truck through the streets of Memphis, tapping the steering wheel and singing *That's all right, Mama!* He was a hero even then. In a sweltering Southern city where the typists undid the top buttons of their damp blouses and jiggled the fabric to let in some air, he delivered fans and air-conditioners. Cool! 'What kind of things will I be delivering if I get the job?'

'Memory,' she mumbled.

Like the corners of my mind, sang Frankie in his best Elvis voice. Christine laughed and told him it was computer memory which was worth a fortune and that's why all deliveries had to be signed for and checked thoroughly.

'If Elvis could do it,' he said, tapping rhythms on his leg, 'so can I.' He grinned at her and she put down the papers.

'You're good,' she said. 'You can do the accent and everything and make your lip go up on one side. I'd like to hear you sing some time.'

Frankie blushed. 'I've got a rehearsal soon. You can come along if you like. Just promise you won't bring your brother. He scares the life out of me.'

'He's fine.'

'He's mental! He just had me by the scruff of the neck out there.' Frankie laughed and pointed his thumb over his shoulder towards the door.

A polar wind suddenly blew from Christine's side of the room. She was staring coldly at Frankie. 'Keep your opinions to yourself, will you,' she said. 'Honestly, I can't open my mouth these days without some bloody man droning on and on about something he has no experience of.' Christine spewed out all the thoughts she had late at night sometimes. The nights when she was angry with the whole world and aching for someone to hold her. She was still Pat's big sister, no matter what happened. He was a kind man at heart, but he couldn't pass a dustbin without kicking it twenty feet down the road.

'Sorry,' he said. 'I shouldn't have said what I did about your brother. I'm the same about my mother. I moan about her all the time, but if someone else tries . . .'

Christine sat up straight and smiled at Frankie. 'I don't

blame you if you think he's a waste of space. He likes to give that impression himself. Sit down.'

'I thought you wanted me to leave.'

'No. No. I was just sounding off, you know. You'll have to get used to it if you're thinking about working here.'

'Well, are you sure that'll be all right? I mean, providing you think I can drive all right. What about all that *Mná na h'Eireann*, all men are bastards stuff?'

'I didn't mean you. I meant men.' She opened the top drawer of the desk and took out a folder. 'So, Frankie,' she said. 'You said you were a mechanic. Did you bring in a CV for me?' Frankie handed it over, not sure what he was letting himself in for. She was every bit as bonkers as her brother. A real drama queen. Very Barbara Stanwyck.

The Old Town Looks the Same

Frankie took three buses from Dublin. It had only been two weeks, but he felt like he was returning from war. As he rounded the corner and came down the hill with his sports bag in his hand, he half expected the women to drop their laundry baskets and cheer him along. For Michael and Hank to break into a trot coming out of their doors to greet him. As he came towards the Palace, he stopped and hoisted his bag on to his shoulder. Two tents, one red and one green, were pitched in a small field. The red tent was larger; the triangular type. A few items of clothing were drying on a bush beside it. A couple of foldaway chairs sat empty outside, the long grass caressing their steel legs. The second tent was smaller and rounded, like a giant caterpillar pupa, and was secured by a network of fine orange ropes. So low on the ground that a person would have to stick their bum up to crawl into it. 'Where did they come from?' he said, as if the tents had just arrived one morning and pitched themselves.

He got his answer as soon as he reached the garage. They came in the battered white camper van with stickers in the back window that was being disembowelled by Michael and a girl with punky hair. She was called Jo and was Michael's new apprentice. In fact, Michael was more keen to tell Frankie all about her and their new residents than he was to ask him how he got on in Dublin. New Zealand. Put a knitting needle through the earth and that's where it comes out. Hazel, Colin and Greg were passing through, heading west, when their van stopped.

Hazel's father was Scottish. Her mother was Thai. Eurasian, she called herself. 'Chinesey' was what Liam called her. She was a physiotherapist from Auckland and was going out with Colin, who was a doctor at the same hospital. He was as large and muscular as she was small; as ungainly as she was graceful. Greg was slender and fair with intensely blue eyes and a few boyish freckles on his nose and around his lips, which were very pale. His light brown hair was thinning at the front and tied back into a ponytail which gave the impression that it had pulled his whole hairline back from his face. He was the quiet one of the three, who dawdled a few steps behind the others, but every bit as friendly. Michael said the whole village would be sorry to see them go.

Eileen had left the door ajar. She seemed pleased to see him. She was in a smart navy two-piece and her hair was freshly done. He wondered if she had dressed up for his return. Did she want him to come back? Was she going to promise him a new start and come to his Elvis concert with a banner that said 'We love you Frankie'? He asked her if there was anything that needed doing around the house. The coal-hole door had been hanging off its hinges when he left, so perhaps he could get stuck into it in the morning. Eileen reached out and took him by the wrist. She got up from her chair and led him out of the back door, turned, pointed and said: 'Look!' A new door with new paint. 'Michael did that, did he?' said Frankie. Eileen was just about to speak when a male voice came ringing around the side of the house.

'Oo-roo, Mrs S!' A man of Frankie's age was standing by them and Eileen did a little skip to stand next to him. He was broad and dark and good-looking and he put his hand around her shoulder, shaking it gently. In his other hand was one of the Tupperware boxes she put her scones in. He had come to return it. 'Ah,' he boomed. 'This must be your son that I have heard so much about. Frank, isn't it?' Both of them were smiling their heads off. Frankie stood there like a halfwit, quite unable to say anything. Had she gone out of her mind? Had she adopted someone else in his absence? Eventually Frankie's Catholic schooling kicked in and he held out his hand. 'I'm Colin,' said the young man, and shook his hand vigorously. One of the blessed New Zealanders, and he had been helping her out. The coal hole was his handiwork, as were the new plugs on the radio and telly. There was nothing else to be done, so Frankie could just sit down and relax. Colin asked him a few questions about the Elvis competition and said that he would see him down at the Palace later on. After he left, Eileen changed into her housecoat and got on with the dinner. All she talked about was the New Zealanders. That Hazel was such a lovely girl. Lovely, and didn't she and Colin make a lovely couple? Lovely, and wasn't Colin kind to fix the television aerial on Mrs Phelan's roof? So kind, and wasn't that Greg a quiet one? Quiet, and he had helped Hank out a few times at the Palace. Greg had made the sandwiches Tuesday lunch-time, and weren't they the best sandwiches anyone had tasted? Raw onion, that's what he used, apparently. Hank should let him at the kitchen more often. His parade well and truly rained on, Frankie dialled Carmel, hoping she would persuade him to come back early, but all he got was her answerphone.

Down at the Palace, Hank squeezed around the bar and

embraced Frankie. Michael rubbed his hands together and asked him what he wanted to drink and Christy gave him a chorus of 'Hound Dog' from the corner. Things were back to comfy normality. Well, nearly. Behind the bar was Greg, the quiet one. He was flipping the remote control on the TV while the beer was pouring. Hank snatched it from him a few minutes later, and throughout the evening the crowd were treated to a strange mix of football and an episode of *The Avengers* where Steed was being chased through a winter woodland by three men in tweed jackets.

Sunday morning, Michael and Frankie got together for a rehearsal. Betty came along with his costume and he darted into the gents' to try it on. Hank and the New Zealanders gave him a cheer when he did a twirl for them. They were leaning over a map, working out their route for the following week. They discussed it while Betty stuck a few more pins in him. Kerry was a dead cert, as they were all into cycling and the Cliffs of Moher, because of a promise that Greg had made to his granny. It turned out that she was from Lisdoonvarna and his father's side were from Mayo. 'A real Irishman,' said Hank, laughing at the way Greg was pronouncing the place names. The funny thing was that Greg really did fancy himself as an Irishman. New Zealand was green and beautiful and full of myth and legend, but there was something missing. Whatever that something was, he hadn't found it in Rome or Tangiers or London. In Ireland he was happy, and he had taken to writing long letters to his parents, telling them things he could never have told them face to face. Hank, for the romantic he was, had a cynical view. 'I call it the Pat's Bar Syndrome,' he said. 'I've spent a bit of time in the States and I can tell you now it's full of places called Pat's Bar where fellas like yourself sit drinking lousy Guinness and eating cabbage and bacon and singing "Galway Bay". All that tourist board stuff.

Sometimes they've had me believing it too. I'd like to see them living here and trying to get a job. The old romance would wear off pretty quickly.' This gave Greg the needle. He remarked that Hank was a fine one to talk, what with his Wild West hall of fame and 'Your Cheatin' Heart' on the juke-box. He'd never been to a Pat's Bar in his life. 'I do make a pretty good Irish stew, though,' he said, and wandered into the kitchen, leaving Hank heavy-hearted. Hazel held Hank's shirtsleeve and said, 'Leave him. He cooks when he's happy and he cooks when he's sad.'

Michael was MC of the karaoke machine again. Their rehearsal was intense. Stop, start, stop, start, like a game of musical chairs. 'Don't Be Cruel' was the number he had chosen for the finals, with 'Return To Sender' as a back-up. 'Don't Be Cruel' was a good showing-off song. Lots of lazy hip swinging and loose phrasing and that lovely 'Hmmm' at the beginning of the second verse. What's more, Gerard Burke had assured Frankie that there would be a group of session singers booked to do the Jordanaires behind him in sequinned jackets. Another thing he liked about it (although he didn't tell Michael) was that it was quick. He could be on and off in the time it took a kettle to boil. Michael thought that Frankie wasn't selling the song enough. He wanted him to move around the stage and reach out to the audience, but Frankie knew what he was doing. 'Nah,' he said. 'You don't understand. The whole reason this song is dynamite is the way Elvis sings it. It's like he's only doing it because he's nothing better to do. Kind of offhand at the beginning. Then, about halfway through, he starts to get into it and bounce around and clap his hands and flop his hair and stuff and then before you know it, he's finished and you're left wanting more. Watch me, Michael.'

Frankie stood in the middle of the stage, the black oblong

of the karaoke machine in place of the Jordanaires. He didn't strike an exaggerated pose. It was more Lady Diana than Elvis, head down and eyes peering up through the strands of hair that hung like a hula skirt over his brow. With the first few bars, he raised his right forearm and snapped his fingers on the beat, the merest ripple coming from his hips. He brought the microphone up to his lips, tucking it close to his chest, as if he were telling it a secret. Just a slight raising of his head allowed him to share it. *You know I can be found sitting all alone. If you can't come around, at least please telephone.* He was down in the dumps, pleading with his girl. Michael moved back and leaned against the wall, looking at Frankie from a distance as someone looks at a large painting in a gallery. How could anyone be cruel to such a contrite little boy? On the next line, he raised his head some more, confusion and mild panic dusting his features. He added Elvis's childish little squeal to the word 'please' in the line *Please forget my past. The future looks bright ahead.* He took a step forward. Just a small step but Michael felt like he was leaping on top of him. When he sang *Baby it's just you I'm thinking of,* Frankie flicked his hair out of his eyes and pointed at Michael, who smiled from ear to ear. From then on, it was exactly as Frankie had said. He started to get into it, to smile and flutter his eyelids and sweet-talk about weddings and wanting no other love. He crossed his heart and blew a kiss and clapped his hands and shook his whole body. It was mesmerising. He even pointed behind him when the Jordanaires went *ooooh,* smiling at them like he was the only person who could really see them. The song ended with Frankie in his opening position, returning to his sulk. Michael clapped his hands above his head. It warranted a fanfare. There was a lot to be said for city living. At the age of thirty-two, Frankie Shaw had at long last learned to flirt.

As they ran it through again, the twanging bass line stretched through the pub like chewing gum. Hazel patted the knees of her jeans and Colin tapped the table-top. A smell was wafting from the kitchen that was so wonderful, it made Hank feel like crying.

On Your Left, Ladies and Gentlemen

Monday, Monday. So good to me, sang Frankie. It was Carmel's CD and it seemed to be stuck in the machine. When he pressed the open button, the CD drawer shot out and shot back in a split second. No time to swap, so the Mamas and Papas it would be for the rest of the morning. It was a hot one with the windows open and the flat still smelling of Carmel's shower gel. She was at work and he wasn't starting until midweek because Christine had a couple of large deliveries to do. It was a whole new Monday feeling. No longer adrift and unemployed, he was happy to potter around and sing hippie songs. At half past ten, he looked up from his book and noticed something catching in the breeze outside the window. It was a postcard on a long piece of string coming from Nancy and Becka's flat upstairs. On the back was a message inviting him up for a coffee. He tugged on it and Becka emerged, her hair dripping down on him. Her face was shaded by the bright sun. He said, 'OK if I come up now?' and turned off the CD.

Their flat was a mess, but had a certain style. Gaudy

seventies furniture was covered in batik fabric and the walls were pink. Posters slid from their Blu-tack in the heat and dust coated the ornaments, but there was one hell of a cocktail cabinet with mirrored doors and an old Terence Trent D'Arby album playing on the turntable. Becka was in a pair of frayed denim shorts and a sleeveless top. He noticed a tattoo of an angel on her arm. 'Coffee?' shouted Nancy from the kitchen as she emptied a half-packet of fig rolls on to a plate. 'Do you want it here or outside?' said Becka, taking him by the hand and leading him to a bedroom strewn with clothes and make-up. The window opened out on to a rooftop. It was only Carmel's bathroom roof, but it offered a new view of the city and sucked up the sun like a sponge. It was set up with a blanket and some cushions and Becka pulled the speakers into the bedroom doorway. Nancy emerged a few minutes later singing *Dance little sister*. Becka took the tray from her and she climbed out of the window. On the tray was a sugar bowl and three mugs, each with a different logo. 'Which do you want?' said Nancy, offering it to him. 'Top Cat, Euro '96 or Dave's Mug.' Frankie took the one nearest to him. 'Who's Dave?' he said.

'Fuck knows,' she said. And there they sat for the next hour or so, looking at the rooftops and listening to records and chatting. Nancy pulled her pink T-shirt dress above her knees and kicked off her sandals. Her legs were a glowing white between the freckles. Becka fetched an enamel pill-box from her dressing table and, with her bracelets jangling, she split a cigarette, lit and crumbled a corner of dope and rolled a joint. Frankie tried not to stare at the procedure, but he was fascinated. It was the first time he had ever experienced drugs close up. When it was passed to him, he pretended it was an everyday thing and inhaled like Jack Nicholson in *Easy Rider*, laughing to hide the cough. Nancy lay back on the cushions, the joint rising like a wick from her mouth. 'Bloody lovely,' she said and Frankie said, 'Yep.'

Halfway through a Madonna album, they started talking about Carmel. The girls were sprawling, lazy-eyed, finishing a second joint, but the dope hadn't had much effect on Frankie. He asked them about Charlie and Nancy grinned. 'He's gorgeous, isn't he?' she purred, cupping her hands behind her head. 'She always gets the gorgeous ones.' Frankie felt sick, but his curiosity was too strong. 'Do you mean Billy?' he asked, flicking pieces of gravel off the roof.

'Who's Billy? I don't remember a Billy,' said Becka, as if she were going through a long list in her head.

'He was her husband,' Nancy sighed. 'That was before you came. He was OK, but not as nice as Brendan or Nick or that one with the American car. What was his name?' They fell silent as they tried to think of it. Frankie's heart had sunk about as low as it could get and the sun was giving him a headache. He put on Becka's mirror glasses and leaned back against the window sill, watching plane trails in the sky.

The doorbell rang. It was Charlie in boy scout shorts and a spotless white T-shirt. He kissed the girls and sat next to Frankie, dangling his legs over the guttering. 'I'm here on a mission,' he said, taking a mug off Becka. 'From God?' she said. 'Nah.' He squinted. 'From Carmel.' Frankie snapped out of his fantasy about pushing him over and watching him plunge, ringlets blowing in the wind.

Frankie couldn't understand what had possessed Carmel to do it. To get Charlie of all people to show him around Dublin for the afternoon. It took until four o'clock to get rid of him. It was like going on a retreat at school with some over-enthusiastic, Simon and Garfunkel-loving priest spouting out parables as you sat, picking grass on the playing fields. Charlie could have been a tour guide. He was far more impressive, far more boastful than the skinny girl who showed them around Trinity College. The anoraks worn by the Japanese tourists were louder than her little voice. People at the next table were listening in to Charlie as they sat in the warm glow of MacDaid's. He had been lecturing Frankie on the great literary pubs of Dublin, pointing at stern photos stuck up all over the walls. If he didn't know absolutely everything, he kept it well hidden. Frankie's only concern was to get as many pints of Smithwicks down his throat as possible. From what he heard, all of these writers spent most of their time getting in some serious drinking. If you can't beat them, join them, thought Frankie. Charlie was trying to beat them. He was spouting poetry left, right and centre. Is that what Carmel liked? Verbal flowers in big, perfect bunches being hurled at her from all directions? Is that what they were up to in her bedroom? Was he reading passages to her from James Joyce as she lay gazing up at him? That's probably why he looked so knackered in the mornings. Reading out all that stuff with no full stops.

It was an effort to get Charlie drunk. His glass was always half full and Frankie had to stare at him impatiently and pat at the change in his pockets until he got the hint. When he finally left, Frankie did a fantastic job of standing up and shaking his hand and thanking him for the interesting history lesson. Yes, he must get around to reading some of those books. Yes, he was sure it would expand him as an artist. What a load of crap! He liked Elvis songs and so did most people. James Joyce never wrote anything very catchy.

Dublin was very musical for a Monday. Mind you, it was a hot day and the Yanks were out in force. An army of bomber jackets and clean sneakers and pink socks. Frankie sat on a step and watched and listened. A bunch of kids were entertaining the crowds with some traditional stuff. They weren't bad. A young boy was pat-ta-ta-pat-ing away on the bodhrán with two spotty girls on fiddle and banjo. The Yanks were lapping it up. Flat caps bobbing up and down in the crowd on Grafton Street. A little further down, two scruffy guys were sitting in a doorway on a car rug. They were doing something angry on guitars covered with stickers. Students jangled by them in long skirts and big boots and there was a smell of strawberries in the air. The traffic was snarled up around St Stephen's Green. People were crossing between the cars. Women in summer dresses and guys in suits with their jackets over one shoulder, and for a split second, Elvis. He was all in black, young and lean, but his hair was long. He was wearing a red bandanna around his neck. He could have walked straight out of his 1968 comeback special. His stride was wide and laid-back as he emerged from behind a bus, but then he stopped, pivoted on his Cuban heel and looked over to Frankie. It was just a glance, but it burned deep into Frankie's gaze. A van went by and he was gone. Frankie leaned back, fuzzy-headed as the music mixed with the usual cries: 'Cigarette lighters. Five for a pound!' and some fella going on about Jesus. The sun came in and out and the sounds came in and out and above him the sheeting flapped on some scaffolding. Suddenly, Charlie was right and James Joyce was right and Frankie wanted to say he was sorry for being so down on them both. This was a poetic city if you opened your eyes. There was room in it for Elvis and Molly Malone and Carmel and Charlie and Thin Lizzy and the Mamas and Papas.

S

Stuck in the Mud

At the theatre, Gerard Burke was smart-casual in his Caterpillar boots and jeans and a cream linen shirt. He made the Elvis impersonators look a bit 'old hat' in their western shirts and black slacks. Frankie was glad he was wearing his delivery driving clothes. He was getting into the swing of things. Christine had stayed in the van with him for the first couple of days, showing him all the short cuts. He had only got lost twice the day before and had completed all his deliveries before the offices closed.

The Elvises had been summoned, this time on the phone, and those that could had arrived in dribs and drabs on a gloomy Tuesday morning. The strange little man with the mirror glasses was the first one there. He was a local. Frankie was second, and attempted to talk to him, but the guy in the glasses just laughed and bit his fingernails. When Frankie noticed that there were words tattooed on his knuckles, he went and sat by himself.

'We've had this idea,' Gerard said when they were all assembled, twirling his stopwatch in front of him. 'Well, it's more of a concept really. We want to do a thing called

"Forever Elvis", create a bit of continuity with what you're doing.' The Elvises looked at each other. Already they were nervous, but when Gerard attempted to line them up like a school assembly, passing a downturned hand over their heads and saying 'Now you, now you,' the rebellion began.

'Hang on a minute,' said the shortest, the bald man who was in a shiny tracksuit. 'You see, this isn't going to work, Gerard my boy. It isn't going to work.' Gerard folded his arms and gave the man a questioning look. 'It isn't going to work because I wear different shoes. I had them made to give me a bit more height.' On the word 'height', the bald guy swung up on to his toes, lifting himself by around two inches and making him equal to the man in the glasses, who was standing to his right. Gerard sighed and pulled him up a place in the line. With that, the Elvis in glasses who now found himself at the end said 'Me too' and stood on tiptoe. He made a fist as he said it. The shortest Elvis flinched, his mind trying to work out how he could build up his shoes a little further. Gerard stood back and frowned, imagining an ever-growing line of men producing stilts and stepladders so that none of them would go down as Ireland's shortest Elvis. Frankie shuffled his feet and considered for a moment that he hadn't given much thought to his shoes. So far, he had worn his smart black lace-ups to the fittings. He needed to find something a tiny bit more Vegas, seeing as all the others were taking it so seriously.

Gerard soon gave up on the idea of filing on like beauty contestants. Plan B was to have all the Elvises standing on different parts of the stage and, one by one, they would be discovered in spotlights, performing a line or two from their songs. This idea had the musical director rubbing his chin and sucking in through his teeth. Gerard marched up and down, not really listening to the technicians. 'That will be nine more specials,' said the lighting guy through a crackling PA system. It went quiet as Gerard mulled the idea over. Frankie looked above him at the confusion of lights and cables. Millions of plugs with white-painted numbers and letters. B73. D19. Someone had to put them there and point them all in the right direction.

Once again, there was discontent in the Elvis camp. The shortest Elvis had elected himself union leader. 'We feel,' he said, 'that it might take something away from our acts if people knew what we were going to sing.' The Elvis in glasses snorted from the shadows. Gerard was close to giving up, but he made one last attempt at placing all the Elvises around the stage, imagining circular pools of light around their feet. They all struck an Elvis pose with their legs splayed. Frankie remembered a playground game called Stuck in the Mud. It was like tag, but if you were touched by the person who was 'it', you would have to freeze with legs parted until someone climbed through. 'OK. OK. How about the opening of "Jailhouse Rock",' said Gerard, regaining some of his earlier confidence. 'You know. *Da dum . . . Pum! Pum!*' He mimicked the guitars and drums and swivelled his hips in time. 'Not bad,' the union leader said, and the others grunted and nodded. With each 'Da dum . . . Pum! Pum!' a new hip-shaking Elvis would emerge until they all rocked together. Bingo! Now Gerard was getting into it, pointing at the stuck-in-the-mud Elvis at the far right-hand corner of the stage. 'Da dum! Don't stop moving now.' Once they had all gone 'Da dum' and wiggled, Gerard had them all singing a line. 'Elvis number one. What's the first line of the song?'

Warden threw a party in the county jail, sang the photocopier salesman from Sligo. *The prison band was there and they began to wail*, sang Frankie, putting his heart and soul into it. He had standards to stick to, even in rehearsal. By the time the first chorus was under way, a wall of Elvises sang together, clicked together, clapped together. Gerard was glowing with excitement, skipping across the stage, his stopwatch bouncing against his chest. *Everybody, let's rock*, sang the Kerry Elvis, who sounded promising. He was young and handsome, but until that moment had never said a word. When it came to his line, the Elvis in glasses was acting even weirder. What came out was a mad sort of roar, sliding up and down the scale, improvising Elvis in an almost jazzy way. 'Now all come to the front of the stage,' said Gerard. 'The ones at the back first. Imagine there's another one there and there. Remember we're two short today.' Frankie plodded forward, trying to get into the spirit. It felt safe to be on stage with other people. He wished they could do the whole contest like that.

There was barely time for individual run-throughs, as the rest of the superstar impersonators were starting to arrive. The Elvises gathered in the corridor that led to the stage door as they waited their turn. A couple lit up cigarettes and one made a call on a mobile phone. As Frankie finished his rehearsal, the Elvis in the mirror glasses came up to him, but didn't say anything. He stood with his hands on his hips and stared until Frankie tried again to introduce himself. 'Wacker,' he said at last in a broad Dublin accent. 'You're a bit good, aren't you? Fancy your chances, then, do you, man?'

'As much as anyone else here, I suppose,' smiled Frankie, moving towards the door. Wacker grabbed him by the sleeve. 'You're better than those bastards,' he hissed, pointing a thumb at the others. 'You've got the spirit, man. The spirit of Elvis. He's with you, man, just like he's with me. I can see him. He's watching us, man.' Frankie thought about seeing Elvis in the traffic jam, but decided not to mention it. Wacker pulled up his mirror glasses and sat them on top of his oily hair. His eyes were an eerie blue. Tinted contact lenses. The word written across both of his fists was ELVIS. Wacker tapped the bridge of his nose with an index finger. 'Me or you,' he said, backing away. 'He will decide.'

'Bloody hell,' said Frankie as he emerged into the daylight. 'Sanity!' He looked at his watch. Time to be getting back to Owen Brothers and another van of memory.

Garlic

There was definitely something new in the air as Frankie walked past the post office. It wasn't the visitors. No more camper van around the side of the Lone Star. No more tents in the field. Garlic, that's what it was. Lovely garlic bubbling in butter, wafting from the back window of the Palace. It was advertised on a blackboard outside the door. TONIGHT'S SPECIAL. GARLIC MUSHROOMS. SEAFOOD PIE. FRESH FOOD SERVED DAILY. Frankie rubbed his eyes. Same village, same pub, new smells and sounds. A parallel universe. Several years before, Hank had flirted with the idea of serving food other than sandwiches, but it had come to nothing. This was quite a departure, and judging from the noise coming from the pub, a successful one.

Incredible! If Frankie had read it in the papers, he still wouldn't have believed it. There she was, looking like a regular, chatting away to Hank with her hand on his arm. Eileen Shaw, sipping a bitter lemon and polishing off a plate of king prawns. Their papery shells and pleading limbs lay crumpled in a dish in front of her. 'Frank!' she said, waving.

'Over here.' She was sitting with her sister, Greta, her knees tucked under the table. 'I wasn't sure if you were coming, so I didn't make lunch. Why don't you get young Greg to make you some of these prawns?' Frankie nodded as Greta's husband, Con, pushed a chair over from another table. It turned out that Eileen popped into the Palace without much provocation these days. Her independence was no longer a novelty to the others. Frankie wondered if it had been done to make him feel guilty about not coming home for two weekends, but there was such enjoyment in her face. When Frankie had reached the house earlier and found it empty – no Eileen, no dinner smells or peas soaking or table laid – he had had the terrible vision that she had died all alone or was up at the hospital. But no. He had come all the way home, cherishing the idea of the rosy reception he was going to get, and she had cleared off to the pub.

Hank looked the same. No he didn't, he was happier. He seemed to enjoy his tiffs with Greg, who had decided to stay for a while longer. The others had rumbled out of the village with little short of a civic send-off the previous Tuesday. Off to the Ring of Kerry. Greg had stayed because after Paris, Rome and London as a threesome, Colin and Hazel deserved a little time on their own. A bit of romance, and who knew what might be the outcome? He planned to join them in a couple of weeks. The whole village applauded him for his selfless act and he was taken in by Hank and installed in the spare room. Yes, the spare room, Michael assured Frankie. Definitely the spare room.

As Frankie ate his seafood, he noticed that 'Dancing In The Street' by Martha Reeves and the Vandellas was playing on the juke-box. The guys were singing along to it. There were more young people than usual and kids ran around the beer garden, stealing chips from their parents' plates. Thirty-two years he had spent in that village, waiting for something to happen. Thirty-two years of Eileen laying the table and 'Your Cheatin' Heart'. He had begun to believe that it would be like that until the end of time. Then he went away for a few short weeks, looking for adventure, and he missed all the fun. A posse really did ride into his little town and chase the ghosts away. Something he and all the sequins in the world could never do.

'Mind what you're doing!' shouted Hank to Greg, who was standing behind the bar, throwing a glass from one hand to the other before putting it under the pump. 'Who do you think you are, bleedin' Tom Cruise?' Greg danced around as he got change from the cash register and handed it to Michael's punky assistant and a couple of her friends. They all cheered, knowing how much it would annoy Hank. 'Enough of that!' he shouted from Frankie's table. 'Or I'll have you all in there doing the washing up.' He sat down next to Frankie and loosened his apron, saying it was ages since they had had a chat. Indeed, when Frankie thought about their afternoon sitting down behind the bar, it did seem like a long time ago. Hank said that Greg could be a pain in the arse, but he was right about cooking. It made all the difference to the place; brought in a few families from Enniscorthy on a Sunday afternoon. When Greg had gone, he was thinking of getting someone full time in the kitchen.

Frankie looked for a hint that there was something more going on than cooking. He liked the idea of Hank and Greg as a double act, chiding each other and flipping the television channels until the doors were closed and it was time to kiss and make up. Greg was not much of a cowboy, though. He was a dance-music junkie, a fitness freak who cycled to the coast every morning on his racing bike and knew everything there was to know about *Star Trek* and nothing about John Wayne. Anyway, his little posse had left town and he was soon to follow them. It was best if he didn't leave a broken heart behind him like all the cowboys did.

∫

The Geometry Set

The finals loomed large. Frankie rehearsed in the lounge and among the little fishes in the bathroom. He sang in the delivery van with his backing tape blaring from an old radio cassette of Carmel's. In the big, noisy city, he could be as loud as he wanted. Funnily enough, it was Carmel who was quiet all of a sudden. She seemed to disappear to a world within herself. Frankie hadn't lived with her long enough to know whether it was something that happened from time to time. He worried that she was grieving for her mother and he couldn't help her. Nancy and Becka were away on a last-minute bargain holiday to the Greek islands, so he just sat in with her and didn't pry.

Work started every day at eight in the morning when the drivers gathered in the Owens' yard and drank coffee and tea. On the days when there weren't nine o'clock deliveries to be made, he tinkered around with the vans or tidied up the yard. If not, he was off into the traffic with a pile of delivery notes attached to a clipboard. They were pink on top for the office and white on the bottom for the client. They were signed, printed, timed and dated daily by receptionists in blazers, who smiled and chatted for a while. Computer deliveries were usually 'back door', with an intricate set of coded keypads and metal shutters to be navigated before he could push his trolley into the building. Those places smelled of paper and sour milk and the men were quiet and signed the delivery notes in tense, microscopic handwriting. There were days, though, when things took a lighter turn. A consignment of musical potties had the staff of a mother and baby shop in a party mood. They invited Frankie to join them as they poured diet cola into the bowls, sending the tinny strains of 'Congratulations' and 'Baa Baa Black Sheep' around the stockroom.

Christine was excellent. At the office, she was on the phone, mainly, but sometimes she would come and sit with him while he was working on one of the vans. She was good to talk to, although she never gave much away about herself. Frankie presumed that she was in most nights because she watched every soap opera going and gave him blow-by-blow accounts of the heartbreaks and triumphs of her favourite characters. She got quite passionate about certain storylines and Frankie had a feeling that they were close to home, but he didn't ask. Pat was out of sight most of the time and, looking at the rosters on the office wall, Frankie reckoned that Christine was keeping them apart. The other drivers were nice. Frankie was friendly with a couple called the Beechys, who were in their late fifties with grown-up sons. They were the ones who reminded him about Christine's birthday.

It was on a Friday, so the idea was to meet up after work and go for a drink. When Frankie got back from his rounds, he looked at her through the window. She was standing talking to Pat. There were a few cards lined up on the window sill, looking from the outside like a lower set of milk teeth. He stood with his clipboard and his keys in his hand, thinking about his shoulder bag which was tucked behind the hat rack. Inside was Christine's present, and he wasn't sure whether to give it to her right away, or wait until he was in the pub. Either way, it was going to be an embarrassment. Why hadn't he bought her something less personal like a mug or candlesticks? Why did he have to get carried away? Pat was leaning against the filing cabinet when Frankie came in and put the delivery notes on Christine's desk. He nodded as Frankie retrieved the bag, but twitched as he came closer to the window where Christine was standing, holding up a compact and applying a pink lipstick. She looked over her shoulder at Frankie and smiled, then angled the compact mirror so she could see Pat. As he started to move, she snapped the mirror shut, put her handbag over her shoulder and said 'Right, then' and reached for her jacket.

It was a large pub with a square, central bar. The others had bagged a table against a back wall and they gave a little cheer as Christine approached. On the table was a collection of presents, so Frankie added his, glad that he had waited. Mr Beechy bought a round and they all raised their glasses. Over on the other side of the pub, there was a karaoke machine and the first performers of the evening were lining up. While a girl sang 'My Guy', Christine started to unwrap her presents. Pat spotted a couple of friends and moved over to the bar and Frankie looked nervously at his package, wrapped by Carmel with twirly ribbons. She was saving it till last, glancing at it as she unwrapped the others. She did get a mug from one of the drivers and some bubble bath, and a new coffee filter machine from the Beechys. At last, her hands rested on Frankie's gift. She looked over at him and smiled and he looked in the other direction. She unfolded the paper carefully and slowly lifted the present out. It was still wrapped in a layer of blue tissue paper and one of the lads made a joke about pass the parcel. Frankie was dying of embarrassment, knowing what was to come. He'd had this idea that Christine was the kind of woman who did not spend money on herself. Never treated herself to luxuries. She wore a little make-up. He had seen her putting it on in the rear-view mirror of her car some mornings. But, no matter what, she wore earrings. Bright coloured earrings. Frankie had persuaded Carmel to sell him one of her hand-made treasure chests. A trinket box with a shiny gold padlock and Carmel's trademark seaweed patterns and shells on the side. It was purple and gold and deep green. The lining inside was black velvet and Carmel had painted Christine's initials on the lid in tiny gold letters. Frankie had thought it would be practical. Now he sat, frozen to the spot, watching Pat as he stood and shared a beer with his friends. He was praying that he wouldn't look over and see it. 'Aaah!' said the crowd at the table as Christine held it up to the light, running her fingers over it. 'Frankie,' she said breathlessly. 'My sister made it,' he snapped. Pat hadn't noticed, so he managed to smile at her and mumble, 'Thought it might come in handy for your earrings.' She took off the pair she was wearing, two wooden parrots, and put them inside. Over on the other side of the pub, the music continued with a man singing 'Born To Be Wild'.

Pat waved at a girl he knew and was just about to move towards her when Christine shouted out to him. 'Look at all my lovely presents, Pat.' He turned around and his eyes settled on the box. Frankie hugged himself and crossed his legs. 'Lovely,' said Pat, shrugging his shoulders. Frankie leapt up from his seat like a scalded cat. 'Drinks?' he shouted. 'Now you're talking, lad. Now you're talking,' said Pat, slapping him on the shoulder. As he waited for the round, a tenner in his hand, Pat introduced Frankie to his friends. They were both enormous and wore black T-shirts and had swallow tattoos on their necks and heavy gold bracelets. They were called the Macallan brothers and they had been at school with him. 'He's our mate,' they kept saying, pointing to Pat. In the end, Frankie bought them a drink, too. The tallest of the brothers had a cauliflower ear. He thumbed it and said, 'Pat did that, you know.' Pat laughed. 'Yeah, I did that all right,' he said, proudly.

'Boxing?' asked Frankie, leaning casually on the bar.

'Nah,' choked Pat. 'I did it at school. Martin here wanted his ear pierced, so a couple of us decided to do it in woodwork. We made a kind of operating table by pushing two of the benches together, then we cut a length of wood, so it went right under his earlobe, supporting it, you know. Then we got a compass from a geometry set and a hammer and wham!' Pat mimed the operation with gusto and the brothers rocked with laughter. They nudged him into continuing. 'The problem was,' he spluttered, 'that the compass got stuck in the block of wood. Wouldn't budge. We all tried to get it out, but it was like the sword in the fuckin' stone. Anyway, the more we wiggled, the more blood came out. You wouldn't believe how much blood can come out of your ear, and all the time Martin is yelling the place down.' Martin screamed in remembrance, cupping his earlobe in his hand. Frankie looked over his shoulder. Christine was looking at him and she raised her eyebrows and smiled. One of the brothers nudged Frankie, who asked: 'Em, so how did you get it out, then?' The three men nodded and Pat continued. 'Well, we turned Martin over and tried knocking the back of the wood with the hammer. The point was sticking through, you see. We were a bit scared that we might break his nose, but he was all right. It was only bruised.'

'Earlobe was a right mess, though,' grinned Martin. 'It swelled up like a grape.' He pushed it forward so Frankie could get a better look. Christine came up to them, holding on to her third gin and tonic. 'Hello, birthday girl,' said Pat, and put his arms around her shoulders and gave her a squeeze. 'Who's my girl, then? Who's my girl?' She smiled tiredly and said, 'Well then, Frankie, are you going to sing for me tonight?' She motioned towards the karaoke. Frankie shoved his hands into his pockets, but Pat and the brothers cheered so loudly that he had to move to stop himself being deafened. He weaved through the crowd. Men and women in leather and denim jackets, holding bottles of beer. A tall Indian man handed Frankie a thick book of song titles. He scanned through it with Pat looking over his shoulder. There were loads of rock and roll songs, from 'Peggy Sue' to 'Tutti Frutti'. He struggled to find an Elvis number that wouldn't make Pat think it was some kind of serenade for Christine. She would hate it if there was a fight. He settled for 'All Shook Up'. It wasn't ideal, but at least it was upbeat.

The Owen Brothers staff moved over to his side of the bar and clapped as he stepped on to a small platform. Next to him was a television screen with a cheaply made Japanese video overlaid with the song lyrics. The music started and Frankie realised that he felt safer there than he had all evening. He was a little drunk and Elvis, his best friend in the whole world, was there to ease the pain. He couldn't look at Christine, or at Pat, so he let his gaze wander over the line of glasses hanging from the top of the bar, all catching the light. The ceiling was ornate and died orange with cigarette smoke. Fine cobwebs were twirling around the lamps.

I'm proud to say that she's my buttercup.
I'm in love. Hmmm. I'm all shook up.

They were clapping along and Pat was telling people to shut up and listen. His gruff voice cut through the melody as Frankie wiggled his hips. Over by the door stood a man in a black shirt and a red bandanna. It was the Elvis of the traffic jam, and before Frankie could blink, he was gone.

5

The Tide Went Out

Christine put the jewellery box on her dressing table. She still had her jacket on and her handbag over her shoulder. All the way home, she had been imagining it there, sitting pretty between the perfume bottle and the mirror. The glass top of the table was dusty and the whole room needed a clean, but she was too drunk and too happy to care. It had been a great night with the presents and the good wishes and Frankie singing his Elvis songs for her. Even Pat had warmed to him. She knew he would. Her brother was the king of hollow threats. Just before it broke up, she had seen Pat singing a Thin Lizzy song with the Macallan brothers and begging Frankie to join in. Frankie had been a sport, although he looked pretty scared. He would get over it. She thought he had a lovely voice, even when Pat was grabbing him by the shoulder and sticking the microphone up his nose and singing: *Man, when I tell you she was cool, she was red hot. I mean, she was steaming!*

Christine flopped on her bed and undid her jeans and her blouse. She wiggled out of them and threw them over into the corner next to the wardrobe. She didn't care that the curtains were half open and that her room was overlooked by the flat opposite. 'I'm shameless,' she said, secretly doubting whether anyone would be that bothered about seeing her half naked on an unmade bed. Her bra and knickers didn't match and they were grey from washing. Things had been different when she was with Brian. She never had a hair out of place. Always clean and stylish, apart from the times she had to hide from the world. It all seemed so long ago, now. She had tried to forget him, but it was hard. She had Pat to remind her every day. It was as if he were carrying Brian around piggyback and all the emotions that went with him. They were so alike. Both hurt and victimised and fools to themselves, and lovable, sometimes. She had often thought that if she found a different type of man, one like Frankie, let's say, she wouldn't know what to do with him.

She went to her wardrobe and hung her jacket up. She pulled out a pink silk shirt and sat on the bed looking at it. It was time she threw it away. She had worn it last when she was with Brian. Still smarting from a slap on the cheek, she had told him to leave once and for all. She had said it before, but something of her passion must have touched him. He had burst into tears, totally wrong-footing her. She had hated herself for melting. She had never thought that he could cry but they were real tears. She held him and felt them on her shoulder. She heard him saying, 'Don't leave me, Chrissie. Don't ever leave me. I'm so sorry.' He had said it a hundred times before. Later, when he was asleep, she had seen the blouse in the light from the bathroom. His salty tears had stained the fabric, leaving a mark like the tide leaves on a beach. She had hung it as it was in the wardrobe, and though his promises were like piecrust, his tears were preserved. They had come in handy sometimes when she was missing him and forgetting the reason it had ended. It was comforting to know she had been cried over.

Something to show her grandchildren, like a rose pressed between the pages of the family Bible. Fat chance of her ever having grandchildren. Not the way she was going. Not unless they came through the post. She put the shirt back on its hanger. Maybe next week.

The Green Room

Charlie made a dramatic exit. He nearly slammed the door off its hinges and his arm was in the wrong sleeve of his jacket. 'Thanks a lot!' he said at the top of his voice. Carmel emerged from the bedroom a couple of minutes later. She made her way into the lounge, where Frankie was watching a video of Elvis in Las Vegas. She flopped down beside him in her dressing gown. 'Silly arse. Did you see the way he stormed out like his pants were on fire or something?'

'What's up?' Frankie didn't take his eyes off the screen.

'I only asked him to change a bloody light bulb.'

'What? And he's gone off to get nine more artists to help him, has he?'

'That would be right. No, he just took offence at the way I asked him.' It went quiet. 'Well, I was looking up at the damn thing. It reminded me. I didn't realise he took everything so seriously.'

'He's the sensitive type.'

'You would have changed the light bulb for me, wouldn't you?'

'I'm the sensitive type too, remember.'

Elvis was singing 'Suspicious Minds'. 'I'm sorry, Frankie,' she said. 'You know. About Charlie. Him and me. It must have done your head in.'

'It did a bit.'

'It wasn't serious or anything. Just a bit of fun, really. Sorry.' Frankie nodded and Elvis mumbled something into the microphone. 'There I go again,' she said. 'I'm always doing the same stupid things and then saying sorry. It's like Billy, you know. I married the poor guy even though he was completely wrong for me. My mother thought he was brilliant and I thought, "Oh my God, I've finally done something right. I've got this really cute boyfriend." It was like I was trying to convince myself that it would be all right. Of course, now I realise that my mother probably liked him because it wasn't you and she wouldn't have to explain things. Poor Billy. God, if he knew how screwed up I was about the whole thing. I just sat there waiting for him to let me down. It probably goes back to when Daddy left. I probably blamed myself, so I do the same thing to everyone who gets close to me. I need to talk to Daddy. See him. Not now. I'm still too much of a mess. I should try and find some space for myself. Oh, don't worry, I'm not trying to get rid of you.' She patted him on the knee. 'You and Charlie, all in one day. That would be good, wouldn't it? God! I don't know why I'm telling you all this. Maybe I do. I feel like I need to explain. Well, not explain, because I think you're the only person who understands. Does that sound stupid?'

'No.' Frankie could hear the tension in Carmel's body. It affected her voice and her breathing. It was exactly the same thing that happened to him when he was trying to say what he was feeling.

'I was pregnant once, you know.' Frankie looked at her, but he didn't say anything. Carmel was staring down at her hands, picking paint from under her fingernails. 'I talked

myself out of it. That's what Billy said. I told him to keep
it a secret until it was really obvious. I didn't even tell my
mother or anyone. I was so scared that if I said anything,
if anyone said "congratulations", I'd just lose it on the spot.
Anyway, it was fine for a while. Couple of months. I was
talking myself into it, you know. Just like I did with Billy.
Like "we'll have a baby and everything will be brilliant". I
just got on with work, but I came in one day and there was
this terrible smell of paint. I went into the spare room and
there was Billy and three of his mates doing it up in this
yuk green and they all smiled at me as I came through
the door and I knew that they had known all along. I was
just so angry. I could remember thinking, "Right. I'll show
him. I'll teach him to go behind my back and tell all his
friends. I'll lose the baby now, and then he'll be sorry." I
mean, what was the matter with me, Frankie? It was like
the baby didn't matter. Looking back, I'm glad that I did lose
it. Didn't think so at the time. God! It was so awful. Anyway,
it would have ended up as a right basket case with me for a
mother. I really feel that everything happens for the right
reason. That it all makes sense in the end. It wouldn't have
worked with us anyway, you know. I'd have dropped you
just like I dropped him. One day, we'll look back at what
happened and it will be all right. It's almost all right now
because we can talk about things and it has made us even
closer. It means that we will always be there for each other.
That's really brilliant, isn't it?'

The lounge of Carmel's flat was like a paper collage,
layers of two-dimensional pictures pasted on top of each
other with no air or life in between them. Motes of dust
froze in the air and the television had no sound. It was a
blob of light in the corner. They were both silent. Frankie
was looking at his socks.

'So, Frankie. Will you come and visit me in the mental
hospital?' She smiled and rubbed her nose with the back

of her hand. 'Anyway, now you know. You had a lucky escape.' Carmel was reaching over to the coffee table for her cigarettes. 'Anyway, I've decided to go without. Live a single life for a while, until I get my head sorted out. Celibate. No complications.'

'Famous last words!'

'No, I'm serious!' She laughed. 'It's always a complete disaster. A clumsy great mess. God! You wouldn't believe some of the nerds I've come home with, thinking it would be like *Love Story*. It's so ridiculous when you think about it. Sex, I mean.' She lit a cigarette and looked over at him. 'What about you, Frankie? What's this Christine woman like? You seem to get on pretty well.'

Frankie was glad of the change of subject. 'Christine?' he said. 'No way! I mean she's a nice woman, but she's . . .' He stopped for a moment. Trying to sum up Christine was quite a job.

'What? Is she funny-looking?'

'No. She's all right, you know. She's definitely got a hard side to her, though. You wouldn't want to get too close. Anyway, even if I was entertaining the idea, which I'm not, there's her brother to contend with. Honestly, if I get within twenty foot of her, he walks in the door. It's like he's got radar, or something.'

'Oh, I'm sure he's not that bad. It's probably all an act. I bet you anything that in a few weeks you'll be friends with him.'

Frankie shook his head. 'Carmel, I'm not kidding you. He's the kind of fella that eats light bulbs as a party trick. He's bananas.'

There was a knock on the door. A sharp, purposeful knock. It was Charlie, still red in the face. 'Hi,' he said, pushing past Frankie. 'I've just come to get my keys.' Carmel's head came over the back of the sofa. She wiped her eyes so that she could see Charlie properly. When Frankie got up, she had started to cry. Not big sobs, but a constant dribble of tears which met under her chin. Charlie didn't see her. He knocked on the door of her bedroom and Frankie said, 'It's OK, there's nobody in there.' The keys were on the bedside table. He swooped them up so violently that they flew out of his hand and landed on the duvet. 'Have you been standing outside all this time, Charlie?' He didn't reply. Frankie felt so sorry for him. How was he to know what was going on in Carmel's head? Imagine leaving so angry and so hurt, only to realise that his pockets were empty and that he would have to skulk back in and run the risk that she was sitting there laughing at him. Frankie wanted to pat him on the back and tell him that he was a nice man. He had been wrong about Charlie. Jealousy really stank. On the way out Charlie did see Carmel. Her blotchy face and the tissue in her fist. Frankie was glad. He wanted Charlie to think she was crying for him and the break-up of their affair. Perhaps it would have made him feel a little better. A little less rejected.

∫

Angel

It arrived at the office in a brown paper package. His instant stardom. Unwrapping it, Frankie shivered. He traced a clean fingertip over Betty's handiwork, the seams and the sequins. It wasn't the best Elvis suit in the whole world, but Frankie adored it, because it had been made with love. The previous Tuesday, he had finally found the shoes to match, chunky white ankle boots with a zip up the side. Just in the nick of time, too, as there was a photo session planned for that afternoon. For the first time, all the Elvises would be together in one place. Posturing in the sunshine on St Stephen's Green. Frankie had bought some make-up, too, and a sponge bag to put it in. He had told the shop assistant that he was buying them for his sister who had broken her leg and couldn't get out much. The boots had a bit of a heel, so he decided to try them with the costume.

'So, what do you think?' He stood in the door of Christine's office in all his finery. He made her jump. 'Christ,' she said, 'I thought you were the angel of the Lord there. Come to bring me glad tidings.' She looked him up and down. His hair was wet and combed back from his face. The suit was blue-white. Dazzling. Flared trousers with a triangle of silver sequins stretching from the hem to just under the knee. Around his waist was a wide belt, fastened with a rectangular silver buckle with writing on it. His shirt was studded with little silver starbursts, exploding all over his chest and up his arms. Christine put her hand up and shaded her eyes. Peering out through the haze of light, Frankie's face was gentle. A lock of hair above the centre of his forehead worked its way loose and sprung back into a curl. The silence made her nervous. 'Looks good,' she said. 'I mean, in an Elvis kind of way.' She ran her finger across the big belt buckle. 'Where did you get that?'

Frankie grinned. 'You won't believe me. My cousin made this. It's a plate off an old tractor we had out the back of the garage. It's amazing how it cleaned up. You don't think it's too much, do you?'

'Well, I thought that was the general idea. It's a couple of days to the contest, Frankie. Why are you all dolled up now?'

Frankie put the sponge bag on the desk and sat down beside her. 'It's the photographs today,' he said, 'and I had to make sure it fitted. Anyway, I'm glad I did. It seems that the zip has got broken. See.' He turned towards her, wiggling the zip fastener, which was stuck halfway down his chest.

Christine squinted. 'Come into the light,' she said. She put her hand on his chest and pushed him gently towards the window. She could feel his ribs through the scratchy white fabric. She moved her hand downwards. 'Brrrrum,' she said. 'God, you're skinny. It's like a xylophone. I hate men who can just eat and eat and never put on a pound.' She had her head right up against his chest, trying to see in behind the zip. 'I think it's just the fabric.' Her hair was brushing against his flesh and he could feel her breath. She was wearing perfume. He could smell it in the warmth coming from her body. She wiggled the zip. He looked out of the window. Pat was crossing the yard towards his lorry in a dirty old pair of jeans and a sweatshirt.

'I hope he's not going to drive that thing.'

'Hm?'

'Pat. He's just staggered over to the rig like Dean Martin.'

'He'd better not be drunk or his life won't be worth living. Now, hold still. I think I have it.'

Frankie looked down at her. She was wearing a blue jumper and the neck had slipped to one side on it. She pulled her hair away from her face and tucked it behind her ear. That was when Frankie saw the scar. A large, white, uneven scar like a crescent moon which ran from a point about two inches below her ear to the top of her shoulder blade. 'How did you get that?' he said, running a finger over it. Christine let go of the zip and pulled the jumper over her shoulder, flicking her hair forward. She didn't look up at him. 'Sorry,' he whispered. 'I didn't mean . . .' Christine breathed out heavily.

'No, I'm sorry. I know you didn't.' She put her palms flat on his chest and looked up at him. The scar was hidden by her earrings. 'Some fella did that a couple of years back. With a broken beer glass.' He wanted to touch the scar again. Touch it gently, so she would know he didn't think it was ugly. Her fingers closed around the zip again and she smiled nervously. 'Don't worry, Elvis,' she said. 'You won't have to spend the rest of your life in this.'

Pat was in the back of the cabin, propped up on one elbow. He was peering out from under the little curtain at the office window, listening to a tape of Queen's greatest hits. 'What the . . . ?' he said as Christine pulled the zip down to Frankie's waist. He was grinning all over his face and squeezing her shoulder. Pat's mouth went dry and his heart started to pound. She used to smile like that with

Brian at the beginning. Oh, they never stopped smiling. He got a bottle of whisky out of the glove compartment and swigged. As Freddie Mercury sang 'Crazy Little Thing Called Love', Frankie peeled off his white sequinned shirt. He held it out in front of him and Christine took it in her hands. The glow from it lit up her face and her hair. 'Let's have a look, now,' she said, running her fingers along the zip. 'Here's the problem, see, that little thread. Hang on, I'll bite it off.' She pulled the piece of thread out and dipped her head down. Pat peeled the wrapper back on his Mars bar. He was just about to take a bite when he saw Frankie and Christine disappearing under the window frame.

They both said 'sorry' at the same time, then started to laugh. They sat on the floor and rubbed their foreheads. 'I'm always doing that,' said Frankie. 'Cracking my head off someone else's. Laurel and Hardy used to do it all the time, but it didn't look like it hurt. Bloody does, doesn't it?'

'Here.' Christine handed him the shirt. 'You'd better get up now and get out of that suit before you get it all creased.' There was a muffled clunk from outside the window, but neither of them paid it much attention. Frankie slipped the shirt back on and tried the zip up and down a couple of times. 'Magic,' he said. 'Thanks, Christine.' Pat came into the room at an angle of forty-five degrees, like his legs couldn't keep up with his head. 'Take your hands off her,' he spat, pushing Frankie back against the window so that the sequins clattered on the glass. 'Pat,' said Christine. 'Why the Charles Bronson impersonation? I was only fixing Frankie's shirt for him.' Pat had Frankie in an armlock and was dragging him out of the office. Christine tried to pull them apart but Pat's training as an athlete won hands down over Christine's diet of chocolate biscuits. She followed a few steps behind. Frankie had given up wriggling because his arm hurt too much. 'Just because you set me up with one lunatic,' she yelled. 'Are you listening to me? Look, there's nothing going on with him. Is there, Frankie? Never in a million years. Put him down, Pat.'

'I'm not going to hurt him. We're just going to have a little chat, aren't we, Elvis?'

Frankie nodded and Pat relaxed his grip so the soles of Frankie's feet were flat on the floor again. Pat had calmed down by the time they got to the lorry. The door of the cabin was still open and Queen were singing 'We Will Rock You'. The heavy beats and the audience clapping on the tape cracked around the yard, bouncing off the walls. Pat leaned against the side of the container. 'Fresh meats from a happy herd' written in vivid green next to a cartoon cow. Normally Frankie would have run ten miles in the opposite direction, but he was in his luminous magic suit that nobody could touch. He was Elvis the Invincible. Elvis the Indestructible.

'You know, Frankie,' said Pat. 'I could break every bone in your body.'

'Oh yeah?'

'Tough guy, are you?' Pat rolled up his left sleeve.

'Not in the slightest. I wear make-up, remember?' Frankie patted him on the arm. 'Now, come on. I know you have a job to do later on. Why don't you get some sleep? Christine is safe with me. I promise. She's just a friend.' Elvis the Reasonable.

'You don't fancy her, then? Not even a little bit?'

'Well, er, no.'

'There was a little bit of hesitation there, wasn't there?' Pat stuck a shaking finger in Frankie's face. 'Something I learned in the boxing ring. Never hesitate. Just go straight in.' He demonstrated with a few sharp punches in Frankie's direction. 'Mess around for one second and the other fella will flatten your nose out for you.'

'Is that what you're going to do?' Frankie tried a cold, hard stare.

'I've done it before, you know. Done much more.' Pat's face was getting closer. 'The last fella who went out with Christine used to be a friend of mine. Bastard put her in hospital. Shall I tell you what I did to him? Shall I?' Frankie nodded. 'I put *him* in hospital. Gave him a taste of his own medicine and I rubbed his nose in it.' Bubbles of spume were forming at the corners of his mouth. Frankie imagined Pat rubbing medicine all over some guy's nose. 'Look, Pat,' he said. 'I told you. I'm not interested in going out with Christine.'

'Are you sure?'

Frankie shrugged and cast his eyes up to heaven. 'Yes!' he shouted. 'God! You're worse than my mother, Pat. I immediately feel like I've done something wrong every time you come into the room.' Frankie stepped back. It was the suit talking.

Pat closed his eyes. 'I know,' he said gently. 'I know. I know. I know.' He said it a little louder each time and as he said it for the third time, he turned and smashed his forehead against the side of the lorry. Smashed it again and again.

'Jesus! What are you doing?' Frankie stepped forward then back then forward again and placed his hand on Pat's shoulder. He looked over to the window. Christine was on the phone. Pat carried on banging his head. 'Come on,' said Frankie quietly. 'Let's go and sit down or Christine will worry about you. She does, you know. She worries about you all the time.'

Pat turned around. His head was scarlet. 'I'm going in the back,' he mumbled. 'I can't bear her looking at us.' He swung himself up like a monkey on a length of rope. Frankie looked around the yard. He waved at Christine through the window and started to walk back to the office, but stopped when he heard a violent banging from the back of the lorry, shuddering its metal walls.

The container was piled to the ceiling with cardboard boxes with the same cartoon cow on the sides. Pat was flailing about in the middle of them, picking up tin cans, which were dropping like bombs from one of the boxes and rolling all over the floor. Frankie was a superhero. He pushed Pat aside and told him to sit down, then single-handedly stopped the avalanche, catching cans in mid-air and stacking them neatly in a corner. 'If you'll excuse me, Pat,' he said, 'I have to be getting along. I have things to do.' There was a slight Southern drawl in his voice. Pat staggered to his feet, holding one hand up. 'Frankie,' he said, patting him heavily on the arm. 'You're a fuckin' gentleman. I mean that. I do. Fuckin' brilliant man. Sorry I, you know, em . . . Sorry.'

'That's all right. Now come on, I really must go and get changed now.' Pat didn't let go of his sleeve. He twisted the fabric in his fist and Frankie felt a couple of the sequins popping from their threads. He followed Pat to the boxes like a child being led by the ear. They sat down and Pat put an arm around his shoulder. 'I'm sorry, you know,' he said. 'I want to say I'm sorry. I was being a bastard back there. Fuckin' bastard. Sorry about the language. I don't mean any harm. I think that you and Christine are brilliant. No. I was well out of order back there. Accusing you of, well, you know. You see, I get so angry with people.' He looked down at his knuckles, which were scarred and callused, and for a moment he was still. 'Now, go off to your meeting,' he mumbled. 'Christine is looking forward to seeing the finals. You know, I reckon she likes you.' Pat slapped Frankie on the shoulder. It made him cough.

Frankie climbed down from the lorry. The sun was shining. He headed back to the office, brushing off his Elvis suit. It had survived its first hurdle without a smudge. Christine was leaning against the door frame of her office as he came down the corridor towards the toilets. She bit a smile off her lips as he headed towards her. 'He's OK,' he said, pointing in the direction of the yard, and Christine said, 'Yeah.'

Hamburger Heaven

Around St Stephen's Green, the traffic swirled and screeched and rumbled in Frankie's chest. From the shopping malls, women emerged with brightly coloured bags and click-clacked in their smart leather shoes towards the Grafton Street throng. The Green could be approached from all sides, so Frankie slipped through the nearest gate and made his way over lawns and balustraded bridges towards the centre. It was a perfect day with the dappled sun dancing on the water and the roses all bursting into bloom. The sunlight smelt of vanilla and the shade smelt of pine needles. 'Wait up,' said a voice behind him. It was the little bald Elvis, whose name was Bob, except now he wasn't bald. He was wearing a glossy black toupee which completely transformed him. He didn't look like Elvis, but he did look like an Elvis impersonator. 'It's good,' said Frankie, gesturing towards his head, and Bob smiled. Shoulder bags in hand, they arrived at the centre of the Green. A few of the others were there, including Gerard and Patricia the Producer, who were sitting on one of the fountains eating ice lollies. There were two photographers and a couple of journalists and behind them, under a tree, Frankie spotted a television film crew. 'Gentlemen!' Gerard sprang up, faltering as a lump of glossy orange ice slid from his stick and splatted on the ground by his suede trainers. 'Hey, look at you!' he grinned at Bob's shiny pompadour. 'Fantastic!'

Jerry from Sligo waved at them from one of the benches. He was sitting with his wife and had a little girl on his lap. Frankie and Bob were guided through the trees to where a Winnebago was parked. Outside, a man in a gold blazer was having a smoke. He was pretty sharp, although his ginger eyebrows looked strange with his black hair. Gerard introduced him as the contestant from Cork and they chatted for a while. The Winnebago was their dressing room, but it was occupied. They could hear a mumble of voices from inside. After a couple of minutes, the door opened and another Elvis stepped down. Jim, the winner of the Cavan/Monaghan heats, was the tallest and chubbiest so far. He was in a white jump suit with bootlace-style straps criss-crossing his chest and an enormous phoenix-from-the-ashes belt buckle. He had been to Graceland six times, and once he had made a woman faint because she thought he was a ghost. They all laughed at that because he was the least ghostly person they could imagine, unless, of course, Elvis had just gone on eating the hamburgers on the other side. Frankie moved towards the back of the caravan, but the big Elvis said, 'I'd hold on if I were you.' He dropped his voice to a whisper. 'There's the weirdest guy in there.' Frankie had a fair idea who it was and decided to wait until the van was vacant.

Back on the green, the cameras were in position and the Elvises sparkled like a bunch of Glitter Barbie dolls. The film crew were from the local TV news and the journalist was from the *Irish Times*. Patricia was filling them in on the details of where everyone came from and what they did for a day job. Frankie tried to sneak a peek at the others and realised that they were all doing the same, sizing up each other's hair and faces and bodies and jump suits. It was plain that they were all taking it seriously. There wasn't a patch of denim to be seen. Just as Frankie had expected, the other jump suits looked like professional jobs. They were in cotton rather than nylon, and featured diamante studs and detailed, beaded embroidery and brocade. Frankie felt small and tatty and stood at the back, but the photographers pulled him forward. Patricia came up to him, hugging a clipboard to her chest. She smiled at Frankie and put her finger under his chin and said: 'Come on. You look great.' He looked up at her through the wisps of hair on his forehead. 'Thanks,' he mumbled. She turned her hand over and gave him a playful punch on the jaw. 'Honest,' she whispered. 'You look fit.' She backed away, still smiling at him over her shoulder. Gerard arranged them for a series of group shots, trying not to make them look like Elvis United FC. Frankie stood at the front, smiling like Patricia had told him, obscuring the larger, flashier guys. Wacker stood beside him in a powder-blue studded suit with matching chunky-heeled boots. He kept nodding and clicking his tongue at Frankie and saying, 'All right, man?'

When the photographers had finished, the TV crew moved in. They weaved between the Elvises, getting them to do a quick hip shake or lyric to camera. Frankie could feel the heat on his neck and on his face as they approached him with the steadicam and a hairy microphone that looked like a moon boot. A young man, who he had seen covering all the 'wacky' stories on the news, came up to him and asked him his name. Frankie heard the quivering of nerves in his own voice as he answered. They asked him to sit apart from the others on a bench and talk to them some more. He looked over at the other Elvises. Some were in groups, talking to each other, but the rest were looking at him, wondering why he had been chosen. In the front line was Wacker. He paced up and down like a little patch of sky, his mirror glasses reflecting the greens of the trees and the grey of the tarmac. The reporter was very enthusiastic about the whole thing. He admitted to being an Elvis fan, but one who couldn't hold a note. He asked him about the Palace and his job and what his friends thought about the contest. As the sound man squatted and the cameraman stood squarely, Frankie warmed up and laughed and chatted as if they weren't there. He even sang a few notes of 'Don't Be Cruel' and the interviewer clapped along. As the film crew moved back to the fountains, Wacker came up to the reporter and shook his hand and stuck his thumb up and grinned into the camera.

Frankie queued outside the Winnebago with the others to get changed. He told them about what the reporter had asked him and said that it probably wouldn't be used anyway. Wacker pushed his way towards him, tugging on his sleeve. 'Hey,' he said in a hushed voice, looking like he was about to give away a secret, 'why don't you and I split? We could be waiting here for hours.' Frankie raised an eyebrow and said, 'What? On the bus? Like this?'

'I'll give you a lift, man,' grinned Wacker. 'I have my van around the corner.' Frankie was just about to say a polite 'no' to him, but realised that the sooner he got back to the yard, the sooner he could finish his work for the day. He knew that Christine was overstretched. He bit his lip and turned to Wacker. 'You don't have to drop me home, I work just over by . . .' Before he could finish, Wacker said: 'I know where you work, too' and grinned. For some reason, what Wacker said did not seem strange. Frankie, coming from a village like Loughfergus, was used to everyone knowing where he lived and worked. He didn't realise how spooky it was coming from a man he had only met three times before in one of the busiest cities in Europe. He just shrugged his shoulders and headed off with his fellow 'would-be celebrity' into the swirling traffic. Later, he would curse the magic suit for not making him more streetwise.

These Spring Rolls are Soggy

Frankie was expecting a rust bucket, but it turned out that Wacker had his own business supplying hot hand towels to Chinese and Indian restaurants. With the job came a small laundry and a smart new minivan. Wacker pulled the keys from his bag and threw them up in the air a few times as they approached it, singing all the way. The front seat was cluttered with paperwork which he gathered up in his arms and handed to Frankie. He moved around to the back, leaving the passenger door open, and unlocked the rear doors. 'You couldn't put them right in the back there, could you, on top of the silver boxes?' Frankie went to lean forward but remembered, just in the nick of time, that he was wearing his white suit, so instead he climbed in, squatting and keeping the soles of his shoes flat on the floor of the van. He walked right into the trap. A trap with lights and warning signs all over it. Wacker hit him in the small of the back, the doors slammed and that was that.

He was thrown on to his face as the van moved off, and he put his hands out to protect himself from the heated steel boxes in which the steamy, plastic-wrapped flannels were stored. He attempted a couple of kicks at the door, but all that did was send sharp pains up his leg. He crawled over to a pile of used cloths which were damp and strongly scented with lemony cologne, but they were cleaner than the rest of the van and soft on his knees and elbows as they bumped along. As there were no windows, he had no idea where Wacker was intending to take him. All he did know was that he felt queasy. It always happened in cars when he wasn't looking out of the window. As a child on the school bus, he just needed to take one look at a friend's music magazine and he'd be reaching for the plastic bag which his mother had put at the bottom of his satchel just in case.

Eventually, they came to a halt and he heard Wacker's footsteps coming around the side of the van. 'What's going on?' shouted Frankie, angry at how polite he still sounded. The footsteps stopped, turned and headed away, the chunky heels scraping concrete. Frankie strained to hear anything, but it was quiet apart from distant cars and radios. Next, there was the loud shuddering of a garage door being closed. A lock-up, that's where he was. One of a million lock-ups around the city at the backs of housing estates. Somewhere he could starve and die and never be found. The smell of his rotting flesh would be drowned out by lemon cologne. All they would discover was an Elvis suit. Nylon lives for ever. What a way to be remembered. He could feel sweat breaking out all over him, clammy on his back and hot under his arms. He fished around for an unwrapped cloth, opened it and pressed it to the back of his neck.

As he sat and hugged his knees, his bottom damp from the flannels, he heard a door clicking open and the footsteps returning. There was a jangle of keys unlocking the back door and suddenly there was light. Silhouetted against it like a phantom was Wacker, and glinting in his hand was a gun. At first, Frankie thought it was a joke gun, like a cigarette lighter, but as his eyes adjusted, he realised that it was small but real. A derringer. A pistol used by riverboat gamblers in the olden days of the Mississippi. Elvis was reputed to keep one tucked in his boot at all times, even when he was on stage. Wacker had certainly done his homework. He turned Frankie around, stuck the gun in his back and led him to the rear of the garage, through a door and up a flight of stairs.

Frankie couldn't believe that it was real. He didn't feel scared at all. Wacker wasn't exactly terrifying. How could he be in a powder-blue jump suit and mirror glasses? The flat smelt stale, like old laundry, and was filled with warm light from the orange curtains that covered every window. It was a shrine. A museum of memorabilia. A fire hazard, to say the least. Against every wall were piles of magazines and records and newspapers, some yellowing and some sealed in plastic. The hall was lined with guitars and gold discs and framed song copies and paintings of Elvis in his Vegas suits and a few of Jesus in his crown of thorns. Frankie made a mental note to put JFK back in the triple frame at home. He was led into a bed-sitting-room with sixties wallpaper and a stars-and-stripes bedspread and about five million other things, all Elvis. It was hard to find the tackiest. The only non-contender was the stereo system, which was state of the art. Wacker pointed to a leopardskin print chair and Frankie sat down, still trying to take in the surroundings. Working on the Scooby Doo theory that all villains are desperate to explain themselves, he leaned back, crossed his legs and said: 'Now, Wacker, what's this all about?' Wacker paced around, polishing the gun on his studded sleeve. The beads clattered against the metal. 'Never you mind, man. Never you mind,' he said.

'Look, you can't just grab a man off the street and keep him hostage. What do you plan to do? Kill us one by one so that you can win?' He laughed and attempted to get up from the chair, but Wacker swung round and pointed the gun at him again. Keeping it pointed, he pulled a roll of thick tape and a pair of scissors from a shoe box. 'I don't play God, man,' he said, heading for Frankie with the tape over his arm like a bangle. 'I just do what I'm told. You broke the rule, you see.'

'Oh, for God's sake,' moaned Frankie as Wacker bound his wrists with the tape. 'What rule did I break, in your expert opinion?' He still thought it was all a bit of a joke. He felt sure that Wacker was going to untie him soon and reveal the hidden TV camera. He hoped he hurried up because he was allergic to Elastoplast and this stuff was twice as bad. Wacker sat down on the bed and finally took off his glasses. Frankie noticed a collection of pill bottles on his bedside table and they didn't look like vitamins. He was following the Elvis road, stone by stone. 'What?' said Frankie again as Wacker leaned back on a red velvet cushion and cupped his hands behind his head. The gun was nestling in his groin and his eyes were an alien milky blue thanks to his contact lenses.

'You're doing this for yourself, aren't you, man? Not for him. You should be doing it for him.' Wacker looked up at a portrait of Elvis in a suit similar to the one he was wearing. 'I thought you were all right at first, but then I heard you with the gentlemen of the press, Frankie, talking about your little village and your job, but you never mentioned him. How could you have done that, man? You're only here for his glory, you know. If it wasn't for him, who would you be? Nobody, that's who. A tuppenny-ha'penny mechanic from the sticks.' He looked flushed with the emotion of his little speech and near to tears. Frankie remembered how at school the nuns made them all write AMDG at the top of the margin in their exercise books. It meant that the work on each page was dedicated to the glory of God. To Wacker, entering the competition had nothing to do with winning a trip to Graceland. It was a passion play. AMDE. All my day for Elvis. All his life, too.

∫

Chalk and Cheese

The bigger they are, the harder they fall, or so the saying goes. Hank stepped out of the deep, dark crater he had formed in the bar and slipped into the garden It was 5.30 and the pub had been locked since lunch. The table where he settled his coffee cup was rickety and splattered with bird droppings. When he swung his legs up on to it, he felt the softness of the rotting wood under his heels. His shirt buttons strained and he gave his stomach a consoling pat. Things would be fine. They had been fine before. The coffee burned his lip and brought tears to his eyes, so he focused on a couple of ashtrays on a far table. He didn't dare look around at the bare wall by the drainpipe where the racing bike had been for so long. He was afraid that its shape would still be there. Just a ghost burned into the bricks by the sun, like the pale area under the diver's watch on Greg's arm.

By now the bike with its purple panniers would be somewhere up in County Clare, chained to the back of the camper van. After all, that's what Greg had come for. He was a tourist. He never intended to stick around.

If only things hadn't ended the way they did. So clean. No upturned tables or shattered glasses or whisky streaming down the walls. More than anything, Hank wished that he could know someone well enough to break up with them properly and to see that they were hurting too. But Greg was gone without a whimper and it was business as usual. And business was booming.

There was a ton of food to be prepared for the evening and the washing up from lunch, yet there he was sinking a cup of coffee he had warmed through in the microwave. If Greg, the lord and master, had still been around, there was no way Hank could be sitting there. By now, Greg would be arranging garnishes on plates and he would be grating the skin of his knuckles into a mountain of cheddar. This was luxury. Peace and quiet. He stood it for another five minutes, then went inside and turned on the juke-box. Then he turned on the TV so that he could see that little square of movement out of the corner of his eye.

It was all his fault. Things had been so easy. After years spent trying to charm the pants off tall Midwesterners, Hank had managed to share his home with another man. A man who didn't make him nervous. A man whose company he had come to enjoy. But one false move . . .

He had got used to the sound of Greg early in the mornings. The swish of the bike on the wet road then the clatter up the stairs then the chug of the plumbing as he took a shower. Hank never did anything foolish such as coming out of his bedroom door accidentally on purpose to catch Greg emerging in a towel with his little radio playing into his armpit. No siree bob, that's not the way buddies behave.

So how could he have read things so wrongly? He should never have assumed that Greg was the slightest bit interested in men at all, let alone him. He was always so rude, making jokes about the decor and his clothes. Saying that steel guitars sounded like the death cries of a million mice. And anyway, what would Hank want with a guy who wore skinny T-shirts and cycle shorts and lifted tomato tins to improve his arm muscles. Cowboys do not wear tracksuits, not for anyone.

God knows what came over Greg that night. It hadn't been the food, because neither of them had done much more than pick at the raw ingredients. The Palace had been full every night. Cars were parked up as far as the old social club and the new menus had been delivered that morning. They were struggling to keep up with the demand, even with Christy's wife, Polly, helping out. It hadn't been the wine because neither of them had found any time for a drink. It wasn't the dancing either, because that had been the night before.

Whatever it was, it happened as Greg came through the door of the kitchen with the last of the dishes from the abandoned tables. He had taken in the blackboard and wiped it off. The cloth whizzed over Hank's shoulder and landed damp and chalky by the sink. Hank was standing, scraping a rim of cheese from the large dish they used for seafood pie. Greg was singing along to the tune on the juke-box. 'Your Good Girl's Gonna Go Bad.' There was something about the way he danced around to it, camping it up, willing Hank to turn around fully and look at him. Hank felt the familiar collywobbles and stayed facing the sink. They should have just finished the dishes and said goodnight.

But they didn't. Hank turned around and smiled and suddenly it was like this was their first introduction. 'All right there, buddy?' said Greg, putting a hand on Hank's shoulder. Then there was the look. The look that went on for ever as the steam curled around them. Then a moment of confusion and embarrassment. Both of them clattering about and discussing the groceries for the following day.

Hank mentioned Frankie and the plan for the finals. He was going to the show with Michael and Betty and dropping in on Carmel for tea. Greg said that he would hold the fort and they washed a couple more dishes. Then Hank shrugged and said: 'Unless you want to come along with me. See a bit of Dublin, maybe? I could get Brede to look after things here. I mean, if you want to?' Oh, how he longed to lasso those words and rope them back in, but Greg just smiled and moved a little closer so their arms knocked against each other as they washed and dried. 'Yeah,' Greg said at last in a strangely shaking voice. 'You, me, Dublin. Could be nice.' They both grinned as they lifted the last of the pans from the water, then their arms were empty. The record finished, the juke-box clicked and then fell silent.

Neither of them moved for a moment. Greg sniggered and plunged his hands into the soapy water. Hank felt the crackle of the suds brushing his cheek and his heart hit a banana peel. They didn't kiss. They stood and held each other. Hands pressing against backs and squeezing shoulders. The feel of each other's earlobes against their necks. After they separated, Greg stayed as silent as ever. Hank was frozen. That slender, gentle man had squeezed him up like a tube of toothpaste. His ribcage felt bruised from the inside and looking at Greg as he blushed and trembled only made it worse.

It was the longest night. Hank lying with the covers all bunched up under his chin, knowing Greg was just the other side of a brick wall. He was afraid to move or to go to the bathroom in case Greg heard. Hank wondered if he was lying in there looking at the doorknob, scared out of his wits that it would turn, catching a moonbeam, and reveal a fat, bearded man wearing only a Stetson. He lay there making elaborate plans about what he would say the next morning. He would tell him to forget it ever happened. Anything so long as they could carry on being friends. The

Palace had suddenly felt aptly named and he didn't want it to be just a sign over a door again.

But there was no such conversation. Greg's swishing tyres came a little later than usual in the morning. Hank woke and went downstairs to fix breakfast for them both. The salads were already made, sitting ingredient by ingredient in their separate ice-cream tubs, sealed and fresh. The menus had been written not just for one day, but for three. The order forms had been filled for the wholesalers. And Greg's things had gone. No note. Just lists. Later, as he tried to pick his heart up off the floor, Hank found a pink and yellow 'Goodbye Good Buddy' written on the chalk board with a smiley cowboy face underneath. Hank fingered the two stubs of chalk, fighting the urge to paint his own face with them into a sad, dusty clown.

Saucy

The microwave pinged in the kitchen. Wacker emerged a few seconds later carrying a tray with two bowls on it and two cans of Coke. He had changed out of the pale blue suit and was now all in black with a red bandanna at his neck. Frankie realised that he was looking at the Elvis of the traffic jam. At the time he hadn't noticed, perhaps because, in spite of his common sense, he wanted to believe it was a sign. Wacker must have been following him for a couple of weeks. Frankie felt as if his guardian angel had flown away out of the window, leaving him at the mercy of a very uptight goblin.

Wacker put the tray on the floor and moved over to a wall of records, colour coded and protected by plastic outer sleeves. He stood with his hands on his hips and grinned up at them. 'What do you fancy?' he said to Frankie, who was gazing down at the mixture of Chinese leftovers in the bowls. Perks of the job, he imagined. 'You can have anything you like, as long as it's Elvis. Sun, RCA Victor, Gold Series, singles, albums, eight-tracks, anything. Go on. Try me!' He beckoned to Frankie with his ring-covered fingers, daring him to come out with some obscure recording that Elvis himself would probably have been happy to forget. Frankie thought for a while, then said: '"Moody Blue". On blue vinyl?'

'Easy,' said Wacker, springing into action and running his fingers along the middle of three rows of albums. 'You're going to have to try a little harder to catch me out.' He lifted the record up, wiped it with an antistatic cloth and lowered it gently on to the turntable. As the first few bars sounded, Wacker crouched down and picked up one of the bowls and a set of snap-apart wooden chopsticks. He pulled himself up close to Frankie, knelt and lifted a mouthful of glow-in-the-dark sweet and sour pork to his mouth. 'Open wide,' he said, and Frankie's eyes crossed as he watched it getting closer and closer to his face. It was red hot and Frankie had to open his mouth and let some cool air in as the sticky sauce sizzled on his tongue. 'Sorry, man,' said Wacker, and he blew on the next mouthful. Frankie saw it coming. Wacker sprayed orange globules all over the front of Frankie's suit. Neither of them said anything. Wacker slowly lowered the bowl to the carpet and backed away. He disappeared into the kitchen and came out with a damp J-cloth. 'Let me,' said Frankie. 'I could rinse it through with some soap. Look, you can stand behind me with the gun if you want.' Wacker stroked his chin, the cloth balled in his fist. His heel caught on the bowl of food and catapulted it up his own trouser leg. Frankie bit back a laugh as Wacker hopped and swiped at his foot with the cloth. The record finished.

By nine thirty, Frankie was very uncomfortable. Wacker had let him go to the toilet, but had bound his wrists even tighter afterwards. The stain had dried on his shirt and he had been listening to Elvis non-stop for nearly four hours. Frankie loved the King, but there can be too much of a good thing. Overriding the kidnap situation was Wacker's euphoria at having a fellow Elvis fan in his grotto. He was falling over himself, pulling out LPs and EPs and singles and playing half a verse of each before finding something better. On top of that, there were the many exhibits in the Wacker Museum to be contended with. Frankie's feet were encircled by knick-knacks. Everything from five-hundred-dollar Elvis dolls to a supposedly authentic cufflink and a replica TCB lightning-flash diamond brooch. Wacker was taking care of business for the man in the sky.

It was nearly time for their five minutes of fame. Wacker turned on the TV and pulled his armchair up next to Frankie. The ruched lampshade which sat like a party hat on an Elvis-head base threw stark shadows around the room. The sports results finished and on came the local news. A fire in a warehouse took up almost the entire broadcast, but then the presenter cracked a smile and they knew it was time. The reporter was seen climbing through the undergrowth like a jungle explorer looking for gorillas. He looked over his shoulder at the camera. 'I have been told,' he whispered, 'that there is a whole colony of them in this neck of the woods, and if we're very quiet, we might just catch them.' He parted a few leaves with his hands and there they were. In came an Elvis song as the camera stalked them. Wacker was suddenly in close-up, grimacing. As he watched himself on the screen, Wacker bit his nails and rocked back and forth. He glanced over at a photograph of Elvis on his mantelpiece every few seconds, as if he were looking for the King's approval. Frankie was trying to spot himself in the background, but it was difficult. Out of focus, they all looked alarmingly similar, and he began to think that the reporter had a point with his wildlife angle. Then, there he was, sitting on the bench, chatting away casually. Frankie found it difficult to watch himself. It made him feel sick, but at the same time it was exciting. He wondered whether Carmel was tuning in, and Christine. By now, they would be wondering where he was. He couldn't even ask them to tape it for him, so he could send it to Michael. It might be the last-ever photograph taken of him. They could be showing it on the missing-persons broadcast in a few months' time. He could hear the voice-over saying: 'Frankie is a quiet man who enjoys dressing up as Elvis Presley at weekends.' They were so sad, always, those missing-persons shows. Pictures of teenagers in their pyjamas, opening Christmas presents and smiling into the camera, clean and sleepy. Totally different from the pierced and painted faces of the kids on the bridges and in the shop doorways. Frankie heard himself singing to the reporter and watched his hair moving in the breeze. It wasn't a bad epitaph.

It was time for bed. Frankie settled down on Wacker's deep-pile carpet. He was given a pillow and covered with an unzipped sleeping bag, but his hands were still tied behind his back. Before Wacker turned off the light, Frankie had a view of the flat from floor level. Over a wheatfield of cream twisted wool, he could see tumbleweeds of fluff clumping under the bed, dust-covered slippers, plates died orange by dried baked beans. Wacker removed his outfit and slid into bed in a black satin jockstrap. 'Night, man,' he whispered. 'Give us a shout if you need anything.' He talked as if they were boys and Frankie was sleeping over and they were going to lie awake for hours, letting out Coca-Cola burps and talking through their favourite film plots. But it was to be a different kind of night. After an hour, Frankie was woken by his shoulder, which had gone to sleep. He turned on to his back, but it wasn't long before his hands, which were jammed into his buttocks, went to sleep as well. On top of that, the dusty carpet was making his nose itch and the only way to scratch it was to jam his face into the pillow and nod. He wriggled back and propped himself up against the side of Wacker's bed, watching distant car lights sliding over the curtains, and tried to think what would be the sensible thing to do. The bedroom door was shut and the handle was high up, so trying to escape was bound to be noisy and, therefore, futile. The butt of the gun was pressed into Wacker's curled, sleeping hand. He knew that they had a final rehearsal at ten thirty in the morning and that if they missed it, alarm bells were sure to sound. He thought about Joe Shaw, former superhero, recently demoted. What would Joe have done? The high point of the night was imagining his father hogtied in an Elvis suit in the bedroom of a madman. With Joe's luck, he would have been kidnapped by a woman and after a few hours she would have untied him. He would have spent the night in her bedroom, all right, but they wouldn't have slept. Frankie thought about Carmel and Christine and wondered if they were lying awake thinking of him.

Carmel lay awake and thought of Frankie, because his bedroom was empty. 'Lucky bastard!' she said. Christine was awake because she had to work late, covering Frankie's deliveries. 'Selfish bastard!' she said.

The Old Dears

At twenty to eleven, Eileen Shaw and her sister Greta walked into the Coffee Lounge in Enniscorthy. They were ten minutes early. They were always ten minutes early so that they could get one of the chairs with a decent back on it. The others were like padded milking stools and played hell with the spine after a few minutes. The boy with the red face was behind the counter and he nodded to them and smiled as he did three mornings a week, and Greta said, 'He hardly looks old enough to be working,' as she did three mornings a week. They kept their jackets on and their handbags on their laps. The room was as crimson as the sacred heart from wallpaper to carpet to seat covers. The other tables were empty and the strings of Mantovani swooped and soared through the dusty air.

Eileen looked out of the stained-glass portion of the window. It made the people and the cars change from one lollipop colour to another and the raindrops made them wiggle. A couple walked by hand in hand as 'Some Enchanted Evening' reached its climax. She closed her eyes for a second and found herself wishing that it was

Frankie with Carmel. After all, there was nothing wrong with the girl. She wasn't Eileen's first choice, but then, he went out with that Margaret for a couple of years and Eileen had thought that she was a right drip with her plastic hairclips and her bitten nails. She knew how keen Frankie had always been on Carmel, even when they were children, but it seemed so one-sided. She couldn't bear the thought of it blowing up in his face. What would it have been like if Joe hadn't loved her back? Eileen didn't mind that Carmel was still married to Billy Stevens. She knew that not all marriages were happy ones and that she and Joe had been lucky. So many women of her generation had endured long years with bullies and drunkards or men they didn't love who had made them pregnant, because there was no alternative for them. So many good men had been terrified to touch the wives they loved for fear of bringing yet another child into the family. Nobody dared question it in those days for fear of being outcast and shamed and refused admission to the church. These were the things they talked about three mornings a week, and the lad behind the counter thought they were swapping scone recipes.

The others had arrived now. Josie was wearing a purple plastic mac that dripped on the carpet next to the point of Kathleen number one's umbrella. Kathleen number two wore a lot of make-up. There was always a little rim around the bottom of her chin where the powdered pink met the sallow beige of her neck. Seeing Eileen, they begged for the latest news on Frankie. They couldn't believe that the young man who had tinkered around with their boilers and fixed their broken light fitments was about to stand on a stage in a shining white suit and sing to every man, woman and child with a TV.

'What does he look like in his costume, Eileen?' they said. She took a sip from her coffee and said: 'Lovely. Like a knight in shining armour. Betty did a marvellous job with it.' She couldn't look at Greta, who knew full well that she was lying. She had seen the suit, all right, but only at Betty's, where it had hung on a womanly dressmaker's dummy, its sequins swirling over the flattened breasts. At the time, she had winced at the thought of her son in such a ridiculous get-up. The other women nodded to each other and Eileen kept smiling, daring them to laugh at her little boy. 'What's he singing again?' said Kathleen number two, and Eileen tried to hide her panic as she realised she didn't know. She couldn't even hum a few bars. '"Don't Be Cruel",' said Greta, and for a moment Eileen thought she was telling them off. How dare they be so cruel. Rubbing in the fact that she hadn't paid any attention to the most important thing in Frankie's life. It pained her that she couldn't stand there like a mother should and cheer him on. There was something that felt almost disloyal about it. Disloyal to Joe, perhaps. 'You must be proud,' they said. 'Yes,' she said. 'Very proud.' She meant that bit. She was bursting with pride about Frankie in general. He was doing a far braver thing than his father ever did. Oh yes, Joe Shaw was a fine singer, a better one than Frankie even, but he was content to be a big fish in a small pond. She wondered what Joe would have thought watching Frankie on the television. He would have been scornful as he always was when deeply cut. He would have been secretly proud too, but not about the white suit. They would have been together on that one.

Greta changed the subject. Scandal came at them from every angle these days, so they were often hard pressed to cover everything. Politics, child abuse, divorce, wayward priests and the EU. Their circle narrowed as the young lad switched on the electric soup cauldron in the corner and wiped down the stainless steel surfaces. The things that had been swept under the carpet for so long were now bursting out of the newspapers and the television screens, fuelling the discussions of Ireland's quiet revolutionaries.

Intelligent women like Eileen and Greta had begun to realise how many questions had gone unanswered. They were women of faith, all of them. Strong faith that could stand a bit of questioning.

The young man behind the counter didn't hear them. He noticed how they all asked for a cup of coffee and had milk instead of cream because cream was difficult to digest. They didn't like the taste of the coffee. They never had done for all the time he had worked there. They whispered to each other: 'It's an awful price, isn't it, and always half cold by the time you get it to the table. That's because of the cups, great big thick things.' Yet they came three mornings a week and talked and fought over who was going to pay for it and gave him a smile and a wave on the way out. He mentioned them to his grandmother once and she asked him if he really and truly liked the taste of beer and if any of his friends had much to say for themselves at the end of the working day. That was the trouble with old people sometimes. They stored up all the smart answers until you had your guard down.

Ladies and Gentlemen, Wacker Has Left the Building

The cassette was on auto-reverse, pounding his eardrums. Moaning and pleading: *Trrrreat me like a fool!* He had to turn it off or he would die. He was lying on the bed with his hands and his feet bound. He could hardly breathe, as blood was running down the back of his throat and blocking his swollen nostrils. Wacker had gone to the rehearsal. The clock on the video said 10.55. By now, all the Elvises would be doing their *Jailhouse Rock* number and looking at the empty halo of light where Frankie should have been. He knew he should move, but he was in too much pain.

From half past four in the morning, Frankie had watched that clock flashing away minute after minute, trying to take his mind off the throbbing in his arms and the prickly rash. Wacker's Elvis alarm clock had gone off at seven. He sprung out of bed and slapped Frankie on the back, saying: 'All right, man?' He untied Frankie from behind with the chilly snout of the gun pressed into his windpipe and the sharp blades of the scissors coming together against his wrists. Frankie was too scared to move a muscle. As he struggled to his feet, he felt the gun sliding down his spine to the small of his back. Wacker locked the bathroom door from the outside. Frankie looked in the toothpaste-splattered mirror. His face was drawn and the stains on his shirt glowed just as bright, even when he dabbed at them with wet toilet paper. The suit smelled stale and it was making him itch all over. Even if he did escape, he wouldn't have time to wash and dry it. He would have to stand on stage steaming with water dripping from his flares.

Wacker made breakfast in a black satin Chinese dressing gown. The gun was in his pocket and every time Frankie tried to make a move, he pulled it out, quick as a flash, twisted and gripped it with both hands like Starsky and Hutch coming around a corner. His eyes were brown without the lenses and he wore chunky black glasses like Buddy Holly. He didn't let Frankie have a knife. He cut the fry-up into little squares and made him eat them with a spoon. 'Thanks, Wacker,' he said. 'You've really changed my life. From now on, everything I do, I do for Elvis. I promise.' He smiled, but Wacker just nodded forlornly into his bacon and said, 'Sorry, man. It ain't gonna work. I mean, if it was me, I'd let you go in a flash, but Elvis, he knows.' Wacker sawed away at his fried egg, the gun and the knife clinking together in his hand. 'Last night he came to me and said, "Wacker, I want you to look after this boy for me. He's lost the faith. He had it all right at one time, but he's lost it."' He reached out and held Frankie's free hand. 'He asked me.' Wacker's grip tightened. 'He asked me to hold your hand. He doesn't want you to be afraid. He said: "Do this in memory of me." He loves you.' A tear rolled down Wacker's cheek. 'Elvis loves you, man, and so do I.' Now Frankie was scared. Wacker was getting Elvis all mixed up with something else. Still holding his hand, he led Frankie back to the chair in the lounge. He took the roll of tape. 'Please,' quivered Frankie. 'Isn't there something else you can use?' Wacker pulled down the sleeves of Frankie's shirt to cover the rash on his wrists. He bound the last of the tape around them tightly, so that Frankie could feel the backs of the sequins digging into him through the fabric. The cardboard inner tube from the tape rolled over the floor in front of them. Wacker's hands clasped Frankie's shoulders, the gun stroking his neck. 'This will be your first test, man,' he whispered, his breath rippling Frankie's hair. 'I think you're ready. Are you ready?' Frankie nodded. Wacker tapped his shoulder with the gun and headed for the door. He stopped and looked back at him, then disappeared into the corridor. In the seconds that followed, nervousness gnawed away at Frankie's stomach like acid. His legs jittered when he thought about getting up. He heard the door click at the bottom of the stairs and some rattling about below. He decided to use his trump card. The one thing that always worked on *Mission Impossible*. It was the old ploy when the captive pretends that he has escaped and then hides behind the door and jumps on the kidnapper when he comes in to look for him.

He stood there, heart thumping, waiting for Wacker, knowing that the vacant chair would be in his eyeline. The room was orange again with the sunlight through the curtains. The lights from the graphic equaliser undulated as Elvis sang the last few lines of 'I Just Can't Help Believing'. There was a creak as Wacker started up the stairs again. Nearer and nearer he came, and Frankie's hands balled into fists, squeezing the tape into his prickling skin. Wacker started to sing along with Elvis. He paused at the top of the stairs and his voice trailed away to nothing. He saw that the chair was empty. Frankie held his breath. He heard Wacker's head turning slowly, his hair brushing against his collar. He raised his leg, so that he could kick the door and charge at Wacker with his head down. Wacker took a step forward so that he was on the threshold. It's now or never, thought Frankie. *It's now or never*, sang Elvis.

Wacker, in a split second, whirled around and karate-kicked the door back with all the force he could muster. It came towards Frankie in slow motion, a brown chipboard tidal wave crashing against him. Against his knee and his face, the handle hammering his nose and sending his head cracking back into the wall behind him. He slid down like string, seeing only brown wood, then blackness.

10.59. Now, by Frankie's reckoning, Bob the bald Elvis would be launching into 'The American Trilogy'. Frankie tried to wriggle forward to the side of the bed. His ankles were bound and chafing together through the fabric of his flares. Wacker's trip downstairs had been to retrieve a long strip of plastic from the machine that wrapped the towels. Now it crackled against the bedspread as he kicked his feet forward and slid into a sitting position. His head swam and he leaned forward to stop himself fainting. After a couple of minutes, he tried standing up, but couldn't keep his balance. His nose had started to bleed again and he licked his upper lip. His suit was already covered in sticky, red rivers. He inched himself downwards, bending his smarting knees until he was sitting on the floor next to his boots.

Elvis started 'Way On Down' and Frankie lay on his side. Like a mucky, sequinned rolling pin, he moved towards the door. Each rotation was agony, sending daggers through his shoulders. He sneezed as the dust and hair and toenail clippings pressed into his face. He mowed down the ornaments that Wacker had lined up for inspection the night before. Reaching the door, he wriggled until he was sitting up against the wall. Tears ran down his cheeks, stinging where they touched the tender skin around his nose. He tucked his feet under him, feeling his heels against the skirting board, and tried to push himself upwards. The muscles in his legs shook violently. He twisted his hands as much as he could, so that his sticky palms gripped the lime-green floral wallpaper. His head came level with the dusty black sideboard, then the shelves with the little Elvis statues posed in a group like a nativity set. Snaking this way and that, he finally made it to a standing position, bracing himself as a wave of nausea passed through him. Repeating his roly-poly movement, Frankie turned, so the planes of his face pressed along the wall again and again like a giant fingerprinting session. The rest of his body followed, the pile of the carpet screwing into the soles of his feet. The light switch by the door got nearer. A grimy, white nose. Behind him, his own nose had at intervals left smears of blood which looked like part of the pattern. The plastic around his ankles was slowly stretching. The plentiful fabric of his flares was slipping out from underneath it and giving him a little more room for manoeuvre. Still, he could only manage pigeon steps. Two inches at most.

The next hurdle was the door handle. He was only semi-conscious when Wacker had left, but he was sure it wasn't locked. He slid down and tried to pull the handle with his chin. He did it, but fell against the door and shut it again. It opened inwards. The second time, he pulled the handle down, hooked his chin under it and pogoed backwards. The door opened, but the pogoing continued with Frankie spinning out of control and landing smack against the stereo system on the far wall. The volume shot up, Elvis screaming: *A hunk. A hunk of burning love* until the walls rattled. Frankie swiped at the knob with his nose, nudging it down to a whisper, then he turned and jumped, sack-race-style, until he was through the door and slapping against the wall of the corridor.

The stairs were steep and covered in a dirty black carpet which was worn away to nothing in patches. He slid down the wall, his back dislodging frames and sending pictures cartwheeling down and crashing against the lower door.

Frankie went down one step at a time on his bottom. As he descended, so did the temperature. By the door, it was cold and draughty. It spurred Frankie on. The lock was a nightmare. He tried his mouth, swirling his tongue around the greasy latch and gripping it in his teeth. He tried it with his nose, too, smearing it with blood and making his eyes run. Eventually, he slid down and lay on his back with his arms turning to pins and needles against his spine. With his feet slippy in their fluff-covered white socks, he manipulated the catch. Every couple of minutes, his toes cramped up and he had to press them hard against the wood to stop them from curling and driving him mad. At long last, there was a click and the chilly air rushed in. He rolled back and kicked the door open. The dark garage beckoned.

It was roly-poly time again, dipping in puddles of oil. Clang! He reached the door. He was so exhausted, it hurt just to swallow. He put his face against the crack and squinted into the light. All he could see were other garage doors and a pile of old car tyres. The crack was only a couple of inches wide, and using all the strength he had left, Frankie could not get it to budge. Every time he heard a car in the distance, he went cold, fearing it was Wacker. A woman's voice shouted: 'David! David, you little bastard! Where are you?' Frankie bellowed for help and kicked the door. Nothing. A chocolate wrapper whirled around the centre of the yard in a breeze, then came to rest on the tarmac.

There was a noise from one of the garages on the other side. The rust-coloured, corrugated door lifted and, like a theatrical curtain call, revealed first a pair of shoes, then a pair of jeans, then a boy of nine or ten. He leaned against the concrete door frame and pulled a cigarette out of his mouth. 'Help!' cried Frankie hoarsely. 'Please help me!' As the boy got closer, the top half of him disappeared from view and all Frankie could see was his mucky trainers and grey school socks. 'Try and open the door.' The trainers moved to the centre of the door and Frankie rolled back as the whole thing shuddered. 'Locked,' said the boy. He knelt and Frankie waited to see his face. It was a tired-looking little face with patches of eczema here and there. His brow furrowed as he examined Frankie's bloody face and the front of his shirt. 'State of you!' he said, and smiled.

'Call the Gardai, will you?' Frankie pressed his lips against the cold, sweet-tasting metal. 'Nah,' said the boy. Frankie rolled on to his back and stared up into the darkness. The woman's voice returned: 'David! David, for the last time!' The boy got up, sighed and sloped off across the yard. Frankie twisted his head to the door. 'Don't leave me!' David stopped at the other garage, then emerged with a brown canvas bag. He pulled out a car jack and squatted at the side of the door near to Frankie's head. 'Mind!' he said, as he cranked up the jack. Air. Sweet Dublin air blew on Frankie's stinging face. After six or seven turns of the jack, the boy stopped, stood back and said: 'Come on then! Indiana Jones!' Frankie performed his last roll, sliding out into the yard. David stood at his feet and tweaked the hems of the glittering trousers with his trainers. He folded his arms, looking around him like he had discovered an alien.

'Untie me,' said Frankie softly. 'Come on, there's a good man. This tape is giving me a rash.' David leaned over and peered at Frankie's wrists. 'Yeah, I get that with plasters,' he said, nodding. 'Itches like crazy. I'll go and get Stanley.' Frankie looked at the sky as David wandered off to find his friend. The deserted yard was blissful. No Elvis music, only the roar of planes overhead. David was back in a flash, but was by himself. Stanley was his knife and its razor blade caught the light. Frankie lay still as David took the knife, pulled out an imaginary hair from his head and sliced it in two. 'Deadly!' he said. He knelt down and took Frankie by the finger. Frankie could smell him. He had the scent of farm-fresh warm milk. Gently and silently, the blade slipped through the layers of tape. Frankie's elbows bent for the first time in hours. He sat up and pulled at the plastic around his ankles. It tore into his numb fingers. David snapped the blade up and down inside the knife. 'What happened to you, then?' he said at last. He folded his arms, rubbing the blade on the sleeve of his sweatshirt. Frankie tried to explain things, but it sounded like a story made up by a five-year-old. David hugged his knees and laughed and blew cigarette smoke out of his nostrils. He found a tatty tissue in his pocket and handed it to Frankie, who wiped the caked blood off his upper lip.

Mindful of Wacker's return, Frankie staggered to his feet and walked around the yard to get the feeling back. The concrete was cool through his socks. When they came level with David's garage, Frankie asked him what was inside that kept him so busy. David wrinkled his nose up. 'Can't tell you,' he grinned. 'Why?' asked Frankie. 'Because then I'd have to kill you,' David said, nudging Frankie's bruised arm. 'Fair enough,' said Frankie. He held out his hand. 'Well, I'd better be off. My boss must think I'm dead.' David tucked the knife in his back pocket and pressed his palm into Frankie's. 'I can give you a lift home if you like, Frankie,' he said. 'I've got a car.' Frankie didn't doubt it for a moment. 'No. I'll be fine, thanks. Look after yourself, now.' David shrugged his shoulders. 'Oh, I'm cool,' he smirked. 'Look at me! It's you I'd worry about, my friend.' As Frankie limped out of the yard, he saw David picking up his tool bag and heading back to his garage, whistling.

Have a Banana

Carmel finally gave in to the twitchy feeling inside her and rang Christine at the office. The answerphone gave out a mobile number and she dialled it immediately. It was hard to keep anything in your head for long in the corridor outside the workshop. From the next room came the *chuga-da-chuga-da* of a printing press. As the dialling tone sounded, low and regular, Carmel wondered if Frankie was with Christine and if they were suppressing giggles before answering. For a flash, she felt the deep heat of jealousy in her lungs, but the phone was answered before she could give it much thought. Amidst the static and the roar of traffic, a voice said, 'Owen Brothers. Hang on.' Carmel grabbed the sleeve of a passing colleague and beckoned some coins off him for the phone. Christine inched the van forward by the roadside so she could get a clear line. She was not in a good mood. Frankie's non-appearance had come as a slap in the face to her, so Carmel's voice was a comfort, especially when she said: 'Ah, you know Frankie. He wouldn't just not turn up. He's not like that.' Neither of them had seen him on the television the night before, but

Mrs Beechy had told Christine about it. She had said that he looked so handsome and that all the young girls would be writing him fan letters. 'Perhaps it's the stardom,' said Christine, staring at the small packages on the front seat of the van. Carmel laughed, crackling the line. 'Stage fright, more like. He's just scared because he's on the verge of something big.'

Frankie was on the verge of the dual carriageway that ran past the airport. Every few minutes, a plane came over his head with such force that he could taste the dust from the road and the long grass whipped around his trouser legs. There were dark, greasy marks all over him and his stockinged feet smarted from the gravel and broken glass underfoot. He had a vague idea where he was, although he hadn't done much driving in the area. He was miles away from the city centre and the theatre and he didn't have a penny on him. If only he had a piece of old card and a pen, he could write 'Dublin Centre' and stand there looking at the oncoming traffic, hoping that someone would take pity on him. He had just seen two lads in khaki get into a car. They had been holding a sign up. He waved and ran towards them, thinking that they might let him have it, but they just waved back. They must have thought he was doing some kind of stunt. A fun run for charity, dressed up as Elvis.

He was getting a stitch in his side by the time a car drew up. The passenger door was flicked open and Frankie looked in. A nun of about sixty-five was leaning over and staring up at him through copper-rimmed glasses. Her white hair fluffed out of her veil on one side where she had been driving with the window down. She was a modern-style nun, in spite of her age. She was wearing a knee-length zip-up habit with a sturdy silver cross around her neck. 'Hop in,' she said.

'Thanks, Sister. I'm on my way into town. Is that where you're heading?' He climbed in. As he shut the door, the sequins reflected all over the car, polka-dotting the nun's habit. 'Em, in case you were wondering,' he said, 'I'm in a show. That's why I'm wearing all this stuff. It's a costume.'

'I thought so,' she said. 'It's a wonderful outfit. Nice and bright for the summer.' Frankie put his hand over the bloodstain as she put the car into first gear. 'This is fun,' she beamed. 'I'm forever being told not to pick up hitch-hikers, but I have met some interesting people.' She turned to him, smiling, and pulled out to the right. A silver Mercedes beeped its horn and swerved into the fast lane. She tutted. Frankie reached around for the seat belt.

'So, are you on your way back from somewhere, Sister?' He reached over and gently released the handbrake as they sped along. Dangling from the rear-view mirror was an identification badge for a carpark. She had written her name on it: Sister Anna Bernada. 'I've been to the races,' she said. She kept turning around and looking at him as she was talking. He looked ahead in case someone stopped suddenly in front of them. 'Yes, yes,' she said. 'They let me out for good behaviour every few weeks.'

'That's nice,' he said. 'By the way, I'm . . .'

Sister Anna Bernada turned to him again and waggled a long, bony finger. 'Oh, I know who you are.' She gave a coy little smile. A 'haven't you been a naughty boy' smile. 'You might think that we are all old fogies, locked away in a convent. A bit out of touch. You do, don't you?'

'Well?'

'We always say that the girls in the school keep us young. Oh yes, we know *Baywatch* and "Ra, ra Paul McGrath".' She was driving in the middle of the road. Passing cars hugged the opposite kerb and drivers waved their arms at her. She nodded and raised her index finger to them in greeting, the way they do in the country. 'I remember your records being all the rage a few years back. I used to have a dance to them myself, sometimes. Now, that surprised you, didn't it? Oh yes, I'm very partial to a bit of a twist.' She patted him on the back of his dirty, bloodstained hand. A nun's pat. Frankie remembered the feeling from his communion class. The way that nuns always took your little hand in theirs and then 'slap! slap! slap!' with the other hand on top until it made your eyes water. You couldn't take your hand away or say ouch, because the poor nun was smiling at you fit to bust and telling you what a good little fella you were.

They swerved through streets that were a hundred shades of grey, save for faded flag colours on some of the houses. 'Oh yes. A bit of rock and roll.' Frankie was looking nervously out of the window, willing the city to sneak up on them around the next corner. His nose left a little triangle of grease on the glass. She glanced at the digital clock on the dashboard and tutted. 'Is that the time, Elvis?' She put her foot down and the car shot forward so fast that Frankie's head slid along the window. He stiffened up and braced his feet against the floor. He didn't have the heart to tell her that he was only a cheap imitation. She was a person who believed in miracles. She'd probably be in the papers next week: 'GHOST OF ELVIS APPEARS TO NUN ON SWORDS ROAD.'

They stopped for traffic lights. Three lanes of cars all glued to the red light. Sister Anna Bernada was trying to get him to sing something. Frankie croaked out a little of 'Love Me Tender' as she revved the engine. As the lights changed they jolted forward and came to a shuddering stop. She had flooded it. A lorry behind them sounded its horn. 'All right. All right,' said Frankie under his breath. She tried to start the car. The lights changed to red again and Frankie put his hand on the steering wheel. 'Leave it for a minute or so, Sister. It'll be grand if you just let it rest.' No such luck. As the amber turned to green, Sister Anna Bernada turned the key and put her foot flat on the floor. The car cut out. Other cars were trying to move around them, changing lanes. The lorry breathed impatiently, tension coming out of the radiator and the headlights. Frankie looked in the side mirror as the lights changed back to red. A large, bald man in overalls was swearing at the blue Fiesta. Mentally blowing it thirty foot in the air and scattering it over the grass verges.

Sister Anna Bernada was nervous. 'Don't worry,' said Frankie, trying to remember the way his driving instructor used to speak. Green went the lights again. The engine was still racing. She slowly released the handbrake and looked in the rear-view mirror. The car crept forward and Frankie breathed a sigh of relief. Sister Anna Bernada looked to her left and to her right. A young woman with a baby buggy was hurrying across the junction in front of them. Sister Anna Bernada touched the brake and the car stalled again.

'Oh, for God's . . .' screeched Frankie. 'I mean, sorry, Sister.' The driver's door of the lorry behind him swung open and the large, bald, neckless driver climbed down. Frankie watched his stomach and his big hands as they moved towards the Fiesta. Fat knuckles knocked on the driver's window. Sister Anna Bernada wound it down and stared into the blue buttons on his overall. The driver leaned down and rested one elbow on the window frame. 'Tell me, Sister,' he boomed. 'Would you be waiting for any particular shade of green?'

Carmel and Christine sat on opposite sides of the desk. They both had their feet up and were holding mugs of coffee under their chins. When Christine had returned to the office, there was a message from Gerard Burke on the answerphone, wondering where Frankie had got to. By the time Carmel had arrived, a state of panic had been officially declared. Pat was out in the van, looking for Frankie all over the city. When he was in the habit of beating people up, someone like Frankie would have been an obvious choice. He had 'victim' written all over him. That went double if he was wearing his make-up.

Christine was complimenting Carmel on the jewellery box she had made when something caught her eye. On the wall above the pinboard, a little cluster of lights danced over the paintwork. Carmel followed her eyeline, thinking it must be from Christine's glass earrings, but then they realised. Carmel leapt up and ran to the window with Christine right behind her. They stood together, breathing on to the glass, their hair painting filigree patterns in the condensation. Frankie was limping through the yard towards them, his sequins cutting the air like cat's-eyes. He was the most pathetic sight either of them had ever seen. In the afternoon sunlight, they ran and stood either side of him like Martha and Mary, propping up his bleeding body, helping him to the door and easing him on to the tatty couch next to the hatrack.

None of them made sense. Carmel and Christine were so choked at the sight of Frankie all battered that they couldn't say anything, either to him or to each other. Instead, they fussed around making cups of tea and wrapping him in coats and car rugs. Either of them could have gone out for food, but neither could bear the thought of leaving him with the other. Frankie was so tired and so bewildered at the two of them fighting over whose jumper to use as a headrest, he too was robbed of words. He just lay and watched a wasp flying up and down a crack in the blinds.

Pat made all the difference. He breezed in, throwing his keys with a clank in the filing tray and leaving his leather jacket in a crumpled hunchback shape in the corner by the door. 'Bloody hell,' he whispered, crouching down next to Frankie and gingerly touching his nose. 'Christine, go and get the kit from the van, will you?' Christine backed away slowly, still staring, like a kid who is sent off to bed in the middle of a good show on the telly. She ran into the yard and Pat nodded a hello to Carmel. Frankie raised his head. 'This is Carmel, my sister. Carmel, this is Pat.'

'I know,' smiled Carmel. 'How are you feeling now? A little better?'

'Yeah,' croaked Frankie.

'He'll be fine,' said Pat. 'I've looked worse in my time. A lot worse!' He smiled over at Carmel. Christine came back and Pat went to work, dabbing away at Frankie's face, flashing a torch in his eyes to check his pupils and expertly applying butterfly-shaped strips of tape to his nose. When he had finished, he went over to the desk and sat straight behind it like a magistrate. 'Now, Frankie,' he said, cracking his knuckles, 'let's hear it. Whoever has done this to you, Frankie, I'll take care of them. They won't be bothering you again.' The girls flashed raised eyebrows at each other and Frankie started.

They sat there white-faced as Frankie detailed his adventures. Pat interrupted a couple of times to ask where Wacker's flat was and to make a few notes. As Frankie mimed his pogo from the door handle, Carmel and Christine bit their lips and looked away, but Pat stayed stony-faced. All hell broke loose, however, when he got to Sister Anna Bernada. 'Oh, come on, guys,' said Frankie, who was choking back giggles himself. 'This is my life I'm talking about. My weird bloody life!' After they had calmed down, they got on to the Gardai, who said they would be over to take a statement. Pat was keen to do their job for them and punch Wacker's lights out, but the others managed to calm him down.

'We'd better give that Gerard guy a ring, too,' said Christine, flipping through the telephone directory for the number of the TV station. Frankie sat up and put his head in his hands. 'Don't bother,' he said. 'I'm finished with Elvis.' They tried to think of what to say. He looked up at them. Carmel smiled. 'You're just tired, that's all.

You'll feel different when you've had a sleep,' she said gently, coming towards him and brushing his hair out of his eyes with her fingers. He pushed her hand away slowly. 'You don't understand,' he said. 'It's not just because Elvis drove Wacker round the bend. He was mad anyway. He'd have been the same way about Madonna or Finbar Furey.' Frankie examined a stain on his knee, rubbing it with his bloody fingers. 'It's . . . well . . . it was like being made to smoke a whole pack of fags at once. The thought of Elvis makes me feel all sick now.'

'It's only one more day,' said Pat. 'It would be a shame, after all you've been through.' Frankie shrugged his shoulders. 'Even if I did want to do it,' he said, 'there's the small matter of my suit.' He took off his shirt and handed it to Christine. She rubbed the fabric between her fingers. 'Oil,' she said. 'I'm sure we could shift that in a hot wash.' Her brow furrowed. 'But then there's the blood. We could try soaking it in cold water first, I suppose.' Carmel nodded. 'You need cold water for blood, especially with white fabric,' she said.

'Who have you been murdering, then?' laughed Pat. The girls tutted and said, 'Women know!' Pat beckoned for them to give him the shirt. He stood in front of Frankie with it, grinning, and held it up. 'Oil? Blood? Takeaway?' He pointed to each of the stains. 'We took one half of Frankie's Elvis suit, and washed it in new Spiffo.' Frankie smiled, and curled up on the sofa. Christine and Carmel grabbed the shirt and whacked Pat over the head with it. As they talked about whether they should chance bleach with the sequins, Pat held his index finger over his pursed lips and pointed with the other hand at Frankie. Glinting beneath a yellow raincoat and a denim jacket, he lay, curled and peaceful and fast asleep.

And the Wind Sings Tammy

Greg wandered to the edge of the Cliffs of Moher, pressing his knees against the black slate walls which prevented tourists like him from plummeting to an anorak-covered death in the waves below. It was eight in the evening and the wind was tearing the ears off him and turning his heart over in his chest. They had come at dawn, but found the cliffs covered in fog, and a glum bunch of Italian children staring out to sea. Shuffling around the packed tourist centre, they had seen postcards of the cliffs in all their splendour and decided to return. Now, the carpark was all but empty. The camper van with its bicycle racks at the back glowed apricot in the evening light. 'Stand by the tower,' said Hazel, pointing her camera at him. She made large spaceman gestures to compensate for the wind, which was carrying her words into the newly harvested fields beyond them. He moved next to Colin and struck a clumsy, smiling pose. 'God! This is so beautiful!' shouted Colin, resting his hand on Greg's shoulder, the fabric of his windcheater flapping and giving off the sound of rapid gunfire. 'Wonderful,' Greg replied. It *was* wonderful.

Wild and awesome and seeming like the very edge of the world.

'I'm freezing, honey,' said Hazel. She hugged Colin and they moved as one down the broad steps towards the carpark. They looked back for Greg, but he had gone walkabout. It was par for the course with him. They hadn't asked him why he had left the Palace so suddenly. They weren't sure if he knew himself. So they climbed into the van and Colin reached for a Thermos of coffee and they sat, painting stick pictures in the fogged-up glass and kissing.

Time to go home. Their adventure was at an end. Hazel and Colin had jobs to go to and families to embrace and a wedding to plan. Greg had to sort his life out. A person could only wander for so long. He wanted to manage a pub, just like the Palace, with food and karaoke and line dances. He wanted it to be in a village like Loughfergus, surrounded by a patchwork of small fields. A place where hawks hung in the sky and cows clumped together on a hill. A place where he could be the person he was becoming with Hank. Before he went and spoiled it all, that is. There had to be somewhere like that in New Zealand. The horn of the van honked in the distance. He took one last long look around him. He couldn't bear to leave. There were probably people in nearby villages with a blood tie to him. Old men who could still recall his grandmother. Greg turned towards the churning water and wished she was with him. He felt like he was at the end of something, like the moment in Road Runner cartoons when the coyote sprints off a rock formation and runs through the air before he realises and plunges into the canyon. He had to run somewhere to stop the ache inside him. The wind chilled the tears on his cheeks and he jogged towards the edge, stepping over the boundary wall and on to the untrodden, emerald grass. Here, the force of the wind was incredible, holding him like strong arms.

'Naaaa-naaaa!' he cried as loud as he could, holding his hands out in front of him, knowing she was there.

He listened to the wind with every part of his body. Between the booms and crackles, he heard a woman's voice. His grandmother, perhaps, or a faraway radio. It was faint and ghostly, but it slowly became clearer. It was a siren. A mythical creature who guided lost sailors and lured them to their death. He stepped forward an inch or two, to where the ground was loose and springy and crumbled into the water. If this was a siren, she had a backing band with a steel guitar and a drum kit. She was singing her ghostly little heart out in a Nashville style. Greg opened his eyes, which he had squeezed shut against the wind, and scanned the horizon. The sun and moon were changing shifts in a pink twilight and she danced in between them. She was pretty, all right. Her hair was golden and piled super-high, one ringlet falling to her shoulder. An hourglass figure swathed in baby pink chiffon with a wide, fifties-style skirt. Around the neckline were gold brocade music notes and her white stilettos trod whirlpools into the sea. As she came towards him, she sang into a gold cordless microphone. Oh, how he had always hated that song:

Stand by your man. Give him two arms to cling to
And something warm to come to when nights are cold and lonely.

He turned and cleared the wall like a hurdle, looking over his shoulder as she melted into a candyfloss cloud. All that was left was the song. Greg ran around the tower. He waved from the top of the steps and Colin flashed the headlights. He plunged his hands into his pockets and started towards them, slowly at first, but getting faster and faster, singing all the way with the siren. In his mind, he was at the kink in the road, halfway down the hill where Loughfergus came into view. He could see the houses with peat fires which sent shimmering smoke out of the chimneys. He was running past the faded, artificial flowers that trembled around the tiny shrine to the Blessed Virgin. Knuckles were knocking on windows and waving at him as he passed them by on his way to the Palace. There it was. The neon sign. The mud-caked rail outside the door where boots and shoes were cleaned off. Helter-skelter, he went down the road to bang on the door, thrilling at the clomp of the cowboy boots as they came down the staircase. Colin wound down the window as Greg rushed towards them with a stupid grin on his face.

The Great Day Dawns

Wacker's flat was empty and the answerphone in the laundry was full of messages from irate restaurateurs whose customers were wiping their hands on the tablecloths. The Gardai had been round the night before, but had found the place deserted. Frankie's bloodstains were all over the wall and the Elvis tape was still quietly playing. They put out a bulletin on the hot-towel van in case he tried to leave the country in a cloud of cologne.

Frankie slept like a log, in spite of being propped up on about a hundred pillows. He knew that the Gardai had laughed their heads off when they left the night before, but he was too tired to care. When he got up, there were hurdles to be negotiated. Number one was the bathroom mirror. It revealed a swollen, purple nose with a small black gash at the top of the bridge. Not as bad as it could have been, but not good either. Better than hurdle number two, anyway. That lurked in a red washing-up bowl on the draining board. Smelling like the school toilets, the suit billowed in cloudy water. Frankie pulled it out and held it up to the window. The water ran fat like honey from the hem.

Some of the sequins had lost their shine and had faded to a dull grey. Those that remained hung limply from their threads. Underneath, the fabric was clean and white, but there were still patches of ground-in oil on the shoulder and the rusty shadow of the blood. He was stirring it about in the bowl with a fork when Carmel came in wearing her Dopey Dwarf pyjamas. Her hair was all messy from sleep and an unlit cigarette dangled from her lips. She sat up on the work surface and looked at him. 'Forget about the suit,' she said, swirling her finger in the water. 'Betty will understand.'

'Do you think I should phone and tell her?' He pulled a couple of slices of bread from a bag as Carmel lit her cigarette. 'She'll be over this afternoon with the others,' she said. 'You could tell her then if you want.' Frankie nodded. The phone rang and Carmel jumped down. Frankie pulled the tractor-plate belt from the window sill and rubbed it with his sleeve. He thought of all the hours he had stood on the coffee table at Michael and Betty's, looking down at the strands of silver in her hair as she fiddled around with pins and cotton. Even then, he could never work out whether he loved the suit or hated it. If it was a glorious outfit or a clever disguise. He couldn't bear the thought of being the only one out of uniform. He would stick out a mile as a casual, fifties Elvis. Carmel's voice was loud from the lounge. He heard her say: 'Just leave him alone for today, will you?'

Gerard had only gone and told the press about Frankie's kidnap. The Gardai had filled him in on the details when they rang him for Wacker's address. This was a gift to the publicity department at the TV station. The papers were already running the story, together with photographs of Frankie taken on the Green. People in Dublin knew Carmel as his sister and one of them could let it slip to a reporter. Eileen, for all her faults, didn't deserve to find out about Joe's infidelity in the paper, so Frankie phoned Christine and Carmel got on to Mickey and his wife Mags. After they had called everyone else they could think of, they took the phone off the hook and got changed. Frankie's first task was to find an alternative outfit for the finals. Because Carmel had the Loughfergus crew coming over, Christine had agreed to go with him.

He got Mrs Desmond downstairs to act as lookout. He imagined himself in the flash of cameras, holding his hand up to his face and saying 'No comment,' and was quite disappointed when she told him there was nobody there but a couple of dustmen loading bags into a cart. Christine met him in Bewleys and after a mug of hot chocolate they headed for the shops. She marched like a sergeant-major, swinging through the crowds with her elbows out at right angles. Frankie dawdled behind her, looking in all the windows until she strode back, took him by the sleeve and pulled him along.

If there was ever a test to their friendship, this was it. Frankie was not a happy shopper at the best of times, but this was like having teeth pulled. He looked glazed as Christine dashed about, picking out things and holding them up against him. She made enthusiastic noises and paid him compliments, but most of the time he was staring at other people and swaying to the piped music. His mind was a blank and, no matter how he tried, he couldn't focus on the competition. In the end Christine threw a cream-coloured polo neck in his face. 'Am I wasting my time here?' she screamed, and stormed towards the door. Forgetting that she had a blue blazer in her hand, she set the security alarms off and the whole shop was filled with bleeping and wailing. Red-faced, she ran back to the cash desk shouting apologies.

Frankie noticed that she got angry in a kind of magnificent way. Her cheeks were flushed and her eyes had an extra sparkle. He had always wanted a temper like that.

One that could blow the dust off any situation. He had tried to be angry a few times, but nobody had noticed. 'Sorry,' he said, hugging the polo neck. He meant to say it quietly, but the sirens were still sounding and he ended up shouting. Shoppers all around them were staring over the rails of clothes, pretending not to look. She hung the jacket on the side of the cash desk and scratched her head. 'What do you want, Frankie?' she said. What he wanted was to still be in Wacker's flat, bound and tied and knowing that the contest was going ahead without him. Out of his control, but he couldn't tell her that. 'I dunno,' he said. 'I mean, this stuff is nice, but it's not like my suit. I felt different in the suit. I don't want to go on without it.'

'Why not? It's a singing contest, not a who's got the best suit contest. You can still sing, can't you, with your nose like that?' She reached out and touched the bridge of his nose.

He turned away. The truth was horrible. 'You don't understand,' he mumbled, prickle-cheeked. 'It's the whole effect. Without the suit, I'm just some stupid delivery driver.'

'And what the hell is wrong with that? Grow up, will you!' She slapped his face. It came out of the blue. It wasn't a hard slap, but it caught him with a loud crack which echoed all over the shop. She drew her hand away. It was hot and shaking. Christine stared at the ceiling. The shop assistant stared at Christine. 'Sorry,' she said. 'But you were sounding just like Pat.' There was a murmur coming from the other customers. They saw Christine as a mother smacking her child in the supermarket. They didn't see that she was hurting more than Frankie. He put his hand on her shoulder and smiled at her. He understood. He picked up the cream cotton polo neck and walked to the counter. The shop assistant was young and sweet and had a badge pinned to her blouse. It announced that her name was

Dearbhla. Frankie joked with her and tried to explain the situation. 'Elvis,' she said. 'Have you been to that place in Temple Bar?'

Dearbhla saved the day. There was an authentic fifties clothing shop just around the corner from Carmel's workshop. It was like stepping into a very big wardrobe, packed to the ceiling with bowling shirts and plaid jackets and bandannas. If Frankie had known about this place all along, he would have lived there. The walls were decorated with rock and roll album covers and a large poster of Marlon Brando in leather. It was hot in there and stuffy and scratchy like new pyjamas. The people who worked in the shop looked like extras from *Happy Days*. Frankie tried on worn jeans and Hawaiian shirts. Christine leaned against a glass cabinet that contained cufflinks and belt buckles and cigarette lighters. To her right stood a giant silver propeller fan in a black metal mesh. It slowly shook its head, shuddering the taffeta prom dresses which hung from a high rail. It caught Christine's hair and blew it away from her neck, where the scar glistened. Every time Frankie came out, she beckoned him to the centre of the shop and stood him in front of a full-length mirror. Pretty soon, there was a pile of clothes that he couldn't live without and he was still trying to find a costume. 'What are you singing?' said a lad with a pointy, gelled flat-top. When Frankie told him, he ducked under the counter, shuffled about with a pile of CDs and found the track. 'Don't Be Cruel' filled even the gloomy, mothballed corners of the shop and guided Frankie to a deep green, single-breasted jacket and a pair of purply-blue jeans. When he showed them on their hangers to Christine, she turned her nose up. They looked like nothing. Too plain to pass a remark on, but the guy behind the counter nodded. Frankie slipped into a cubicle to try them on. Christine looked up as she heard the curtain clinking open. Out walked Frankie and he looked dazzling.

The green brought out the colour of his eyes. His new cream polo neck was tucked into the jeans and the shop assistant shimmied over with a heavy-buckled black leather belt. With his hips jumping along to the tune, Frankie threaded the belt and snapped the buckle. He stretched out his arm to Christine, who stepped slowly towards him, wishing she had learned to jive like her friend Ciara. Elvis sang: *Come on over here and love me. The future looks bright ahead.* Christine stood on his toes. 'You're going to need some new shoes, by the way,' she giggled.

∫

Nerves

Michael called from a phone box in Wicklow. The news of Frankie's kidnap had floated on the airwaves to their car radio. Carmel sat on the sofa with the phone at arm's length and her toes a club sandwich of cotton wool on the coffee table. In honour of Frankie's performance, she had painted the nails glitter-purple and was stranded, surrounded by the deep lounge carpet. Michael raved on through half an Oprah Winfrey show on the telly, clanking coins into the pay phone. He had worked out some new dance steps for Frankie and tried to explain them over the line. Carmel heard Betty in the background saying: 'What are you doing in there?' Poor Michael, he was so worried about his star. He so wanted it to be perfect. Betty was cool about the suit, though.

Half an hour later, Frankie turned up with a bin-bag of clothes and nearly knocked her over with his enthusiasm. She told him about Michael's call and the new dance steps, but wished she hadn't. He paced around, packing and unpacking his bag, putting on records, taking them off again, looking at the clock and starting sentence after sentence, then trailing off. Every time she mentioned Betty and Michael and the suit, he changed the subject and piled more gel on to his hair. Then the woman downstairs turned up and told him that the van he came in was about to get a parking ticket. He ran out like a scalded cat with his bag in his hand and said he was off somewhere and would be back later and if he missed Michael, to give him his love.

After he left, Carmel knocked her cactus into the sink. After three summers of watering the blessed thing with an eye-dropper, she guessed that it wouldn't survive a swim in washing-up liquid. She then spent nearly ten minutes crouched over in the bathroom, trying to fasten her black body. Every time she straightened up, the poppers went again and the fabric flaps sprung up towards her waist. She gave up eventually, knowing she would be walking funny all afternoon, and changed into a denim shirt. Frankie had put a jinx on the day. Filled the air with stomach-knotting tension. When the tape recorder in the lounge chewed up one of his precious Elvis cassettes, she began to think that none of them would make it to the contest alive.

Just before Hank and Michael and Betty arrived, she swooped around the flat, plumping and straightening and looking nervously out of every window. She had bragged about her great lifestyle all the time she had been in Loughfergus. Now, she thought it looked like she was trying too hard. Betty brought flowers and Hank had a bottle of sparkling wine in his hand. In the kitchen, Michael was down on his hands and knees within seconds, looking behind the giant fridge. 'Get out from there,' screamed Betty. 'I've just had that suit cleaned.'

'I've never seen one of these before,' he said. 'Except for on the telly. Does it work OK?' He opened it up and gazed inside, running his fingers along the shelves. He pulled out a couple of supermarket packets. 'Hey, look at these! Mini-tomatoes. And these! Look, they're tiny little potatoes.

The size of marbles. Jesus, Carmel. Where do you do your shopping? Munchkinland?'

Betty sat on one of the stools, her handbag on her lap, as Carmel put the flowers in the vase. She looked up at a postcard of Elvis Presley stuck to a cupboard door. 'I used to keep a picture of him under my pillow when I was at school,' she said. 'He really was a lovely-looking fellow.'

Michael came up behind her. 'Are you talking about me again?' He grinned over at Carmel, who was carrying the flowers through to the lounge. As she came in the door, she saw Hank, leaning against the window sill and looking out over the grey roofs, piled up on top of each other like dishes on a draining board. He looked sad. 'Penny for your thoughts?' she said, putting the flowers on a side table, fluffing them in the vase.

'They're not worth a ha'penny.' He forced a nervous smile and she slid her arms around his large, warm stomach. Hank put his hands on her head, stroking her hair, and they stood there for a moment, happy with the feel of each other.

'Don't mind us.' Michael stood aside to let Betty in with the wine bottle. Hank's hands rested on Carmel's shoulders. Michael came up and tugged at her hair. 'Unhand that woman, Mr Green, or I'll tell Frankie. He'll have your guts for guitar strings.' Hank pulled away and sat down on the sofa with the others. There was an ache in him that had gone away while he cuddled Carmel. Betty poured the wine into Carmel's groovy goblets. 'I wonder how Frankie is feeling now?'

'Oh, I'm sure Christine will be keeping him busy. Keeping his mind off things.' Carmel handed around crisps and peanuts. 'We're probably more worried than he is.'

Betty was looking out of the window, lifting a handful of nuts to her mouth. 'I wonder what it's like back in the village?' she said. 'Brede is down at the Palace and she's put chairs all around the telly so that all the lads can watch it. It'll be the greatest thing since the World Cup. Everyone will be tuning in.'

'All except his mother,' sneered Carmel.

Betty put her glass down. 'Don't you believe it. Given half a chance, she'd be up here watching him. It's all just a load of show, you know, all that tutting and casting her eyes up to heaven.'

'If that's acting, she deserves an Oscar,' mumbled Michael, but Betty put her hand on his knee.

'What do you know, love? You run a mile every time she comes around for tea. She's her own worst enemy, that's the trouble.'

'No. I'm her worst enemy. She hates me,' said Carmel. 'She never liked me, even when we were kids. Now I've snatched Frankie out of her home and put him in mine. I bet you she's got a little wax doll that looks like me somewhere.'

Betty smiled over at her. 'She's just not used to the idea of you and Frankie. It was quite a shock to her system.'

'Me and Frankie?' Carmel bit her lip and looked over at Hank. He shook his head.

'Oh, come on Carmel,' Betty said. 'We know why he came running up to Dublin the minute you left the village. We're not as old-fashioned as you think. I know you're still married to Billy, but what's the sense when things aren't going right? You're just the shot in the arm that Frankie needs.' Carmel coughed. Hadn't they noticed that her things were in one room and Frankie's were in another? No, they were off on a magic carpet ride. She hoped nobody would let something slip and send them tumbling to earth with a crash. 'Cheers, then!' said Michael, and they all raised their glasses. 'Here's to Frankie, and to you, Carmel.' God, it made her want to cry.

Elvis Never Played the Caesar's Palace

Frankie followed his nose. His nose ran all the way home. The white delivery van clattered down the hill towards Loughfergus. In the back, his new outfit hung from a wire coat hanger and his shoulder bag slid over the floor. Three hours earlier, he had been going great, heading for a famous triumph over adversity. Then, all of a sudden, he was up in the air like a flipped beer mat. He just had to get away from all of them. From Michael and his last-minute Arthur Murray dance lessons, Betty and her well-concealed disappointment about the suit. From Christine, who had been acting like Pollyanna all day, and Pat, who was suddenly his dearest chum. Sometimes, too much sympathy can be worse than a slap in the face. He had planned to drive to the coast and get on a ferry. Instead, he had ended up where he had started, where the Wexford Elvis had first played the Caesar's Palace. He pulled over by the church and wound the window down, letting in the cow-fresh air. It was quiet, like Saturdays always were, and there wasn't much danger of seeing anyone. He decided not to drive in, just in case, and took the keys out of the ignition. One of the drivers had left their cigarettes and a lighter on the dashboard. For the want of something significant to do, he pulled one to his lips and lit it. It was four in the afternoon and he had to be at the theatre by seven.

Frankie had never been able to smoke, even when he had wanted to as a teenager. His mates just laughed at him as he coughed and spluttered his way through one of theirs. Age hadn't changed things. He still fiddled around too much, tapping off ash before it had formed and blowing out fat blobs of smoke like a goldfish. His eyes were streaming, but he persisted, thinking that one day it would just happen and he would suddenly be Mr Cool. A slim figure, all in black with a red scarf, was coming up the hill towards the van, but Frankie didn't see until it was too late. He hummed along to the radio, brandishing the cigarette like a conductor's baton. He wiped the tears from his eyes, looked out through the windscreen and froze. His pale, trembling lips said: 'Oh, shite!' He flicked the cigarette out of the window and saw it rolling down the road towards the approaching feet. With a deft movement, it was squished flat.

'Frank!' said Eileen. 'Is this what they've been teaching you in Dublin?' She was on her way to see Joe, as there were flowers in her hand. He opened the door of the van and stepped down. She came up to him, peering at the mark on his nose. 'I hear you've been in the wars.' She leaned back, satisfied that it wasn't life-threatening.

'It's nothing,' he said, unable to look her in the eyes. Together they moved into the graveyard. She walked ahead of him, swishing through the seedy long grass in her black skirt. Joe's grave was dusty and the flowers in the vase were parched and droopy. She blessed herself and murmured a prayer as the pea-green leaves shivered above them. She opened one eye and looked at Frankie, who was reading the other headstones. 'Shouldn't you be somewhere?' she said, taking a bottle of water from her bag and emptying out what was stale in the vase. 'In case you haven't noticed, it's getting on.' She glanced at her watch for effect. It was very small and most of the time she hadn't a clue what it said. 'You don't want to be late for your big night.'

Frankie stood behind her, his hands in his pockets and his back to the sun. 'I'm not going to the finals,' he said. She turned and pulled the new flowers tight to her chest. She was wearing lipstick and her red silk scarf shone in the light. She glowed warm against the cold stone. 'You were right all along, Mum,' he said softly. 'I should never have started all this Elvis nonsense. That thing yesterday proved it to me.' He smiled in the hope of getting one back.

'Oh, great,' she said, all indignant. 'This will all be my fault, I suppose. The whole village sitting around the tables in the pub, all excited, and they find out your mammy won't let you go on. Oh, that will make me very popular.' She knelt forward and shoved the stalks into the vase. They were thin, fragrant freesias which rolled together, leaning over the glass lip.

'I thought you'd be pleased.' He crouched down beside her, his knees still scabbed and smarting beneath his jeans. He held out his fingertips and caressed the petals.

'Well, you thought wrong.' She pushed his hand away from the flowers and held it tightly. 'If you start something, no matter how hare-brained it is, you follow it through. Look at your father.' She patted the headstone. 'He stayed at that factory until he was head foreman. I'm sure there were many times when he would have gladly let someone else sort out the problems.' Frankie looked at the headstone and Eileen looked at Frankie. He seemed so fragile with that purple bruise on his nose. A paler, softer version of Joe, the way he was long ago, when he, too, had dreamed about being a wandering minstrel. She wanted to tell him about some of his father's shortcomings, but she decided to stay quiet. He never said it, but she knew Frankie idolised his father. She couldn't spoil it for him now. She would far rather he saw her as the big bad wolf. 'Don't listen to what I say, Frank,' she said softly. 'Do it for your friends. They've all put money on you. If your father was alive, he'd have put money on you.'

Frankie smiled over at Joe's grave. He was a gambler, all right, living all those years in the same village as Mary and Carmel. Did he have sleepless nights imagining what would happen if it had all come out? Surely he must have been scared, because he loved Eileen. He really did. Frankie had been in love, so he felt qualified to look back. When he did, he saw Eileen and Joe dancing in the living room and he was singing to her over the band on the radio. She was wearing a cornflower-blue dress, a little longer than was the fashion, and she had her head tucked into his neck. His hands stroked the back of her hair as they shuffled around in front of the fire. They had seen him peeking in the door crack, and Joe had called him a spy and yelled at him to go to bed. Frankie realised that now Joe was just a shadow in his mind. He wondered if it was the same for Eileen, whether she had to get out the photograph albums and remind herself.

Eileen got up, brushing off her skirt. Frankie gave her a hand. They passed Mrs Macnamara's grave. There was a dead pot plant on it. He walked over and cleaned away a few blades of grass which had grown up between the little green pebbles. He tucked the pot plant behind the headstone. 'Carmel asked me,' he said, although she hadn't. 'Poor woman,' said Eileen with a faraway look in her eyes. Frankie felt shaky. It would be so easy to tell her the truth about Carmel and end a lifetime of long, uncomfortable silences between them. Perhaps she would fall into his arms. They stood either side of the grave and neither of them moved. They were like the two cars on his Scalextric set. Day after day, they went round and round on their two tracks, only a couple of inches apart. The only way for them to touch was to crash into each other and smash themselves to bits. Frankie looked over at Eileen, but stayed quiet. He was always a boy who looked after his toys. It was the way his father taught him and those things never really go away. Joe was great at playing games, but he liked to win. Frankie usually let him. Joe was the tycoon of Monopoly, the draughts King of Kings. The Bosco of glove puppets.

Eileen longed to go up to him like other mothers and embarrass him with a cuddle. She blamed Joe. He had been such a big man that she had got smaller and smaller in comparison. The incredible shrinking woman. She used to be a bright spark, but when it came to stories, Joe was the one who could tell them and have the whole crowd hanging on his words. Whenever she started a joke, he had finished it and taken it and made it his own. In the end, she used to say: 'No, you tell it, Joe. You're better at those things than me.' When Frankie was a little boy, he had clung to her and brought to her his scraped knees and his hidden treasures and his tears, but pretty soon there was Joe with his football and his visits to the pub and his 'Don't bother Mammy with that now. Be a big man.' After he died, she looked at Frankie and saw a stranger, snookered from her view for too long. A sensitive man who folded his arms and bit his lip when he was upset and went somewhere far away from her when he was happy.

'My white suit was ruined, you know,' he said as they left the graveyard and walked up the hill to the van.

'Thanks be to God,' she smiled. 'I know Betty worked hard, but, well . . .' She wanted to tell him that he didn't need a white suit to shine. She looked at the Owen Brothers logo on the side of the van. 'Are they nice, these people you work with?' she asked, hanging her handbag over her wrist.

'Lovely. I've made some good friends.' He paused with his hand on the door handle. 'You know Carmel?' He looked at her, grinning. She nodded. 'Well, she's a good friend.'

'Fancy!' said Eileen, almost smiling at him. She put a hand up and shaded her eyes from the sun. Frankie glanced up at the steeple and said, 'Just a good friend. That's all. We were more, you know, for a while, but, well, we decided to keep it . . .' He sniggered and looked at the road. 'Well, friendly.' Eileen shrugged her shoulders and Frankie opened the van door.

'Will she be there to see you sing tonight?' She climbed up into the van and ran a finger over the dust on the dashboard. Frankie nodded. 'And the people I work with. Christine, she's my boss. You'd like her, and of course there's Hank and Michael and Betty. They're all up now, having tea with Carmel.'

'And you're here.' She looked at him sternly. 'Sort yourself out.' Frankie started the van and pulled out on to the road heading for the village to run her home. 'Is there a prize if you win?' she asked, holding her bag handles on her lap. He told her it was a trip to Graceland. 'You could visit your Auntie Anne while you're over there,' she said, and Frankie nodded. A nervous shudder went through his stomach. 'Will you be watching, Mum?' He looked straight ahead. 'Oh, I've no doubt,' she sighed. 'I'm baby-sitting for Betty and they'll be glued to it.' Frankie was thinking about slamming the brakes on and swiping her one across the cheek when she shouted: 'Stop!' They were outside the Palace. Eileen was excited. She wriggled, trying to undo her seat belt. Frankie leaned over and clipped it open for her. She was looking at the New Zealand camper van, which was parked beside them. 'They're back!' she said. 'Isn't that lovely? What a shame they've missed Hank.' She turned to Frankie and smiled. 'Well, perhaps they will stay for a couple of days.'

'Yeah, maybe.' Frankie leaned back in his seat, feeling her slipping away once more. She slid down, then turned and looked in at him through the door crack. 'You'd better be off.' She patted the door. 'Or you'll miss your chance.'

'Wish me luck.' He crossed his arms and bit his lip. Eileen looked at him for a while, then smiled. She raised one hand. 'Good luck, Frankie,' she said. She slammed the door, then walked to the door of the Palace. Just before he pulled the van away, she turned back and waved at him.

He was nearly up by the church again when he realised. 'Frankie,' he said, feeling the prickle of tears in his throat. 'She called me Frankie.' He felt like someone had given him the whole world with chocolate sauce on top. For as long as he could remember, he was Frankie to everyone but his parents, and no matter how many times he begged them, they wouldn't budge. Frank was a person Joe created and he knew, right from the start, how he was going to turn out. This Frankie character that appeared was a bit of an impostor and he was having none of it. But today, at long last, Eileen said bollocks to Frank and to Joe and hurrah for Frankie! Fade in the Hallelujah Chorus!

The Girls are Back

The doorbell rang. Carmel was hoping so hard that it would be Frankie, it didn't occur to her that he had a key and would have let himself in. 'Ta-dum!' Nancy fell into the hallway with a clinking bag of duty-free slapping against her shin. 'The girls are back in town!' she roared.

'Hi. How was your holiday?'

'Fuckin' ace!' She was a reddy-brown colour and her freckles had turned into big muddy splatters on her face. She was wearing a long white cheesecloth dress with a wine stain just below the collar. 'Sorry, Carmel, I'm rat-arsed. We were delayed for four hours in Greece. Got wasted in the bloody departure lounge, then they kept giving us all these little bottles of wine on the flight.' She rubbed her left eye with her fist. 'You know what we're like, girl. We were nicking them off all the people who didn't want them. All the pensioners up the back. Becka has gone for a lie-down. You should see the colour of her.'

'Is she brown, then?'

'She's fuckin' navy!' Nancy headed for the lounge. Carmel

surged ahead and squeezed through the door frame just in front of her.

'Nancy. I'd like you to meet some friends of mine from back home. This is Hank and Michael and Betty.' They all stood up and Nancy shook one hand at a time, dropping her plastic bag into a chair. Betty brushed a few crumbs from her skirt and said: 'You look like you've been somewhere nice, Nancy.'

'Greece. For two weeks. It was gorgeous.' She flopped into the chair, mumbled 'Shite' and pulled the bag out from under her. 'Just sat on the duty-free. Can you believe that? Hey, Carmel, you'll be smoking bent cigarettes for the next six months.'

'You've a lovely tan,' said Michael as Hank giggled next to him.

'Well, I did.' Her nose was pink and crusty and her shoulders were divided by a tidemark of peeling skin. 'My brother came and got us from the airport. He was nearly fainting at the colour of Becka, then he says to me, "So, Nance, where's your tan, then?" Cheeky sod! I told him to go and look under my seat in the plane.' She looked over at the sofa. Hank was helping them all to another cup of tea. 'Do you know Frankie?' said Michael, grinning and leaning forward. Carmel was screaming inside her head. 'We've come up to see him sing.'

'Of course!' Nancy sat up in the chair. 'It's the contest tonight, isn't it? Oh God, I hope he wins. He's such a dote, isn't he?' Carmel's hand squeezed Nancy's shoulder.

'Would you like a cup of tea, Nance? We'd just need to put some more water in the pot. Come into the kitchen and give me a hand.'

'Great,' she said. 'A cup of tea would be lovely.' She got up from the chair, kicking over the plastic bag.

Betty cleared her throat. 'I'm the same as you, love,' she said. 'No matter where you go in the world, there's nothing like a cup of tea to let you know that you're home. You can never get a decent cup on the Continent. I think it's the milk.' Carmel pulled Nancy out of the door before she could reply and steered her to the kitchen.

'Let go of my arm,' she hissed, 'or you'll have the rest of the skin off it. What's the bloody panic?' She went over to the sink and gulped down three glasses of water as Carmel spoke.

'It's them in there. They don't know about Frankie being my brother. Well, Hank does. He's the big fella. But the others would drop dead on the spot if they knew. I've been going crazy all afternoon trying to say the right thing to the right person.' Nancy carried on swallowing. 'Are you listening?'

She put down the glass and breathed in deeply. 'Yeah. I'll keep my mouth shut. Oh God, I needed that. My guts are killing me. For the last two weeks we've been drinking this stuff night and day. It tasted like warm nail polish remover. I was going to bring you back a bottle, but . . .'

Hank came in, holding the teapot. 'You'll be needing this,' he said. He came over and put it on the sideboard, then went over to Carmel and put his arm around her shoulder. She leaned her head against his shirt. 'We were just getting our stories straight,' she said, patting his stomach. 'About Frankie, I mean.'

'I thought so.' Hank's deep voice growled through his chest into Carmel's ear. 'It's been playing on your mind all day, hasn't it? I know. There are times when I want to tell Michael, but I think it's best to wait a while. Himself and Betty still think you're sleeping together. Finding out that you're his sister would give them a heart attack.'

They heard a muffled screech from the lounge: 'Oh my God!' It was Betty. Hank, Carmel and Nancy flashed wide eyes at each other. 'Could she have heard from there?' said Hank. The kettle clicked. The three of them stood, frozen to the spot. 'Don't know,' said Carmel. Dry-mouthed, they shuffled towards the door.

Betty was red in the face and had her left hand clamped over her mouth. Michael was leaning against her, his face turned away from the door. 'Sorry,' gulped Betty. 'I know I shouldn't have been so nosy.' Her eyes were red with tears. Michael gingerly held out a clenched fist. Carmel put out a shaking palm. Down fell a little rubber dolly with a key ring coming out of its head. She slowly pulled it towards her and looked down. Nancy let out a yell from over her shoulder. 'Oh, Jesus!' She doubled over with loud, snorting laughter. Carmel rolled the figure in her palm. A grinning little waiter in an apron. Nancy was gasping. Tears rolling down her cheeks. 'It's a present from Becka,' she said. 'Give him a squeeze.' Carmel pressed the figure between her thumb and forefinger. A huge pink rubber penis flipped out from under his white apron. Carmel screeched and dropped it on the floor. 'Er! Yuk! Oh God, that's revolting!'

'It fell out of the bag,' giggled Betty, wiping her nose on the back of her hand. Hank had taken it and was squeezing it again and again. 'Anyone you know?' said Michael, and they all had to sit down.

Snow White

Christine had butterflies in her stomach. The anxious feeling you get when you are going on holiday and everything is packed and all the electrical things have been unplugged and there is still loads of time before the taxi comes to take you to the airport. All afternoon, she had been pacing around the yard, waiting for the van to return, knowing that something wasn't right. Now, she was at the theatre. It was half past seven and still there was no sign of him. A man from the TV company was standing outside the stage door and when she mentioned Frankie's name, he got all animated. He had called everywhere trying to find him. The press were waiting. Christine stood trembling, as the man went on and on. She couldn't hold back the panic any longer. 'What about Wacker?' she said. The man's eyes widened. 'Oh, God!' he said. 'That's it! Oh, what am I going to do?' He bolted inside the building, knocking over a Frank Sinatra who was coming out for a smoke.

She walked around to the front of the theatre and glanced at herself in the shop window next door. She was wearing a long yellow dress she had bought for a friend's wedding. The lace around the collar hid her scar, but she had never liked it. Now she hated it, because everyone else in the crowd was wearing casuals. The Elvis fans were easy to spot. Men with crêpe-soled shoes and big belt buckles. A woman was holding a sign saying 'Come On Sean'. When she moved out of the way, Christine spotted Carmel with three other people. She couldn't bear to talk to them. Frankie wasn't going to show and it was all her fault. Too late. Carmel saw her and pointed her out to the others. Christine waved and moved towards them, but a man pushed past her and knocked her off balance. Trying to steady herself, she got her heel caught in the hem of her dress and fell into an undignified heap on the pavement. She was winded and sat for a second as a space cleared around her. Carmel and her friends were smiling in her direction and the big guy was waving, but none of them were coming to help her. It was as if the wind had changed and they were all frozen in time. A strong hand clasped her from behind and a voice said: 'Oops-a-daisy!' It was Frankie and, as he lifted her, the others rushed forward and embraced him, squashing her in the middle.

They moved together around the side of the building. The Loughfergus crowd were busy asking Christine how Frankie was getting along with the job and raving about Carmel's flat. 'Isn't it lovely? Oh, you haven't seen it? Well, you must pop over some time.' The man from before was on a mobile phone, but he snapped the mouthpiece shut and ran forward when he spotted Frankie. 'Oh, thank God!' he shouted. 'You won't believe the panic I've been in. I thought that lunatic had got you again! Have you any idea how many performers I have to look after tonight?' Frankie came towards him smiling and shook him by the hand. 'Sorry, Gerard,' he grinned. 'I got held up, em, in traffic, I mean.' Gerard tucked the mobile phone into a holster on his hip.

'Well, say goodbye to your fan club and I'll see you inside in about two minutes, right?' Gerard stormed through the stage door. Frankie turned to the others. He shook Hank by the hand, said 'Sorry about the dance steps' to Michael and 'Sorry about the suit' to Betty, who kissed him on the cheek. Christine stood back, but Frankie stepped towards her. 'Good luck, Frankie.' She reached out and patted him on the chest. 'You're a brilliant singer.' He slid his hand up her arm, gripping her by the shoulder, then touching her ear with his fingertips. Her handbag slipped off her other shoulder and she caught it by the strap, jerking Frankie's hand from her face. They both sniggered and separated, then she backed away with Hank, Betty and Michael and headed towards the front of the theatre, dragging her handbag by the strap like a toy dog. Then there was just Frankie and Carmel.

'Well,' she said. 'Here we are again.'

He took his suit and his bag from her hands. 'Yeah.' He looked at her grey-green eyes, which were so like Joe's, for a second too long. She looked away and smiled. 'Sorry,' he said.

'I'm not.' She touched his cheek. 'Not about anything.' She took her hand away. 'Well, you'd better go and get ready or I'll have Charlie Cheesecake in there telling me off.'

Frankie laughed. 'You mean Gerard? He's not so bad. He's just keen, that's all.' He looked towards the stage door. There was a rumble of voices from within the building.

Carmel backed away, but stopped. 'Are you?' she said. 'Keen? I mean, is this what you want?'

Frankie wrinkled his nose and shifted the bag in his hand. He looked over at the outside broadcast van in the yard. 'Sort of,' he said. 'Yeah. It's a start, isn't it?' Carmel laughed at him. 'What?' he asked, laughing anyway. She folded her arms, then unfolded them and put them around his neck.

She hugged him and kissed him on the cheek and said: 'I love you, Frankie.' He was so glad she had waited. That she hadn't told him on the day they found the beach glass or the day she put the pot plant on the grave. 'I love you too, sis!' He hugged her back, wrapping his suit bag around her. It was like catching a butterfly in his cupped hands. Back then, he would have held it for too long, but now he could watch it dance away into the sunlight. Carmel skipped down the alleyway, turning again and again to wave and shout, 'Good luck! Break a leg! See you later!'

The theatre was crawling with people. All the dressing rooms were packed and through the open doors came the smell of sweat and perfume. Outside one, a Dolly Parton look-alike was hyperventilating into a crisp packet and a teenage boy and girl were clomping their way through *Riverdance*. Gerard led him through a maze of passageways and up a flight of stairs. They passed a door with the word 'ELVIS' written on it in chalk. From inside came the sound of thunking guitars and voices singing. At the end of the corridor, there was a toilet and an unmarked door which looked like a cupboard. Gerard fumbled around with a giant bunch of keys until he found one that opened it. A strip light flickered on and revealed a boxroom. Gerard took a step back and beckoned Frankie forward.

A row of Elvis jump suits hung from picture hooks. They twinkled and swayed in the disturbed air. Big suits and small ones. Comet suits. Burning Love suits. Suits with capes and suits with gold buckles. On the floor were seven pairs of shiny white shoes nestling in crêpe paper inside cardboard boxes. It was like Snow White with oversized dwarves. 'Take your pick,' grinned Gerard as Frankie stood mesmerised. After the story of his kidnap hit the newsstands, they had started arriving. Kind-hearted owners of fancy-dress shops and Elvis wannabes who never made it to the finals had been moved by his plight. Frankie was so glad that the reporters had missed him in order to catch the show. He was overcome with emotion and sobbed into his hands. The real killer was a familiar Elvis belt buckle and a little pink calling card pinned to one lapel. Elvis O'Donovan was a prince, all right. Frankie walked into the room and looked at them in turn like a military inspection. His tear-filled eyes turned the diamante into sparkling Catherine-wheels. 'What would Joe say?' he thought as he dabbed the tears with his sleeve.

He knew full well what Joe would say. Frankie remembered driving with him once when he was nine or ten. He had begged Joe to let him have the radio on and sat cringing as his father showed his disapproval of the Isley Brothers and their electric guitars. Next came 'Two Little Boys' by Rolf Harris and Frankie relaxed. Towards the end of the second verse, though, Joe suddenly lunged forward to turn off the radio, mounting the kerb in the process and sending a couple of pedestrians scattering into doorways. 'Bloody rubbish!' he shouted, and they drove on silently, looking out of the window. Even then, Frankie knew it wasn't a matter of musical integrity. It was because Rolf was about to deliver that line: *Did you think I would leave you dying when there's room on my horse for two?* Joe had to put a stop to the emotions that were rising in his throat and save them both from a nasty moment. Frankie wondered what would have happened if they had just gone on listening and perhaps shared a hankie to wipe their eyes. Now, he wished that Joe was there among the Elvis suits, and his friends and his mother and the television cameras. He wanted this moment to be marked, so that he could look back at it when things weren't up to scratch. It didn't matter whether he won the contest or if everybody saw his tears. Gerard glanced at his stopwatch and said, 'Look, I'm going to have to leave you to it. When you've found one that fits, go along to the room marked Elvis.' He patted Frankie on the shoulder and sniffed away a tear of his own before disappearing into the passageway.

A dusty mirror was leaning against one of the walls. Frankie went to work, trying on one suit after another. Most were enormous. He tripped up on the kick-pleated flares and nearly disappeared into the surgical-size collars. One was too tight and got stuck over his hips. He broke into a sweat trying to get it off again. Finally, he reached for Elvis O'Donovan's gift. It was loose around the waist and a tiny bit short, but it was by far the best fit. The shoes he chose were a size too big, but he bunched up his socks in the toes and clomped in them down the corridor. As he opened the door, he was greeted by the others. All eight of them were crammed into the same room, which was sparse and white-painted. They stood around the walls amongst piles of their own casual clothes and chatted and joked with each other. He was scared that they would be cheesed off with all his publicity, but they were just glad that Wacker didn't kill him. They shook his hand and patted him on the back in between combing their hair and spraying themselves with deodorant.

The heat in the dressing room was overwhelming and was playing merry hell with Bob's toupee. He was lowering it for the umpteenth time on to two strips of double-sided tape on his sweaty scalp. On the wall beside the mirrors, a speaker relayed the events on stage. Jerry, who was all made up and wearing loads of jewellery, turned the volume knob down and asked Frankie to tell them all about his adventure. 'Yeah, go on,' said the others. Frankie sat next to Bob and laid out his make-up. He wrapped a scarf around his neck to protect the suit and spoke to them as he applied his foundation. Already, the story of Wacker seemed like ancient history. The Elvises listened as they got dressed. One helped another squeeze his chubby shoulders into his suit and the big Elvis from Cavan lay on the floor to get his zip up. Frankie dabbed the foundation over his nose. It hid most of the bruising, but he had to scrape some out of the pot with his fingernail and smear it over the gash. It stung, but he felt better as the powder went on top and made him look like his old self.

Gerard appeared and told them all to be quiet. One of them would have to sing Wacker's line for him in the Elvis Forever routine. The Cork Elvis volunteered and they went through it a couple of times unaccompanied. By now, Frankie was ready and Bob was pulling a comb through his pompadour, scraping it over the gauze. The air was thick with hairspray and the tension of last-minute panic, so they were looking forward to their call up to the cool stage area. It was the interval and they were on right afterwards. As they shook with nerves, they made a clinking noise. Frankie packed away his make-up bag and washed his hands at a tiny scum-rimmed sink in the corner. He felt like he had a cocktail shaker in his stomach, but it wasn't half as bad as it had been in Kilkenny. Knowing how difficult it was to get in and out of a jump suit, he was glad.

There they were. Eight grown men living eight different lives, dressed in almost identical pantomime costumes. Each one was hoping that he would be the nearest to his idol's image. That the audience would squint and believe themselves to be in Vegas in the early seventies. Frankie looked at himself in Elvis O'Donovan's perfect white suit and thought that he might just be the one to take them there. The dressing-room door was open and from outside came the sound of women screaming at each other. Their shrill voices echoed down the corridor. 'Feckin' bitch!' said one. The Elvises stepped out to have a look. The women were both in their underwear. Elaborate bodices, fishnet tights and high heels. The Cork Elvis, who was cupping a cigarette in his hand, squinted and said 'Madonnas!' then took another drag. The fight was broken up by Angelina the Cheralike and a Rod Stewart in leather trousers. Rod's wig was pulled off by one of the Madonnas and whizzed over the floor like a runaway guinea pig. Angelina spotted Frankie and waved at him. He smiled and was about to wander down and see her, but Gerard appeared to usher them all up the stairs.

Frankie was at the back of the line. In front of him, decorated capes fanned out to grip the handrails. A woman with earphones and a clipboard had a frantic conversation with Gerard halfway up the stairs, then pushed past them. The backstage area was cavernous and lit by bulbs covered with opaque sheets of red plastic. The backdrops from the play hung in layers a couple of feet apart and above them was a tangle of ropes and wires. Brick walls were painted black and splashed occasionally with other colours. Over the floor, thick electric cables were taped down and covered by rubber ramps. Getting across them was an assault course. Tucked into every corner was a technician in jeans and a black T-shirt, and several women with earphones and clipboards darted about looking worried.

Gerard was wired. He was in a skin-tight Adidas shirt and wide-legged jeans. 'Elvises all over here, please,' he said in a hissy stage whisper. They dutifully gathered in front of him and hushed up as he put an index finger in front of his pursed lips. The sound coming from the auditorium was a loud rush of air like a conch shell to the ear. To the side of them, the thick raspberry velvet curtain hung dusty and still. From the pit came the sound of a piano and a guitar being fine-tuned. 'OK,' said Gerard. 'When the curtain goes up, you will already be on-stage in your positions. I've put a load of little crosses on the floor so that the light will be directly overhead. Keep to that spot whatever you do, or you'll disappear altogether.' The Elvises nodded and Gerard beckoned them on to the stage. One by one, they found their crosses and covered them with a foot. They smiled and waved over at each other like schoolboys. They craned their necks when they realised what was hanging from the endless ceiling above them. A giant sign, just like the one in the '68 comeback special. A red light bulb ELVIS with the power switched off. This was Frankie's dream come true. He grinned and looked at the others. It was the same for them, he knew it. Just before they heard the buzz of the safety curtain rising, they shuffled and cleared their throats. A couple prayed and Frankie bit his lip and went over the lyrics again and again. He wasn't feeling nearly scared enough and he wondered if it was the suit. The magic, protective white suit. Gerard stayed with them and watched a woman off-stage. A loud, booming voice made them all jump. It sounded God-like. 'Ladies and gentlemen, welcome back to the National Talent Quest.' There was a ripple of applause from beyond the curtain, followed by a hush. 'For the second half of tonight's show, we are proud to present a tribute to show business's most impersonated superstar. The one, the only King of Rock and Roll. Elvis Presley.' With a droning, the raspberry curtain slowly lifted and the red light bulbs came on, sending rivers of blood across the floor. Gerard raced off to the wings, giving them a double thumbs-up. The bandleader, in a black tuxedo, stood and raised both of his hands. Only the upper half of him was visible from the stage, as if he were in a manhole. Frankie sucked as much air into his lungs as he could, waiting for those two hands to move. He was on the very top of the rollercoaster, bracing himself for the stomach-destroying thrills ahead. Down went the hands. *Da dum! Pum! Pum!* went the band, and they were off.

Warden threw a party at the county jail, sang Jerry in his multicoloured American eagle suit. He was loud and strong but still almost drowned by the cheers of the audience. They were coming like a speeding truck at Frankie, hitting him as he sang *The prison band was there and they began to wail*. He did it, without a slip, and had to force himself not to go on singing. He handed the vocal baton over to the big guy from Cavan and looked ahead at the audience. He was near the front of the stage and could see the outlines of those caught in the lights. He saw their hands clapping together. In front of them, a cameraman semi-squatted like a monster. A creepy Caliban with one eye at the centre of his forehead, slowly turning to examine them all. *Everybody, let's rock*, they all sang, dancing and clicking their fingers. All of Frankie's one days and maybes had become a great big now. In his hand was a microphone, not a hairbrush or a shower head. His audience were not half pissed with pints in their hands and nothing better to do, they were rows and rows of real, live Elvis fans.

Frankie stretched his arms out to the side, almost cruciform, and dropped his head so that he was mimicking Elvis's own interpretation of the song. 'One, two, one-two-three,' went his hips. He wondered if the others were doing it too, or if he was the only one really going for it. He wanted to look up and see if the cameras were on him, beaming him all over the country. Was Elvis O'Donovan watching and wishing that he was there, rather than just his suit? Was Eileen proud? The band were really good, particularly the bass guitar, who got the riffs just right. After the solos were over, they all sang the third verse together. The song drew to a close and they repeated *dancin' to the jailhouse rock* again and again; the audience went mad, hiding their fading voices. *Taadummm!* The band finished with a flourish and the noise took over. Frankie finally knew what Scotty Moore was talking about when he described playing with Elvis. How the teeny-boppers made more noise than a kids' swimming gala in an indoor pool. Elvis could have sung anything he wanted and they wouldn't have known. Frankie waited to bow, looking sideways and taking his cue from Bob. Down they dipped and Frankie hoped Bob's toupee stayed in place. Down came the curtain and on ran Gerard, ushering them off and shouting, 'Fabulous! Oh, you should have seen yourselves!'

They scrummed together, patting studded backs, heavy-breathing, tassels slapping. The Cork Elvis with the ginger eyebrows was first on. His suit was the most elaborate. A very convincing copy of a Chinese dragon jump suit from Graceland. They released him from the scrum and the voice of God came back on. 'And now, our first solo Elvis impersonator is Andrew Bryson from County Cork.' There was a cheer and the curtain went up again. Andrew was singing 'Suspicious Minds', and the opening chords sounded while he was still off-stage. The other Elvises stood with their arms folded and their faces still glowing with the heat, watching him as he left the shadows of the wings and the lights hit him, catching his black hair and buffing it with blue. As he took the microphone from the stand and pulled it up to his mouth, Frankie went out of focus. He was thinking about Carmel and what she had said in the alleyway. 'Is this what you want?' It was what they all wanted. To sing in homage. To swing on a star and carry moonbeams home in a jar, like the old song goes. To stand in a magic white suit and be better off than you are. *We can't go on together*, sang Andrew, his right leg pumping. He gripped the microphone in both hands and moved slowly across the stage, keeping his profile to the audience. He sank into a genuflexion for the slow part of the song, holding one hand aloft, tromboning the microphone from his face and shutting his eyes. He was good, and the crowd were being drawn in. He had the kind of confidence that allowed him to kneel at the front of the stage and know that women in the front row would get up and try to reach him over the orchestra pit. *Because I love you too much, baby*, he sang. The lights flashed alternate rainbow colours at his suit, making it dance even when he was still. Round and round went his arm like a hammer-thrower's, with his hips following suit as the rhythms got more frantic. As the last cacophonous notes faded out, he mumbled: 'Thank you, lazengennelmen! You're beautiful! I love you all!'

'Follow that!' said Bob as the audience went wild.

Frankie hugged himself tightly, pressing his wrists against the diamante belt buckle. 'Is this what I want?' he said to himself, thinking about Carmel and Christine, Michael and Betty, Hank and Eileen. Joe. Something was building up inside him as Enda, the Kerry Elvis, went on. Frankie twitched and walked in circles, brushing past the embroidered arms of his new friends. With every rotation, he got nearer to the door which led to the backstage area. As the first verse finished, he slipped through the door and clattered down the stairs to the stuffy corridor. It wasn't what he wanted.

Glory Glory

In row J, Michael was trying to wedge his front-door key into the coin slot on the bracket that held the opera glasses. None of them had the right money and he was desperate to eye up the competition. The *Jailhouse Rock* opening had them all leaping around in their seats. The overwhelming sensation of Elvis in a hall of mirrors. Carnival mirrors that pulled him into different shapes and sizes. Frankie was like a streak of lightning next to the others, tall and slim in the amazing white suit he had suddenly managed to obtain. Michael finally managed to free the little red binoculars and clamped them to his face. He was scared. The first guy was great and had done all the things he had wanted Frankie to do. Carmel sat next to Hank with her legs tightly crossed, wishing she had gone to the toilet in the interval. Back in row M, Christine was chomping her way through a packet of chocolate-covered peanuts. The woman next to her had gone mad at the Cork Elvis and his gyrations. She wanted to kick her in the shins and tell her to save her energy, because Elvis number four would be miles better.

The Kerry Elvis started well. The lights went right down,

then a glitter ball came from the rafters somewhere, sending little silver specks all over the stage. He was all in black, apart from the diamonds, which flashed in the passing shafts of light. He sang: *Are you lonesome tonight?* and he sounded amazing. Michael sang: *Is your bra strap too tight?* to Betty and she dug him in the ribs with her elbow. A man behind them tutted. The band in the pit sounded rich and the backing singers were perfect. It might have been nerves, but his voice had a little tremble which was very effective. It was stronger when he sang: *Is your heart filled with pain? Shall I come back again?*

Hank bit the tiny wooden spoon that had come with his tub of ice cream. He was trying not to let the song get to him. There was a wonderful feeling coming over the auditorium, as if it were filling with warm, soapy water.

There is something about the Kerry accent which doesn't always lend itself easily to heartfelt prose. When the backing singers started to 'ooh' the melody, and Enda took the microphone out of the stand, a hush came about the hall. When he opened his mouth and started to say: *You know, someone said the world's a stage and each must play a part,* there was a murmur of suppressed laughter. They were all wondering who on earth suggested he tackled that particular song. He wandered around, flicking the mike lead and acting out the speech as if he were Marlon Brando in *On the Waterfront*. The tears were rolling down Carmel's cheeks when he said: *Honey, you lied when you said you loved me,* and by the time he got to: *Now, the stage is bare and I'm standing there,* the backing singers were starting to lose their grip. It's very difficult to go 'ooh' when you're laughing. 'Poor lad,' said Betty, and she clapped loudly when he finished.

Little did they know that Frankie was standing in the empty dressing room, easing himself out of Elvis O'Donovan's suit. He was shaking and sweating and all fingers and thumbs with panic. The cotton peeled away from his sweat-dampened legs. The heavy white shoes were kicked against the wall. He stood for a moment and looked at himself in the bulb-ringed mirror. His underpants were pale pink, thanks to a rogue sock of Carmel's in the washer. The scab on his nose was emerging from the make-up and there was a purple ring under each of his eyes. From the speaker came the voice announcing Bob and the roar of applause. In five minutes, Frankie's name would be called.

Bob was going for the Elvis song to end them all: 'The American Trilogy'. He was short and stocky, so he sang the number that made him feel ten feet tall, which dwarfed everything else with its emotion and glorified a nation into which his own could fit a hundred times. A single guitar played the first plaintive bars of 'The Star Spangled Banner' and Bob stood with both his arms stretched towards the crowd like he was giving them a blessing. On either side of his torso, the blue satin lining of his cape shone bright and iridescent like a half-fanned peacock. Slowly, the arm that held his microphone arced towards his face. He turned to the wings and lowered his head as if in prayer. *Oh, I wish I was in the land of cotton*, he sang in a low, groaning vibrato. Michael fiddled around with the opera glasses. 'God, he's sweating already!' he said, handing them to Hank. Bob got instant brownie points for that. The capacity to perspire rivers was an important part of being an Elvis. Bob wiped his face on the turquoise scarf that was tucked into his enormous pointed collar. He walked to the very front of the stage, flexed his arm, reached up and grabbed a fistful of air. *Look away! Look away!* he sang with gusto. Michael and Hank looked away to the rows behind them. Carmel laughed and Betty pulled at Michael's jacket. 'Bloody children, both of them!' she said.

Glory. Glory. Hallelujah! Bob stretched each word to breaking point and the backing singers wailed alongside him. It was stirring stuff and the audience were loving it. All their attention was focused on little Bob. His movements were slow and measured like t'ai chi. The chains that hung like tinsel from the bottom of his broad belt swayed in the orange light as he kneeled and sang: *So hush little baby*. He was transforming into Elvis before their eyes. The Elvis of the seventies whose movements were no longer frantic; whose limbs didn't thrust. A man who was treading water before the currents finally took him under. Bob bathed in his own *Glory, Glory*. He tucked his fingers into the cape and unfurled himself, flapping blue satin as he turned on his heels and displayed the back of his plumage which was encrusted with gold and sequins. Some people at the front were already on their feet, and others joined them as Bob punched the air, screwed his face up and summoned from deep within him an awesome finish. *His truth goes marching . . . Oooooonnnnnn!*

'Nice one, Bob,' grinned Frankie. The cheers of the audience were distorting as they forced their way through the little speaker in the dressing room. He looked at the white suit which hung from a hook behind him and a shiver passed right through him, bristling his hair and fluttering in his stomach and buckling his ankles. He closed his eyes and grabbed the Formica top of the dressing table. 'God! What am I doing?' he said, laughing and shaking his head. He stopped because it made his nose throb. In Kilkenny, it had been the magic sequins, but now it was time for something much more spectacular. Something like the ghost of Elvis himself. Frankie had come close to hearing it before when he was a lad. That soothing drawl which said, 'Go on, brother, and do it for me.' He opened his eyes, but saw only his own reflection. The suit remained empty and limp. Elvis didn't go where Elvis wasn't needed.

The applause over the speaker died away. Frankie took a good deep breath, shouted 'Shit!' and ran out of the dressing-room door. As his black lace-ups clattered up the metal staircase, he could hear the continuity announcer saying: 'And now, from Wexford . . .' Walls blurred and disappeared as he charged into the blackness of the backstage area. 'Frankie Shaw!' said the announcer as he rounded the rows of scenery and saw the others in a semicircle, looking at him in panic. 'Come on, Frankie. Come on!' they beckoned, holding out the microphone. He stretched out his right hand, grabbed it, feeling their palms on his shoulders, stopped for a second to pull down his green jacket, and stepped into the light. Whoosh! There it was. That rush of adrenalin so big that it could knock a man down. He braced himself and stood, looking out. Naked. He looked up at the golden handrail that ran in a crescent around the dress circle and took in the momentary silence before the song began. His heart was jumping around. He knew this was brave, but he wasn't the only one. Hank was brave just being the only 'out' gay cowboy in Wexford. Betty and Michael were brave to bring up three children. All that love. Christine and Carmel were brave with their work and the battles they fought every day. That was the only difference. Frankie had saved his challenges up like pocket money for this.

The foursome in row J grabbed each other by the arms as they saw him. For a second, they thought he had done a runner, then there he was. Better late than never. Betty cried because he looked so handsome in his jeans and that wonderful plain green jacket. The kind of jacket he had worn to the Palace a million times. The bandleader looked around him, smiled and nodded, and off they went. As the bass line announced the song, the audience, who couldn't have been any warmer, let out a cheer. Now, here was one they could all sing along to. Frankie broke into a little-boy grin, tilted his head and sang. *You know I can be found sitting all alone*. Right away, they swayed in their seats and clapped

on the beat. Michael clapped above his head, hoping that
Frankie could see him. Hank glowed with pride. The only
thing in the whole world that could have made it better
was if Greg had been there by his side. Carmel sat back and
thought 'Who would believe it?' Her big brother up there
on stage. He was beating Joe Shaw at his own game. Not for
him the social club on a Saturday night. Frankie was singing
to the whole damn country. Of course he sounded like Elvis.
He always had, but this was different. He was smiling and
when he smiled, it was his own voice, not an impression.
He wasn't content to do what Andrew or Enda or Bob had
done and turn himself inside out trying to become someone
who was a true original. He was happy for the first time to be
Frankie in the style of Elvis. He bounded around. He rocked
and rolled on the sides of his feet, swinging his hips like a
charmed snake. He smiled and reached out to them all and
said 'Howyagoin'. Carmel wondered if he would take her to
Graceland with him. They could hire a pink Cadillac. They
had planned that trip since they were kids, so they really
should go for it, even if he didn't win. It would be so much
better now they were all grown up, although, bearing in
mind how gorgeous he was looking up there, she should
get some long-overdue therapy first.

> *I don't want no other love*
> *Baby it's just you I'm thinking of.*

And you, and you, and you. They all felt it. Christine's
chocolate peanuts were melting. They were jammed in
between her crossed legs and she didn't even notice that
they had softened in the bag and formed one big nut-filled
cluster. She had been right. He was Frankie the mechanic
and delivery driver from Loughfergus. He had bugger-all
chance of being anyone else.

In a pub just outside Dundalk, a man stood on top of

the bar and twiddled the knobs on the telly. The boxing disappeared and was replaced by the Talent Quest. 'Shut up, will you!' he shouted, clenching his fist at the old men in the snug. 'It's my mate Frankie up there!' Pat got what he wanted. They even stopped serving for the duration of the song. Nancy and Becka had Charlie over. Before he arrived, they had flipped a coin to see which of them would try and make him forget Carmel. To ward off hangovers, they were passing around a giant novelty baby bottle filled with ouzo. They sucked alternately on the rubber teat, following each mouthful with a drag on a joint. By the time Frankie came on, Charlie had forgotten his own name. In a high-rise flat to the north of the city, four children sat with their mother. 'I know him,' said a little boy in Power Ranger pyjamas. 'It's Frankie. The man in the garage! Deadly!' He bounced on the sofa. His mother threw a cushion at him and said: 'Sit down, David, and stop making things up!' Just around the corner, a television blared in a candlelit room. On a *King Creole* duvet cover, Wacker lay in his sky-blue suit, curled on the bed with a pill bottle in his hand and a half-eaten burger by his side. It was cold and so was he.

In the Caesar's Palace, it was warm and garlicky. They sat in rows in front of the telly, cheering and banging a bodhrán in time with the music. Christy waved his football scarf and Hazel stood on a chair. Colin held her hand to keep her steady. Behind the bar, Greg and Brede were elbow to elbow, trying to see Hank in the shots of the swaying audience. From the wall behind them, his face appeared between their two shoulders. A wanted man. Down the road, Michael's three sat around an empty pizza box. Their faces flickered blue in the light from the screen. 'Move away from that telly, now,' said Eileen from the chair. 'There are other people in this room who want to watch besides you.' They wriggled back on their bottoms and sat propped against the sofa. Steven feigned disinterest and bit his fingernail. Elizabeth hugged her knees. Liam climbed on to Eileen's lap and she put down her knitting. He looked up at her and raised a little tomato-sauce-stained finger to her cheek, catching a tear. She put her hand around his waist and watched the Wexford Elvis. For the first time in what seemed like a hundred years, she thought of something good and it happened.

∫

Viva Loughfergus!

Elvis Presley died on the same day as Dickie Quirke the postman, so he was shoved out of the limelight a bit. After all, to the people in Loughfergus, Elvis was just some fat eejit in a white suit. Dickie Quirke was the fountain of all knowledge. He was a tiny, wiry little man with feet like a child and a brain like twelve volumes of an encyclopaedia. Not only did he know what went on behind every letterbox he lifted, he could tell you about the Nile or the French Revolution or the rules of mah-jong. People were always trying to catch him out. The kids called him Mervo the Memory Man. Every morning, his bike was followed by a caterpillar of children, all shouting: 'Hey, Mervo, is it true that Elizabeth the First of England had no hair and wooden teeth? Hey, Mervo, is it true that the astronauts had to do a dump in their spacesuits because there weren't any toilets on the moon?' The only question that would have caught him out was 'Hey, Mervo, when was the last time anyone really talked to you? Asked you how you were getting on?' On 16 August 1977, Dickie Quirke choked to death on a scone and the whole village went into mourning.

Of course, it was Elvis who made all the headlines. Newspapers all over town, on car seats and on the tops of shopping baskets. ELVIS IS DEAD, they all said. 'And so is Dickie Quirke, God love him,' said the woman in the newsagent's when Joe Shaw went in. 'I see someone put poor Elvis out of his misery,' he said to Frankie over lunch. Frankie shrugged and stared silently at his food, because he knew Joe would never understand. Eileen put her hand on Frankie's shoulder and said: 'Now, Joe. He's Frank's favourite and well you know it. We should be grateful he's not into that rowdy stuff like the Macnamara girl.' On his way back to work, Joe tore the sports pages out of the paper and handed the rest to Frankie.

He sat on the wall by the shop and read about Elvis. He was heartbroken. Shattered. For years, he had collected his albums from second-hand shops and jumble sales. There had been no shortage of them. They were always to be found, in between the battered copies of the Messiah and Felix Mendelssohn and his Hawaiian Serenaders. Elvis was the one nobody had wanted to know. Nobody but Frankie. He had sat up in his room, day after day, learning all the words and making up dances and collecting clippings in a scrapbook. He took his records around to friends' houses and sat quietly while the girls argued about whether to play the Osmonds or David Cassidy. When they had finished, he lowered the needle on to his favourite Elvis songs. At first, they pulled faces, but in minutes they were up and dancing. Carmel liked all the quirky sixties numbers and twisted frantically to 'Bossa Nova Baby' and 'See See Rider'. She liked the way it made her plaits swing and slap against her head. Mr and Mrs Macnamara stood, sometimes, in the lounge doorway and looked at them jiving around and they smiled big warm smiles. Smiles that Frankie and his friend Elvis had brought them as a present.

On the day Elvis died, Frankie knew that it would never

be the same. Now, everybody would be buying his records and singing his songs. He might as well go and buy the new single by Thin Lizzy. Suddenly, he wasn't anybody any more. He tore the newspaper up and threw it in the bin. As he walked home, he heard some kids saying that Dickie Quirke's face was bright purple when they found him and his eyes had bulged right out of his head, and that in his wardrobe they had found thousands and thousands of undelivered love letters. None of them believed that bit, because nobody wrote love letters. Nobody they could think of, anyway.

KATE THOMPSON

THIN AIR

To outsiders, the Keane family looks content enough. They live on the beautiful west coast of Ireland where Brigid cooks lunches in a local hotel and her husband, Gerard, produces beef and sport horses on the family farm. Their children seem to be turning out all right and, if their lives are not entirely happy, they are at least uneventful. Until one day when their eldest daughter's horse returns home without her.

Martina seems to have vanished into thin air and no one can explain why. Each member of the family, isolated in their confusion, deals with the crisis in their own separate way. Now that the fabric of normality has been breached, the family will have to come to terms with what they find beyond it.

A remarkable novel with haunting descriptions of the magic and history of the Irish landscape, THIN AIR is a lyrical study of how a family can survive and renew itself in the face of a painful breakdown.

Kate Thompson is the author of DOWN AMONG THE GODS and has written the SWITCHERS trilogy for children. Originally from Yorkshire, she has lived in the west of Ireland for many years.

HODDER AND STOUGHTON PAPERBACKS

'Funny and touching in equal parts
and very enjoyable' EXAMINER

If anyone had owned a horse, it
would have been a one-horse town.
A young girl at the top of the hill
had a half-share of a pony called
Muffin, but that didn't really count.

Welcome to Loughfergus, where Frankie sings karaoke at the
Caesar's Palace pub and Hank, the landlord, daydreams about
riding horses through Monument Valley. Frankie's friends want
him to enter the Wexford heat of the Irish Elvis competition.
Hank's friends want him to rope himself a partner. But they're
happy to be just as they are: wired to the moon. Until Carmel
breezes in from the big city and changes everything.

Sarah Kavanagh is from a theatrical family.
She grew up in England, and now lives in
west London. This is her first novel.

FLAME
Fiction: General

Cover photographs: **Neal Farris/Photon**
Joni Mabe's Travel
Panoramic Encyclo
of Everything Elvis

Author photograph: **Johnny Grieg**

UK £6.99

ISBN 0-340-71262-7

9 780340 712627